KU-175-511

Praise for *The Hummingbird*

Winner of the Premio Strega

'A masterpiece of love and grief . . . Everything that makes the novel worthwhile and engaging is here: warmth, wit, intelligence, love, death, high seriousness, low comedy, philosophy, subtle personal relationships and the complex interior life of human beings . . . magnificent – moving, replete, beautiful . . . what makes the book special is that *The Hummingbird* is such an intelligent meditation on life, family, the human heart and the "dictatorship of pain" that comes with grief' *Guardian*

'A masterpiece of articulation . . . Not since William Boyd's *Any Human Heart* has a novel captured the feast and famine nature of a single life with such invention and tenderness. Veronesi explores, with great humour, how the passage of time both expands and expunges the impact of events. And, he suggests, after the pounding of years it is only an individual's character that determines whether or not the edifice will hold' *Financial Times*

'Instantly immersive, playfully inventive, effortlessly wise . . . A family saga that pays homage to the quiet heroism required by day-to-day existence' *Observer*

'Veronesi originally trained as an architect and, rather marvellously, it shows: the structure is inventive, bold, unexpected – slightly bonkers but elegant, and cohesive . . . [it] conveys life's messy unpredictability: joy and desperation, simple pleasures, moments of transcendence, much reeling and confusion . . . There is a pleasing sense of having grappled with the real stuff of life: loss, grief, love, desire, pain, uncertainty, confusion, joy, despair – all while having fun' *Sunday Times*

'A tender, beguilingly epic novel . . . The complex, subtle design of the novel, with a patchwork of key episodes moving back and forth through time, and its textual variety disguise its saga-like scale, its epic proportions catching you off guard. It's almost only once you emerge from its acutely painful ending that you realise how much of life you have witnessed – the vastness, as well as the richness, of the story' *New Statesman*

'Excellent: Marco Carrera is a compelling main character, a devoted father an oblivious husband, a dutiful son and an inadequate brother. The novel's conclusion is a beautiful study of the resilient bonds of flawed love' *Times Literary Supplement*

'Veronesi's novel has been hotly anticipated by English readers. Life-affirming' *New European*

'A masterly novel, a brilliantly conceived mosaic of love and tragedy. Veronesi creates a thought-rich and ultimately comic meditation on human error and lost chances. It's a cabinet of curiosities and delights, packed with small wonders, strange and sudden turns, insights of great poise and unusual cultural reference points. *The Hummingbird* is an object lesson in authorial control. Veronesi truly knows and loves all matters of the heart' Ian McEwan

'Somehow or other Sandro Veronesi pulls off the extraordinary feat of making you believe he is writing for your ears alone. I cannot tell you what *The Hummingbird* is about because that would be to betray a confidence. But I can tell you it's a mightily clever novel' Howard Jacobson

'I love *The Hummingbird*. A real masterpiece. A funny, touching, profound book that made me cry like a little girl on the last page' Leïla Slimani

'Long considered one of Italy's leading writers, Sandro Veronesi has dazzled both readers and critics with novels that are not only page-turners but profoundly literary. An heir to Italo Svevo, he explores, from book to book, intergenerational conflict, existential anguish and the passage of time. These themes, in Veronesi's hands, burst with vitality. Trained as an architect, he plays inventively with form, producing works that are unconventional, disarming, and profoundly humane. With his latest novel, *The Hummingbird*, he has re-written the family saga. Ardent, gripping, and inventive to the core, it has already been hailed a classic' Jhumpa Lahiri

'*The Hummingbird* is a profound story about the myriad ways in which human passions collide with forces beyond human control. From its first page to its last, it's as full of surprises as it is jolts of recognition. Sandro Veronesi has overcome the ultimate, and most difficult, of any novelist's challenges – created a story of such depth and scope that it can stand unembarrassed alongside life itself. It's a remarkable accomplishment, a true gift to the world' Michael Cunningham

'Reading *The Hummingbird* is a spellbinding experience; it's so clever, funny and deeply moving' Roddy Doyle

'Much more than a novel about a family – which its deceptively unadorned surfaces might suggest it to be – *The Hummingbird* portrays a subtle and intriguing political vision, depicting the reach of history into the lives of people we might well believe are outside history's notice' Richard Ford

'Sandro Veronesi is a writer I have always admired. He's funny, smart, rueful, deeply feeling. *The Hummingbird* stands with his finest work. It's some of the most poignant contemporary writing I know of' Rick Moody

'An extremely beautiful and generous novel about time, family, home, love and loss, passion and pain. Funny, heart-breaking, eccentric, tender and completely brilliant. A triumphant, life-affirming novel. Now I want to read everything by Sandro Veronesi'
Edward Carey, author of *Little*

'Sandro Veronesi's captivating novel is at once a gripping tale of family bonds and a provoking meditation on fate and choice, suffering and endurance, love and hatred, and the elusive nature of happiness. I greatly admired its wit and erudition and its deep charm'
James Lasdun, author of *Seven Lies*

'I have known for quite some time that Sandro Veronesi was one of the most skilful and profound Italian storytellers of the past thirty years. But *The Hummingbird* is the decisive proof of his sensitivity, of his extraordinary strength as a writer'
Domenico Starnone, author of *Ties*

'A book full of that roller-coaster ride that is life itself, a succession of defeats and unexpected ascents. Crucially, this is a novel that has the courage to pass the baton to the new generations: in the sea of cynicism in which we all risk to drown, it gives us a glimpse of a possible new future'
Nicola Lagioia, author of *Ferocity*

'Sandro Veronesi is a gracious, generous and mature writer, and under his guidance the many narrative devices and chronological leaps back and forth (also into the future) grow and mature into a remarkable novel. This piecemeal approach shouldn't work, but Maestro Veronesi is in control: it's a clever structure and the plot twists and turns and thunders along. If you don't yet know the work of one of Europe's finest writers, start here'
Rosie Goldsmith, European Literature Network

'Outstanding. A perturbing masterpiece. Absolute beauty in the smallest detail' *Corriere della Sera*

'No other writer in Italy today can tell a story like Sandro Veronesi' *La Stampa*

'Powerful and seductive' *la Repubblica*

'Reading *The Hummingbird* is like getting on a rollercoaster: it's a vertiginous ride – almost to the point of physical pain – and then you are left in a state of wonder' *Radio 24*

'A great novel, vibrating with life and death, happiness and pain, nostalgia and hope for the future' *Vanity Fair Italy*

'Reading *The Hummingbird* is not just a moving experience: it's almost like a therapy session, a lesson in persevering, in letting go of guilt to find ourselves again' *Huffington Post Italy*

'Everything that has made Veronesi one of the greats is distilled in *The Hummingbird* – just more mature and ambitious' *Esquire Italy*

# The Hummingbird

Sandro Veronesi

Translated by Elena Pala

First published in Great Britain in 2021 by Weidenfeld & Nicolson
This paperback edition first published in Great Britain in 2022
by Weidenfeld & Nicolson,
an imprint of The Orion Publishing Group Ltd
Carmelite House, 50 Victoria Embankment
London EC4Y 0DZ

An Hachette UK Company

3 5 7 9 10 8 6 4

Copyright © 2019 La Nave di Teseo Editore, Milano
English translation © Elena Pala 2021

Extract on p.62 taken from 'Hummingbird', published in *All of Us* by Raymond Carver.
Copyright © Tess Gallagher, 1996. Used with permission of The Wylie Agency Ltd.

The moral right of Sandro Veronesi to be identified as
the author of this work has been asserted in accordance
with the Copyright, Designs and Patents Act of 1988.

Elena Pala has asserted her right to be identified as the author of the English
translation of this work.

This book has been translated thanks to a translation grant awarded by the Italian
Ministry of Foreign Affairs and International Cooperation.
Questo libro è stato tradotto grazie a un contributo alla traduzione assegnato dal
Ministero degli Affari Esteri e della Cooperazione Internazionale italiano.

All rights reserved. No part of this publication may be
reproduced, stored in a retrieval system, or transmitted
in any form or by any means, electronic, mechanical,
photocopying, recording, or otherwise, without the
prior permission of both the copyright owner and the
above publisher of this book.

All the characters in this book are fictitious, and any resemblance
to actual persons, living or dead, is purely coincidental.

A CIP catalogue record for this book is
available from the British Library.

ISBN (Mass Market Paperback) 978 1 4746 1748 2
ISBN (eBook) 978 1 4746 1749 9
ISBN (Audio) 978 1 4746 1750 5

Typeset by Input Data Services Ltd, Somerset
Printed and bound in Great Britain by Clays Ltd, Elcograf S.p.A.

www.weidenfeldandnicolson.co.uk
www.orionbooks.co.uk

To Giovanni,
Brother and sister

I can't go on,
I'll go on.

Samuel Beckett

# One might say (1999)

The Trieste neighbourhood in Rome is, one might say, one of the focal points of this story that has many other focal points. The neighbourhood has forever oscillated between elegance and decay, luxury and mediocrity, privilege and insignificance, and that should suffice for now: no point describing it further, because describing it at the start of the story might turn out to be tedious, or even counterproductive. At any rate, the best way to describe a place is to describe what happens in it, and something important is about to happen here.

Let's put it this way: one of the key events in this tale of many tales takes place in the Trieste neighbourhood, in Rome, on a mid-October morning in 1999, and specifically at the corner between Via Chiana and Via Reno, on the first floor of one of those buildings that, as promised, we won't bother describing here. Except what is about to happen here is a decisive and – one might say – potentially fatal event in the life of the main character in this story. 'Dr Marco Carrera, ophthalmologist' reads the nameplate on the door – the door which, for a little while yet, separates him from one of the most crucial moments in a life full of many other crucial moments. Inside his practice – as it happens, on the first floor of one of those buildings (etc.) – he is writing a prescription for an old lady suffering from ciliary blepharitis. Antibiotic eye drops: follow-up medication after an innovative – revolutionary even, one might say – treatment consisting of N-acetylcysteine drops instilled in the eye, which for many of his patients has already averted the main complication of this condition, namely its tendency to become chronic. Outside, however, destiny is lying in wait in the shape of a little man named Daniele Carradori. Bald and bearded, he possesses a magnetic – one might say – gaze, which will shortly be directed at the ophthalmologist's eyes, instilling in them first disbelief, then anxiety and finally sorrow – none of which his (the ophthalmologist's) science will be able to cure. The little man has made up his mind by now, a decision that has brought him to the waiting room where he is currently sitting, looking at his shoes, not taking advantage of the many magazines on display on the coffee tables (brand-new magazines, not the stuff from last year that falls apart when you pick it up). No use hoping he'll change his mind.

Here we go. The door opens, the old blepharitic lady walks out and turns to shake the doctor's hand, then heads towards the reception desk to pay for the treatment (120,000 lira) as Carrera pops out to call in the following patient. The little man gets up and comes forward, Carrera shakes his hand and welcomes him in. Nestled in the shelving unit next to the trusty Marantz amp and two mahogany AR6 speakers, a vintage Thorens record player (now obsolete but one of the best in its time – that is, a quarter of a century ago) is playing Graham Nash's *Song for Beginners* at a very low volume. The enigmatic record sleeve – propped up against the above-mentioned shelving unit and picturing the above-mentioned Graham Nash holding a camera against a rather obscure background – is the most eye-catching element in the whole room.

The door closes. Here we go. The veil separating Dr Carrera from the most devastating emotional shock in a life full of many other emotional shocks has fallen.

Let us pray for him, and for all the ships out at sea.

# Poste restante postcard (1998)

Luisa LATTES
Poste Restante
59–78 Rue des Archives
75003 Paris
France

Rome, 17 April 1998

Working and thinking of you

M.

# Yes or no (1999)

– Good morning. My name is Daniele Carradori.
– Marco Carrera, good morning.
– Does my name ring a bell?
– Should it?
– Yes, it should.
– What did you say your name was?
– Daniele Carradori.
– Is that my wife's therapist's name?
– Correct.
– Oh. I'm sorry, I never thought we'd meet. Please, take a seat. What can I do for you?
– You could listen to me, Dr Carrera. And once I've told you what I have come here to tell you, perhaps you could decide not to report me to the National Order of Physicians, or worse to the Italian Psychoanalysts' Association – which, as a colleague, you could do quite easily.
– Report you? Whatever for?
– Because what I'm about to do is forbidden and severely punished in my line of work. I had never even dreamed of doing something like this, ever in my life – I had never imagined I could even *conceive* of such a thing – but I have reason to believe you are in grave danger, and I am the only person in

the world to be aware of this. Therefore, I am here to inform you, even though by doing so I am breaking one of the most sacred rules in my profession.

– Goodness! I'm listening.

– I'd like to ask you a favour first.

– Is the music bothering you?

– What music?

– Never mind. What did you want to ask me?

– I'd like to ask you a few questions to confirm what I've been told about you and your family: it would help me exclude the possibility that the account I've been given is somewhat misleading. I think it is unlikely, but still: I cannot completely exclude it. Do you understand?

– I do.

– I've brought some notes. Kindly answer me only 'yes' or 'no'.

– All right.

– May I begin?

– Please.

– Are you Dr Marco Carrera, aged forty, raised in Florence, with a degree in medicine from La Sapienza University in Rome, specialising in ophthalmology?

– Yes.

– Son of Letizia Calabrò and Probo Carrera, both architects, both retired and living in Florence?

– Yes. My father is an engineer, though.

– Oh, right. You have a brother named Giacomo, a few years younger than yourself and living in the US, and – forgive me – a sister called Irene, who drowned in the early 1980s?

– Yes.

– You are married to Marina Molitor, a Slovenian national working for Lufthansa?

– Yes.

– You have a daughter, Adele, aged ten, currently in year 5 at a state primary school near the Coliseum?
– Vittorino da Feltre primary, yes.
– And was Adele, between the age of two and six, convinced there was a thread attached to her back, which prompted you and your wife to seek the help of a child psychology specialist?
– Manfrotto the Wizard . . .
– I beg your pardon?
– That's the name he used with the children.
– I see. So it is true you went to see a child psychologist?
– Yes, but I don't see how this has anything to do with—
– You do understand why I'm asking these questions, don't you? I only have one source, and I am verifying it is a reliable one. It's a precaution I have to take, considering what I came here to say.
– That's fine. But what have you come here to say?
– A few more questions, if you don't mind. These will be of a slightly more intimate nature, and I'd like you to answer with the utmost sincerity. Do you think you can do it?
– Yes.
– You gamble, don't you?
– Well, not anymore.
– But in the past, would it be fair to say you were a gambler?
– Yes.
– And is it true that up until the age of fourteen, you were much shorter than other kids your age, so much so that your mother had nicknamed you 'the hummingbird'?
– Yes.
– And that when you were fourteen, your father took you to Milan to undergo an experimental hormonal therapy, after which your height went back to normal and you grew over six inches in less than a year?

– In eight months, yes.
– And is it true that your mother was opposed to the treatment, and taking you to Milan was the only time your father exercised some authority as a parent, seeing as in your family – and forgive me for reporting this exactly as it was reported to me – 'no one gives a fuck about what he says?'
– Ha! That's not true.
– It's not true that your mother was opposed to the treatment, or that no one gives a fuck about what your father says?
– It's not true that no one gives a fuck about what my father says. It's just what people think, especially Marina. They're such completely different characters, my father and her, that most of the time—
– You don't need to explain anything to me, Dr Carrera. Just answer me yes or no. Is that all right?
– Yes, fine.
– Is it true you have always been in love, and for many years have engaged in a relationship with a woman named Luisa Lattes, currently liv—
– What? Who told you that?
– Guess.
– Never! It's impossible, Marina could never have told you that—
– Only answer yes or no, please. And do try to be honest. Are you, or could you have led your wife to believe that you are still in love with this Luisa Lattes, yes or no?
– Not at all!
– So you're not secretly seeing her when you happen to attend a conference in France, or Belgium, or The Netherlands, or anyway not far from Paris, where Ms Lattes lives? Or during the summer, in Bolgheri, where you happen to spend the month of August in two neighbouring holiday homes with your families?

– That's ridiculous! We see each other every summer at the beach with our children, that's true. We talk a little, but we've never dreamt of 'engaging in a relationship' like you said, let alone meeting in secret when I travel for work.
– Look, I am not here to judge you. I'm only trying to understand if what I've been told about you is true or false. It is false, then, that you and this woman are secretly seeing each other?
– False, yes.
– And can't you entertain the idea that your wife might believe this is true, even though it isn't?
– Of course I can't! They've even become friends. They go riding together, I mean the two of them, alone: they dump the kids with us men and ride around the countryside all morning.
– That proves nothing. You can befriend someone and spend time with them every day precisely because you are morbidly jealous of them.
– Yes, but that's not the case here, believe me. Marina is not morbidly jealous of anyone, I'm faithful to her and she knows it. And now will you please tell me why I'd be in danger?
– So you haven't been writing to each other for years, you and this Luisa?
– No!
– Love letters?
– Not at all!
– Are you being honest, Dr Carrera?
– Absolutely!
– I'll ask you one more time: are you being honest?
– Of course I'm being honest! Will you tell me—
– In that case I apologise, but contrary to what I believed – strongly believed, I assure you, or I wouldn't have come

here – your wife lied to me and so you are not in danger as I thought, therefore I won't bother you any longer. Kindly disregard my visit and above all don't mention it to anyone.

– What? Why are you getting up? Where are you going?

– I apologise again, but I have made a serious mistake. Goodbye. I know the wa—

– Now look here. You can't come here, tell me I am in grave danger because of something my wife told you, cross-examine me and then just leave! You better tell me what's going on or you bet I will report you!

– The truth is I shouldn't have come at all. I always thought I could trust your wife and I have formed a detailed opinion about her condition precisely because I have always believed her. Based on this opinion and faced with what I thought was a very serious situation, I decided to act outside the limits of my profession's code of ethics. But now you are telling me your wife has been lying to me on a key issue, and if she lied to me about this she probably lied about many other things, including those that led me to conclude that you were in danger. As I said, it was my mistake, and I cannot but apologise once again, but ever since your wife stopped coming to see me, I have been wondering about—

– Wait, what? My wife has stopped coming to see you?

– Yes.

– Since when?

– Over a month ago.

– You're joking.

– You didn't know?

– No.

– She hasn't been to see me since our last session on . . . on the sixteenth of September.

– But she tells me she's still seeing you. On Tuesdays and Thursdays at 3.15 p.m. I pick up Adele from school as always, because Marina is with you. I'm meant to pick her up this very afternoon.

– I'm not at all surprised she's lying to you, Dr Carrera. The problem is, she lied to me too.

– Ah come on, she lied to you about one thing. And then, forgive me, but aren't lies supposed to be more revealing to you therapists than the truth that is being concealed?

– Says who?

– I don't know, you . . . people. No? Since I was little I've been surrounded by people in therapy and I've always heard that setting, transfer, dreams, lies, all that stuff matters precisely because that's where the truth hides. What's the problem now if Marina made something up?

– No, if this story about Luisa Lattes is only a fantasy of hers, that changes everything, and it's your wife who is in danger.

– But why? What danger?

– Look, I'm really sorry but it's no longer appropriate for me to be talking to you. And don't tell your wife I came here, I beg you.

– Do you seriously think I'm going to let you go after what you've just told me? Now I demand—

– No point threatening me, Dr Carrera. Feel free to report me, if you wish: I deserve it, considering the mistake I made. But you can never force me to tell you what—

– It's not a fantasy of hers.

– I beg your pardon?

– What Marina told you about Luisa Lattes is not a fantasy. It's true, we're seeing each other, we write to each other. Except it's not a relationship, and I'm certainly not being unfaithful to my wife: it's just our own thing and I wouldn't know how to define it, and I can't understand how Marina knows about this.

– Are you still in love with her?

– That's not the point here. The point is—
– Forgive me but I must insist: are you still in love with her?
– Yes.
– You met in Louvain in June?
– Yes but—
– In one of your letters from a few years ago, did you write to her that you like the way she dives into the sea from the shore?
– Yes but how on ear—
– Did you and Ms Lattes take a vow of chastity?
– Yes but, honestly, how can Marina know about this? And why don't you just say what you have to say instead of going round in circles? There's a marriage at stake here, for fuck's sake! A daughter!
– I'm sorry to say this to you, but your marriage has been over for a long time now, Dr Carrera. And there will be another child shortly, but it won't be yours.

# Sadly (1981)

Luisa Lattes
14 Via Frusa
Florence 50131

Bolgheri, 11 September 1981

Luisa, my Luisa,

No, not mine sadly, just Luisa (Luisa Luisa Luisa Luisa Luisa Luisa Luisa Luisa): I ran away, you say. It's true, but after what happened, for those long, unimaginable days I was racked with guilt, and I wasn't myself anymore – I was no one. I went into some kind of a trance, I thought it was all my fault, because I was with you while it happened, because I was happy with you. I still think it is my fault.

Now they're all saying it was God's will, or destiny and all that bullshit, and Giacomo and I were at each other's throats, and I blamed him, and I can't even look my parents in the face. If I ran away, my Luisa – no not mine sadly, just Luisa (Luisa Luisa Luisa Luisa Luisa) – I ran in the wrong direction, like those pheasants I saw in a forest fire once, back when I was a fireman: terrified of the blaze, they leapt up and, instead of flying away from it, they flailed towards the flames, getting closer, too close, until they fell in. The fact is, I didn't realise I'd run away: there were so many things to take care of – all of them terrifying – and there was that ridiculous Montagues and Capulets farce that made it impossible for me to venture past the hedge (of course it was possible, Luisa, I'm not denying it, Luisa Luisa Luisa Luisa, but I was beside myself, Luisa), and so I didn't, and didn't even say goodbye.

And now I'm here, alone, and I mean truly alone: everyone has left, they say they'll never come back, sell the house, never set foot on a beach again, never go on holiday again. And you all left too, and I venture past the hedge all the time, now, and no one can see me, and I go to the beach, to Mulinelli, behind the dunes, and there's no one there and I should be studying but I'm not even pretending, and I think of you, I think of Irene, of the happiness and the desperation that crashed down on me at the same time and in the same place and I don't want to lose either of them, yes I want them both, but I'm afraid I'll lose them too, lose this pain, lose the happiness, lose you, Luisa, like I lost my sister, and maybe I've lost you already because you say I've run away and sadly that's true, I've run away but not from you, I've only run away in the wrong direction like those pheasants Luisa Luisa Luisa Luisa Luisa I'm begging you, we've only just begun don't you die too, and even if I've run away wait for me forgive me hold me kiss me I haven't run out of things to say I've run out of paper,

Marco

# The eye of the storm (1970–1979)

Duccio Chilleri was a tall and gangly boy, quite gifted at sports, although not as gifted as his father thought. Black hair, horsey teeth, so thin he seemed to be always in profile, he had a reputation for bringing bad luck. No one could tell exactly how and when that rumour had started, and so it felt like it had always followed him around, just like the moniker that came with it – The Omen. During his childhood, he had another nickname: 'Blizzard', after the ski brand, because of the way he always triumphed in local skiing competitions.

Like most things, that rumour did indeed begin somewhere – namely during one of those very skiing competitions, a giant slalom regional qualifier at the Zum Zeri – Passo dei Due Santi ski resort, in the Tuscan–Emilian Apennines. Duccio Chilleri had finished second in his category in the first round, behind the favourite, a smug little boy from Modena named Tavella. The weather conditions were appalling. Despite the strong winds, the run was shrouded in fog, to the point that the judges seriously considered cancelling the race. Then the wind relented and the second round got the go-ahead, even though the fog had thickened. As they waited for the race to start, Duccio's father (who was also his coach) massaged his legs, urging him to charge down the run, go in for the kill and beat that Tavella. When he got to the starting gate, ready to pounce down the now nearly invisible run – his father telling him he could do it, he could win, he could beat Tavella – Duccio Chilleri was heard uttering the following words: 'He's going to fall anyway, and hurt himself too.' Duccio finished with the best time and then it was Tavella's turn. No one saw exactly how it happened because of the fog: all they heard was a horrifying scream coming from the run-off after a steep incline. The judges rushed there to find Tavella on the ground, unconscious, with half a pole sticking out of his thigh (the gates were still made of wood back then and sometimes the wood snapped). A pool of blood glimmered like red lacquer in the milky blur of snow and fog. Tavella didn't bleed to death only because the pole, having gone through his leg muscle, had barely brushed against the femoral artery. It became the most serious accident in the history of that ski resort, destined to be remembered for many seasons to come – together with Duccio Chilleri's words.

Thus began his reputation as a jinx: it happened all at once and with no hope of redemption. No one had even bothered making a connection between the accident and his childhood moniker (Blizzard), which effectively already placed him within the same ominous karmic field better exemplified by his adult nickname. Nor had anyone speculated on the origin of his surname – quite rare in Italy and only present in certain parts of Tuscany – which, rather aptly in his case, sounded like 'killer'. (Had they made that connection, they would have been wrong anyway: his surname probably originated from a consonant swap with the more widespread 'Chillemi', a family name which could boast a noble branch in Lombardy, and a more prevalent common branch in Sicily.) Either way, no one cared – which goes to show just how easily and casually the rumour spread, to what point his new reputation went completely unchallenged. He was a jinx and that was that.

As he transitioned from Blizzard to The Omen, the wealth of friendship he'd built through his sporting prowess began to slowly dwindle and at the age of sixteen Marco Carrera was the only friend he had left in the whole of Florence. They had sat together in primary school, played tennis together, skied together until Marco stopped competing, and even though they now went to different schools they still saw each other every day. They spent a lot of time listening to West Coast folk rock (The Eagles; Crosby, Stills, Nash & Young; Poco; The Grateful Dead), which they were both obsessed with. But above all – *above all* – what had cemented their friendship was the discovery of gambling. In all fairness, Duccio was the real fanatic, Marco simply went along with his friend's passion, and together they enjoyed the thrill of freedom – or of liberation, one might say – which gambling brought to their lives. Neither of them, in fact, belonged to a family that had ever harboured that demon, even in days of old: no great-uncle plunged into poverty by the fascist aristocracy's baccarat tables, no nineteenth-century fortune squandered by a great-grandfather who'd lost his marbles in the Great War. Quite simply, gambling had been *their* discovery. Duccio, in particular, used it to escape the gilded cage his parents had built for him: the prospect of frittering away their wealth in casinos and gambling dens appealed to him at least as much as the prospect of accumulating it had appealed to them. And at any rate he was fifteen, sixteen, seventeen: how much can you possibly squander at that age? As generous as his weekly allowance was (about twice as much as Marco's), it's not as if those sums could chip away at his family's fortune. At worst, when he was going through a bad streak, he might run up a few debts at Mondo Disco, the record store on Via dei Conti where he and Marco would stock up on imported music – debts that he'd easily pay off himself in a few weeks, without his parents even noticing.

The fact is, most of the time he won. He was good at it. When he played poker with friends in those harmless Saturday-night games where you'd win 20,000 lira at most, there was simply no contest. This, compounded by his new reputation as a jinx, meant that he was soon banned from attending. Not Marco though, he was not banned, and for a while he continued to play (and to win) until he decided to abandon those harmless games and follow his friend on to a more professional route – horse races to begin with. Being a minor, Duccio Chilleri couldn't get into gambling dens, let alone legitimate casinos, but the bookmakers over at the Le Mulina racecourse never asked for ID. He had a real talent for that too, and he didn't leave anything to chance: he would skip school and spend entire mornings at the racecourse, watching horses trot with phlegmy old men who initiated him to the secrets of the racing world. And Marco would join him, time and again, for those precious morning lessons, or in betting shops in the afternoon, or back at the racecourse again in the evening. They'd bet on horses they'd researched, or on the favourites in the fixed races they heard about. Once again, more often than not, the two friends would win.

Unlike Marco, however, who had always kept this venture of his from his family, and who hadn't neglected other friends, or sports, or girls (i.e. all the hallmarks of the successful life everyone believed he was destined to), Duccio used gambling to permanently sever all links with his middle-class future. As humiliated as he'd felt upon discovering his new reputation, he later learnt to draw strength from it. Despite his former friends avoiding him like the plague, he'd still see them every day in school – and because Florence isn't Los Angeles, he'd also bump into them in town, in cinemas or cafés. On those occasions, Duccio had learnt that anything he said would take on the sinister undertones of a curse.

As implausible as that sounds, in the 1970s people did indeed believe that Duccio Chilleri was a jinx. Marco didn't, of course, and the question everyone ended up asking him was always the same: 'Why do you still hang out with him?' His answer was always the same, too: 'Because he's my friend.' And yet, even though Marco would never have admitted it, his real motives were perhaps less honourable. First, as we said, there was the gambling. With Duccio, Marco experienced unparalleled adrenaline highs, earned good money and discovered an underworld that his elegant mother, his meek father, and his siblings could never conceive of (Irene was four years his senior and completely absorbed by her boy problems; Giacomo was only a little younger than him and destructively competitive). The other reason he still spent time with Duccio was hopelessly narcissistic: he alone could be forgiven for fraternising with an outcast. Perhaps because he was so smart, so friendly, so generous; whatever the reason, Marco had enough clout to ignore the herd's rules and get away with it – and basking in this power was extremely gratifying. Truth be told, as the years went by and the shared interests their old friendship was built on vanished one after the other, these were his only surviving ties to Duccio Chilleri.

Duccio, in fact, had changed and – as Marco suspected was the nature of all change – he had changed for the worse. In terms of physical appearance, he'd become quite unpresentable: a white froth had begun to gather at the corners of his mouth when he spoke, his jet-black hair was greasy and dandruff-laden, and he seldom washed properly. As time went by, he lost all interest in music: Britain was back on the scene (The Clash, The Cure, Graham Parker & the Rumour, the shimmering world of Elvis Costello) but he didn't care, he didn't buy records anymore and didn't listen to the tapes Marco made for him. He didn't read books or newspapers, only *Horse & Hound*. At the same time, his vocabulary had descended into expressions that were completely at odds with his age: 'groovy', 'all righty' or even 'okey-dokey', 'crumbs!', 'don't mind if I do', 'tickety-boo!', 'wet my whistle'. Girls didn't interest him, everything he needed he got from the whores over at Le Cascine.

Marco still cared about him, but as a friend Duccio Chilleri had become rather unsustainable – and not because of his reputation. On the contrary: Marco kept obstinately denying those rumours, especially when he was with a girl he liked. When his girlfriends started enumerating the accidents, calamities and bouts of rotten luck brought about by Duccio's mere presence, he would counter by saying, How can you believe that? Look at me, for Christ's sake! I hang out with him. Nothing ever happened to me!

But by then Duccio Chilleri's reputation was too deeply ingrained, and his critics had come up with an argument to refute Marco's defence: the eye of the storm. It went like this: just as those who find themselves at the centre of a devastating tropical cyclone will suffer no damage, the same was true of those, like Marco, who kept in close contact with The Omen. The slightest deviation from the centre – a casual encounter, a car ride, even just waving hello from a distance – and you'd end up wiped out by the cyclone like one of those unfortunate coastal villages.

# This thing (1999)

Marco Carrera
c/o Adelino Viespoli
21 Via Catalani
Rome 00199
Italy

Paris, 16.12.1999

I got your letter. Oh, I got it all right. I got it and no one noticed. It's a tough letter, Marco, and I don't know what to say, as usual.

You're right – I'm not happy, but that's nobody's fault, the fault is all with me. No that's not right, I shouldn't have said 'fault', maybe I should say 'thing' rather than fault.

I was born with this thing, I've been carrying it around for thirty-three years and it's nothing to do with anyone else, it's just the way I am.

So what do you want me to say? I could tell you that now you'd really have a chance to see if what you wrote to me is true. You're clean, and blameless, and free as a bird now: you can start from scratch, you can even make mistakes if you want to (you can always go back, after all).

But not me, Marco, my situation is completely different – I'd have to turn my life upside down, it would all be my fault, and then perhaps I really wouldn't be able to find peace anymore. But I know you'll understand, because you're like me: we love in the same way, you and I, we're terrified to hurt those around us.

I think you're the best part of my life – the part without all the lies, the deceit and aggravation (the phone is ringing, it's you, now I'm about to lose it), the part you can dream of, even at night, because I still dream of you.

Will it remain a dream? Will it happen? Will anything happen? I'm here, waiting, I don't want to do anything, I want things to just happen by themselves. That's rather shitty logic, I know, because nothing ever happens to me – but I can't make a decision, not about this thing, not right now.

Maybe I've been practising doing nothing all these years, so I can succeed at this thing. What thing? I don't know, I don't know, I'm not making any sense, I'll stop now.

Luisa

# A happy child (1960–1970)

Throughout his childhood, Marco Carrera hadn't noticed anything. He hadn't noticed his parents were fighting all the time, he hadn't noticed his mother's hostile indifference, his father's exasperating silences, the hushed-up quarrels at night, their voices lowered to a whisper so the children wouldn't hear (and yet his sister Irene did hear them and took a perverse pleasure in meticulously recording every detail in her memory). He didn't know the reason behind those rows, those fights that were so transparent to his sister. The reason was that his mother (a southerner called Letizia, meaning 'joy', which couldn't have been further from the truth) and his father (a northerner who was true to his name, Probo, which meant 'honest') were simply not made for each other, despite both of them being expats of sorts in Florence. They had practically nothing in common; in fact, there were perhaps no two people less alike on the face of the earth. She was an architect, all abstract thought and revolutionary ideas; he was an engineer, all calculations and practicality. She had been sucked into the vortex of radical architecture; he was the best scale model builder in central Italy.

Marco hadn't realised that underneath the flabby, affluent bubble he and his siblings were being raised in, his parents' relationship had failed: it only produced bitterness and guilt and resentment and recrimination and provocation and humiliation and resignation. That is to say, he hadn't realised his parents didn't love each other at all, or at least not in the most common sense of the phrase 'to love each other', which implies reciprocity. There was indeed love in their relationship, but it was entirely one-sided: unrequited love; heroic, dog-like, unshakeable, unspeakable, self-harming love; love his mother was never able to accept or return, but couldn't reject either, seeing as no other man in the world could ever love her in such an all-consuming way. And so that love had become a tumour, a malign, burgeoning lump that tore her family apart from the inside and kept Letizia nailed down to the unhappiness that had surrounded Marco Carrera from the day he was born.

He hadn't realised that unhappiness oozed from the very walls in his house. He hadn't realised there was no sex in that house. He hadn't realised that his mother's many obsessions – architecture, design, photography, yoga, psychotherapy – were just an attempt to find balance, or that those obsessions included cheating on his father, rather clumsily at times. Her lovers were selected from the ranks of those intellectuals who (perhaps for the last time in history) were putting Florence back on the international scene: the 'high priests' from Superstudio and Archizoom and their followers. Although older than them, she still considered herself part of that group and she was wealthy enough to be able to spend time on her young idols' initiatives without making a penny in return.

Marco didn't realise that his father knew about these infidelities either. He had gone through those years completely oblivious to everything, and for this reason alone his was a happy childhood. What is more, because he (unlike Irene) had never doubted his parents and had failed to understand that they were anything but role models, Marco actually looked up to them. He structured his identity around an assortment of traits he'd picked up from one or the other – those very same traits that had proved utterly incompatible in his parents' attempt at a relationship. What did he pick up from his mother as a child, when he knew nothing? And what from his father? And what, conversely, would he end up rejecting for the rest of his life, once he understood everything? He inherited his mother's anxiety but not her radical ideas, her curiosity but not her craving for change. From his father he learnt patience but not prudence, the ability to suffer, but not to suffer in silence. He had his mother's eye, especially for photography, and his father's craftsmanship. On top of that, growing up in that beautiful house (i.e. having sat, from birth, on those chairs, fallen asleep on those armchairs and sofas, eaten at those tables, studied on those desks lit by those lamps, surrounded by those modular bookshelves, etc.) had given him a sense of arrogant superiority typical of Italian middle-class families in the sixties and seventies: the feeling of living, if not in the best possible world, at least in the most beautiful. And the proof of that achievement lay precisely in all the stuff his mother and father had accumulated (the gulf that separated his parents, in fact, instantly dissolved when it came to choosing furniture).

This, rather than nostalgia, was the real reason Marco Carrera would always find it so hard to part with the objects that had surrounded his family, even when he learnt the truth about them, and even when his family, technically, did not exist anymore. Because those objects were beautiful, *still* beautiful, beautiful *nonetheless* – and that beauty was the spit that held his parents together. After their death, faced with the painful prospect of selling the family house on Piazza Savonarola and everything in it, he ended up cataloguing those objects one by one (while his brother, firmly clinging to his decision never to set foot in Italy again, instructed him to 'get rid of them' over the phone).

As a result, Marco wound up stuck with those objects for the rest of his days.

His father's obsession with tidiness (which, in fairness, Probo never demanded of anyone else, but which remained an absolute, intimidating and – towards the end – even violent neurosis) made Marco an unabashedly unkempt individual. His mother, for her part, was responsible for his unconquerable aversion to psychotherapy, which would become a key trait of all his subsequent relationships with women. All the women in his life, in fact, starting from his mother and his sister Irene, and then on to friends, girlfriends, colleagues, wives, daughters (in short all of them bar none) would invariably end up in the grip of various psychotherapists. This only confirmed – as a son, brother, friend, boyfriend, colleague, husband and father – what he'd grasped from the off: that exposure to 'passive psychotherapy', as he called it, is seriously harmful. None of these women, however, seemed to care, not even when he started actively complaining about it. Every family, they'd say to him, every relationship causes damage, to everyone: considering therapy more harmful than say, chess, was just prejudice. And perhaps they were right, but because of all the suffering it caused him, Marco always felt justified in believing that psychotherapy was like smoking: it wasn't enough not to do it yourself, you also had to stay away from those who did. Unfortunately, the only known defence against passive psychotherapy is to go to therapy yourself, and on that point he had no intention of yielding.

# An inventory (2008)

To: Giacomo jackcarr62@yahoo.com
Sent: 19 September 2008 16:39
Subject: Piazza Savonarola inventory
From: Marco Carrera

Dear Giacomo,

You keep ignoring me and I keep writing. I intend to keep you informed of my efforts to sell the house on Piazza Savonarola and rest assured I won't be deterred by your silence. The news is I called Piero Brachi (remember him? The guy from STUDIO B where Mum and Dad bought all our furniture) and I asked him for a valuation of all the pieces in the flat – he's retired now, and manages an auction website specialising in design from the sixties and seventies. As I thought, there are a few gems in there, and the total estimate is really rather impressive (especially considering that, for all the calamities that led to the collapse of our family and consequently to that house being abandoned, those pieces are mostly in excellent condition). Many of them, says Brachi, are exhibited at MoMA. We need to decide what we want to do with them when we sell the house, because apparently we won't get a higher price for it if we leave them where they are. We could give them to Brachi himself to sell off little by little on his site, or divide them up between the two of us based on what we need or like. Do please give some thought to this, Giacomo, because as I'm sure you realise it's not just about the money: this is all that's left of a life and a family that are no more, but that you and I were a part of for over twenty years – and though things went the way they did there's no reason, believe me, to 'get rid of them' like you said the last time, rubbing salt in the wound. I mean, even Brachi was moved, seeing all those beautiful things he'd sold us: I can't believe you don't care about having a say in what's going to happen to them. I promise there won't be any arguments, I will do exactly as you say, if only you'll acknowledge that it's not fair to just throw them out. Things are innocent, Giacomo.

I'm attaching the inventory Piero Brachi sent me with a separate valuation for each item. It's very dry and impersonal, as I requested and as I imagine you'd prefer, even though he knew many intimate details about each of those pieces: who it was bought for, in what room it was, etc.

**Furniture inventory for the house on Savonarola Square:**

**2 x two-seater 'Le Bambole' sofas,** metal, grey leather, polyurethane, by Mario Bellini for B&B, 1972 (€20,000)

**4 x 'Amanta' armchairs,*** glass fibre and black leather, by Mario Bellini for B&B, 1966 (€4,400)

**1 x 'Zelda' armchair**, Rosewood-tinted wood and tan leather, by Sergio Asti and Sergio Favre for Poltronova, 1962 (€2,200)

**1 x 'Soriana' armchair,** steel and brown aniline leather, by Tobia and Afra Scarpa for Casina, 1970 (€4,000)

**1 x 'Sacco' armchair,** polystyrene and brown leather, by Gatti, Paolini and Teodoro for Zanotta, 1969 (€450)

**1 x 'Woodline' armchair**, heat-bent wood and black leather, by Marco Zanuso for Arflex, 1965 (€1,000)

**1 x 'Amanta' coffee table**, black glass fibre, by Mario Bellini for B&B, 1966 (€450)

**1 x '748' side table**, brown teak, by Ico Parisi for Cassina, 1961 (€1,100)

**1 x 'Demetrio 70' side table**, orange plastic, by Vico Magistretti for Artemide, 1966 (€150)

**1 x 'La Rotonda' table**, natural cherry wood and crystal, by Mario Bellini for Cassina, 1976 (€4,000)

**1 x 'Dodona' modular bookshelf**, black plastic, Ernesto Gismondi for Artemide, 1970 (€4,500)

**2 x 'Sergesto' modular bookshelves**, white plastic, by Sergio Mazza for Artemide, 1973 (€1,500)

**1 x 'O-look' ceiling light**, aluminium, by Superstudio for Poltronova, 1967 (€4,400)

**1 x 'Passiflora' table lamp**, yellow and opal Perspex, by Superstudio for Poltronova, 1968 (€1,900)

**1 x 'Saffo' table lamp**, silver-coloured aluminium and glass, by Angelo Mangiarotti for Artemide, 1967 (€1,650)

**1 x 'Baobab' lamp**, white plastic, by Harvey Guzzini for iGuzzini, 1971 (€525)

**1 x 'Eclisse' lamp**, red metal, by Vico Magistretti for Artemide, 1967 (€125)

**1 x 'Gherpe' table lamp**, red Perspex and chrome steel sheets, by Superstudio for Poltronova, 1967 (€4,000)

**1 x 'Mezzachimera' table lamp**, white acrylic, by Vico Magistretti for Artemide, 1970 (€450)

**3 x 'Parentesi' ceiling lights**, metal and plastic, Achille Castiglioni and Pio Manzù for Flos, 1970 (€750)

**12 x 'Teti' ceiling/wall-mounted light fixtures**, white plastic, by Vico Magistretti for Artemide, 1974 (€1,000)

**1 x 'Hebi' reading light**, metal and white corrugated plastic, by Isao Hosoe for Valenti, 1972 (€350)

**3 x 'Telegono' table lamps**, red plastic, by Vico Magistretti for Artemide, 1968 (€350)

**3 x 'Graphis' desks**, wood and white lacquered metal, by Osvaldo Borsani for Tecno, incl. drawers, 1968 (€3,000)

**1 x 'TL 58' table**, core plywood and solid walnut, by Marco Zanuso for Carlo Poggi, 1979 (€3,000)

**3 x 'Uten.Silo 1' wall-mounted storage units**, red, green and yellow plastic, by Dorothee Becker for Ingo Maurer, 1965 (€1,800)

**4 x 'Boby' storage trolleys**, propylene and white, green, red and black printed ABS, by Joe Colombo for Bieffeplast, 1970 (€1,000)

**7 x 'Modus' swivel chairs**, metal and plastic, several colours, by Osvaldo Borsani for Tecno, 1973 (€700)

**4 x office chairs**, chrome steel and leather, by Giovanni Carini for Planula, 1967 (€800)

**7 x 'Plia' chairs**, aluminium and clear plexiglass, by Giancarlo Piretti for Castelli, 1967 (€1,050)

**4 x 'Loop' wicker chairs**, France, 1960s (€1,200)

**4 x 'Selene' chairs**, beige polyester, by Vico Magistretti for Artemide, 1969 (€600)

**4 x 'Basket' chairs**,* steel and beige rattan, by Franco Campo and Carlo Graffi for Home, 1956 (€1,000)

**1 x 'Wassily Modello B3' chair**, brown leather and chrome-pleated steel, by Marcel Breuer for Gavina, 1963 (€1,800)

**1 x drafting machine with spring counterweights**, wood with iron arms, by M. Sacchi, CEn for M. Sacchi CEn Ltd., 1922 (€4,500)

**2 x vintage bedside tables**, brown teak, by Aksel Kjersgaard for Kjersgaard, 1956 (€1,200)
**1 x 'Sciangai' coat stand**, natural beechwood, by De Pas, D'Urbino and Lomazzi for Zanotta, 1974 (€400)
**1 x 'Dedalo' umbrella stand**, orange plastic, by Emma Gismondi Schweingberger for Artemide, 1966 (€300)
**1 x 'Valentine' typewriter**, metal and red plastic, by Ettore Sottsass and Perry A. King for Olivetti, 1968 (€500)
**3 x 'Grillo' telephone sets**, by Marco Zanuso and Richard Sapper for Siemens, 1965 (€210)
**1 x 'Cubo ts522' radio**, chrome steel and red plastic, by Marco Zanuso and Richard Sapper for Brionvega, 1966 (€360)
**1 x 'Totem' integrated Hi-Fi sound system**,* by Mario Bellini for Brionvega, 1970 (€700)
**2 x 'FD 1102 n.5' wired broadcast receivers**, by Marco Zanuso for Brionvega, 1969 (€300)
**1 x 'RR 126 Mid-Century' record player**,* with integrated speakers and amp, Bakelite, beige wood and plexiglass, by Pier Giacomo and Achille Castiglioni for Brionvega, 1967 (€2,000)
**1 x 'Penny' record player**, Musicalsound, 1975 (€180)

Items marked with a * were valued at less than 50 per cent of their market value because they were either malfunctioning or not in good condition.

Total estimated value: €92,800

Do you see, Giacomo? That house is a museum. Tell me what you want to do with this stuff, and I'll do it. But don't tell me to get rid of it.

Oh, I hope you noticed that in terms of those starred items, we're even: we broke a record player each . . .

Hugs
Marco

# Planes (2000)

1959 – the year he was born – was also the year passengers travelling by plane outnumbered those boarding ships for the first time. Marco Carrera had known that piece of trivia for as long as he could remember: it was a historic event according to his father, an avid reader of sci-fi books where transport was imagined in the skies rather than on solid ground or water. As is often the case with things you have always known, Marco Carrera ended up underestimating this bit of information, cataloguing it as one of his father's harmless fixations.

As it turned out, planes (and flying in general) were one of the most powerful core constituents of his fate. Having previously missed several opportunities to come to terms with this fact, Marco eventually did realise the truth – at the age of forty-one, in one of those mornings that only exist in Rome. Sitting in one of the most beautiful spots in the world, namely outside the so-called 'Granarone' by Palazzo Caffarelli (and specifically on the wooden fence under the pine trees on Via di Monte Caprino), he was reading the shameful accusations that his now ex-wife Marina had fabricated in her deranged divorce petition. Though fairly unremarkable from an architectural perspective, the Granarone is spectacularly situated, overlooking as it does all of the south-western side of the Campidoglio hill down to the Tiber. From there you can see the ruins of the temples of Janus, Juno Sospita, Spes, Apollo Sosianus and Sant'Omobono, as well as the republican-era colonnade in the Forum Holitorium, together with the whole of the San Nicola in Carcere basilica, the Tarpeian Rock, and three quarters of the Theatre of Marcellus. (Incidentally, in the Middle Ages this whole area became pastureland for goats – *capre* in Italian – hence the name 'Monte Caprino'.) Palazzo Caffarelli was built on top of that hill towards the end of the sixteenth century by the Roman aristocratic family of the same name, then purchased (hill and all) by the Prussians in the nineteenth century. The Prussians went on to add several buildings including the aforementioned 'Granarone', which housed the Germanic Institute of Archaeology. The whole area was then repurchased by Rome city council in 1918, following the demise of the Prussian empire. And so it was that in the early 2000s, one of the most beautiful spots in the world ended up housing the city's legal department, including the archive where all court proceedings were filed. That means that anyone being sued or taken to court in Rome had to go there, to the Granarone, to be notified. At which point (it is only human) as soon as they came out of the building, oblivious to the astonishing beauty around them, these people would immediately tear the sealed envelope to read its contents – maybe leaning against a tree, or sitting on the ground or, like Marco Carrera that morning, on the wooden fence. Three other wretched men like him were standing nearby, engrossed in their respective letters: a very young mechanic in his overalls, an elegantly dressed gentleman with his motorbike helmet still on, and a greasy, rough-looking type with grey hair. The mechanic's summons was clearly of a similar nature to Marco's: he could be heard commenting out loud ('that fucking bitch!'), seemingly threatening to beat up the innocent sheet of paper shaking in his hand. And yet, for all his aggression, he looked scared rather than angry – just as Marco Carrera would before long. Because reading his summons on that wondrous morning, surrounded by beauty and history, after months of uncertainty he finally learnt just how hell-bent his ex-wife was on getting rid of him, and how she planned to do it.

After Plan A had been defused by her therapist, Marina had been forced to fall back on Plan B, which – while certainly not as violent – was just as vicious: a divorce petition featuring just about every possible allegation that could be conceived against a husband and a father. All completely unfounded, of course. But as it was, before he could bring a case against her for the extramarital pregnancy that had now almost reached full term – or for the fact she had not allowed him to see their daughter on a regular basis, not to mention the rest of the foul play (Plan A wasn't even worth bringing up in court, her therapist would never have testified) – in short, before he could make these claims against her, he would have to defend himself against the allegations of physical and psychological violence, false imprisonment, battery and abuse, repeated adultery, death threats to Marina's entire family in Slovenia, non-compliance with marital duties, tax evasion, breach of planning permission – the lot. All of it made up (the tax evasion was hers, actually – he had only tried to cover it up. And as for the planning permission, his parents were responsible for the extension of the holiday home in Bolgheri back in that terrible summer when his sister had died, that is 1981, that is twenty years earlier, that is seven years before he and Marina had even met). All of it made up then and strung together by a shoddy narrative peppered with equally made-up details (where the devil is famously to be found), except for one episode that had actually taken place. An insignificant episode, of course, in that preposterous context, but real nonetheless. An episode that had clearly been thrown in with all the lies to remind him that, even though he was being horribly slandered, he was not completely blameless. An episode that occurred when Adele was still sleeping in her cot, so ten years before. In the summer. In Bolgheri. An episode that had been buried deep in the recesses of Marco's memory, but that was clearly still there – and as he read Marina's account of it in the summons, the scene came back to him in all its burning authenticity.

July.

Early afternoon.

Half-light.

Curtain billowing in the sea breeze.

Frantically chirping grasshoppers.

He and Marina are dozing in their bedroom (the one, as it happens, that was built without planning permission in 1981). Next to the bed, on Marina's side, the baby is sleeping in her cot.

Fresh sheets. Fresh pillow. Fresh newborn smell.

Peace.

All of a sudden, a deafening noise. Thunderous, protracted, disastrous, frightening, terrible, apocalyptic noise. In an instant, Marco Carrera goes from floating in and out of sleep to shaking and gasping for breath, adrenaline pumping through his heart, propped up against a pine tree outside their bedroom's French window. That lasts for about five seconds, maybe ten, after which Marco understands what happened and at the same time realises he's bolted out of the room leaving his wife and daughter behind, so he hurries back inside and hugs Marina, who has also woken up with a start and is sitting on the bed, still confused and terrified. He tries to reassure her, to calm her, to explain what happened. The baby, luckily, had remained peacefully asleep throughout it all. He'd been out five seconds, maybe ten . . .

That episode had been virtually erased from Marco's memory, but that morning – conjured up by someone else's recollection – it stood before him intact and vivid as on the day itself: the only true fact in an orgy of lies. According to Marina, he 'cowardly abandoned her and the baby in the room, fleeing alone as soon as danger was detected, which on that occasion was caused by a military jet breaking the sound barrier above them: a harmless occurrence which might have been far more serious and threatening'.

And that was true.

Naturally, his wife's divorce petition failed to mention that it had only been a knee-jerk reaction, and that in fact he had only been away for five, maybe ten seconds (let's say fifteen, for God's sake!). It implied, on the contrary, that he had deliberately run away, and that he had been away long enough to escape, alone, from the impending danger, leaving his wife and baby daughter to fend for themselves, which of course was a very unfair account of the events of that day. That said, the petition also failed to mention what crossed his mind in those few unguarded seconds, before he regained his composure and started behaving like a husband and a father again. It didn't mention where his thoughts had leapt to in that sudden, mad bout of terror. That was his one true shortcoming out of all the shortcomings Marina had in fact fabricated, and the one she couldn't actually be privy to.

And that's when Marco Carrera realised that his father's fixation with planes and the year he was born was not a fixation at all, but a prophecy. He had never given it much thought before – not when he narrowly escaped a plane crash, nor when he married a flight attendant, believing she had escaped that very same crash – but he realised it now, pleading guilty to a single charge out of the hundreds that had been pressed against him. It wasn't so much that he had run away when a military jet from the nearby air base in Grosseto had generated that sonic boom – but rather what he had thought for those few seconds, overwhelmed by fear, as he gasped for breath propped up against a pine tree, anxiously looking at the hedge separating him from the neighbours' garden.

Make it ten seconds: Luisa Luisa Luisa Luisa Luisa Luisa Luisa Luisa Luisa Luisa . . .

# An enchanted sentence (1983)

Marco Carrera
12 Piazza Savonarola
Florence 50132
Italy

Paris, 15 March 1983

Hi Marco,

I imagine you must be wondering who's typed you an entire letter (including the address on the envelope) from Paris. Maybe you went straight to the end to inspect the signature, or flipped the envelope (where I only put my initials, however) or maybe – and that's my favourite option – you immediately sensed it was me. Either way, it is me. It's me writing from Paris, Marco, on my father's typewriter. Yes – I know I haven't been in touch since we moved here.

What am I up to? How am I doing? I'm studying. I like the place I go to every day to study. And so on. I'm not writing to tell you about school.

I think of you often. You're the only Italian I find myself thinking of, together with another guy I can't quite get out of my head. I think of him when I'm sad and of you when I'm happy. And not just when I put on your red jumper, like I did today. I think of you especially when I'm in a taxi, in the small hours, of how you liked to go buy freshly baked bread but were afraid of bumping into your mother and her friends. I think of you when I'm in a taxi on my way home from a party, late at night, tipsy, and I feel like 'merrily wasted potential'. That's what you called me once.

I'd never been in a taxi before. I don't think I was ever in a taxi by myself in Florence. I had no idea how wonderful it is to be in a taxi at night. Flagging it from the pavement, like they do in films. I knew nothing at all about taxis. For instance, I've learnt that if the 'Taxi Parisien' sign is orange it means the cab's taken, and if it's white it's free. And when it is white, I swear, all you have to do is lift your arm and they stop. Extraordinary. But maybe you knew this already? Of course you did. Not me though, I didn't know. And once I'm in, and I've just given my address to the driver, and he starts the car, and we're gliding through lit up and deserted streets and squares, I begin to feel that all the things I've done in the long night that's just come to an end start disappearing: gone are the faces of the guys I've danced with, drunk with, smoked with, gone are their platitudes, everything goes, and I feel good. It's in those moments that I find myself thinking of you. I feel all the unnecessary things slipping away from me and I realise that if you remove all the unnecessary things from my life, all that's left is you.

And yet it's not easy to think about you. Especially after what happened. And I have very few things, so very few memories to hang on to. The one I almost always conjure up is of you sitting on my sofa in Bolgheri, your Walkman and headphones isolating you from the world, while my friends and I eat ravioli. Maybe it's because it's late, or because I'm in a taxi, but that seems like a nice memory.

And I dream of you too, sometimes.

I dreamt of you last night, for instance: that's why I'm writing to you, reverse-breaking the promise I extorted from you (I can't even remember why) never to write to me again.

It was a beautiful dream, Marco. Crystal-clear. Serene. Shame I woke up halfway through it. I remember it well because I wasn't able to get back to sleep afterwards, and I mulled it over for hours. I was lying in a hammock in some sort of Mexican-style patio with a huge ceiling fan slowly spinning, and you were perched on one corner of the hammock, dressed in white, pushing it back and forth with your legs. We were playing a strange game, laughing in a way that's hard for me to explain. You were challenging me to say some sort of enchanted sentence and I couldn't. It was a very strange sentence, I wrote it down as soon as I woke up: 'When I was eighteen the Benedictine friars taught me to speak, and I learnt it all in just one week.' I swear that was the sentence. And I couldn't say it, I kept getting it wrong, and the more I got it wrong the more we laughed, and the more we laughed the more I got it wrong. In the end, we were laughing so hard that you couldn't say it anymore either. And then your father turned up – inscrutable as always – and we asked him to say it, and he tried and got it wrong. I can't tell you how that made us laugh, and after a while he was laughing too, because he kept trying and getting it wrong. He just couldn't, there was no way around it: he'd say 'When I was eighteen the Franciscan friars . . .' or 'learnt me to speak . . .' It truly was an enchanted sentence and we were crying with laughter. Then I woke up. It sounds like a silly dream, but I promise it wasn't. And there was no awkwardness at all between us. Not even with your father. Everything was effortless. But then again, it was a dream.

Still mesmerised by my dream, I got up, went out, went to the gym (I go to the gym now) and witnessed a wonderful phenomenon: it was snowing, but the sun was out. I swear. Under the Arc de Triomphe the flakes were coming down thick, heavy, sodden – but from there onwards the sky was clear and bright, and Notre Dame, in the distance, glistened in the sun. And that wasn't a dream anymore, it was real. And this is a rambling letter, I know, but it doesn't matter. I only hope it won't make you feel awkward, that it won't cause any 'imaginary' problems. (I've just realised that the last time I saw you was in that gym, centuries ago. An awkward encounter.) That's why it's important to keep thinking about you when I'm in a taxi, and if possible to keep dreaming of you like I did last night. Besides, if I'm dreaming of you it means I'm sleeping. I'm so fed up with insomnia, you know, and with thoughts of that other guy sneaking in on me every now and again.

Hugs (if I may)
Luisa

# The last night of innocence (1979)

When they were about twenty, Marco Carrera and Duccio Chilleri started hitting casinos abroad – in Austria mostly, and Yugoslavia – but after a while the long road trips meticulously planned by Duccio (complete with pit stops in brothels and restaurants) had lost their shine for Marco. Aside from the fact that those ten to twelve hours cooped up with Duccio in his Fiat X1/9 had become too much to bear, he felt the need for more professional outings, entirely focused on optimising gambling outcomes: no messing about and no whores. In fact – as we saw – while The Omen still enjoyed spending time with him, the appeal of just hanging around with Duccio had long vanished for Marco. All that was left was the thrill of showing up to casinos accompanied by such a formidable partner – with his slick roulette systems, his supernatural intuition for craps, his animal instinct for blackjack. Therefore, one day Marco took the matter into his own hands and decided that for once they would travel by plane, even though Duccio was afraid of flying. It took him four entire evenings to overcome Duccio's aversion to 'iron birds', using the very same rational arguments – ironically – that he used with his other friends to neutralise their fear of The Omen. In the end he brought him round, and on a fragrant May afternoon the two friends turned up at

Pisa airport planning to spend the long weekend in Ljubljana (they'd driven to that same casino the year before, and won big). The journey would be long too: Marco had hunted out a low-cost charter flight operated by a Yugoslavian carrier called Koper Aviopromet, which for some reason broke up the Pisa–Ljubljana route with a mystifying stop in Larnaca, Cyprus. As a result, the journey took four times as long (while the cost of tickets was mysteriously cut in half).

Duccio Chilleri was very nervous. Marco had given him a couple of sedatives he'd pilfered from his sister's private pharmacy (always well-stocked with psychoactive drugs), but his friend's anxiety showed no sign of abating. Once they'd found their seats, Duccio became uneasy, pointing at the worn-out seats and overhead lockers – which, in his opinion, were clear signs that the aircraft was not being maintained properly. But what terrified him most were the people who kept boarding the plane. The wrong sort of people, he kept saying, doomed people. Look at them – he kept saying – they look dead already. Look at him, look at that other one, they look like they're getting ready for their own funeral. Marco kept telling him to relax, but The Omen grew increasingly agitated.

Suddenly he leapt up and, as passengers kept boarding the plane, he started shouting, asking if there was anyone famous on board – a footballer, an actor, a VIP of any kind – anyone living the good life. The other passengers looked at him bemusedly as they shuffled along the aisle to find their seats and someone asked him what his problem was. You – said Duccio Chilleri – are my problem, because you're dead already and you want to kill me too. Marco grabbed his shoulders, pulled him back into his seat, and did his best to calm him down. Braving the stench emanating from Duccio's jacket, he hugged him while also trying to placate those sitting around them, who were beginning to get annoyed. Everything's fine, he told his friend. Sure – replied Duccio – we're all going to die and that's just fine. Eventually, his face hidden in his hands, muttering and holding back his tears, he stopped bothering the other passengers and seemed to resign himself to his fate. But when a group of boy scouts boarded the aircraft the situation took a sudden turn for the worse. Duccio shot up from his seat: No! Not the bloody boy scouts! He stepped into the aisle to block the first one, a heavy-set, hairy boy who looked particularly ridiculous in his scout leader uniform. Just where do you think you're going? The boy looked confused – maybe he thought Duccio was a flight attendant, because he showed him his boarding pass. Get the fuck out of here! Run along now, chop-chop! Marco got up again to placate him, but this time Duccio Chilleri had completely lost control: he grabbed and shook the terrified boy scouts' heads (Murderers – he shouted – get out!), and when a few of them started fighting back, hurling insults and shoving him, Marco Carrera realised the weekend in Ljubljana was over. Pretending to be a doctor (he was only a second-year medicine student), he diagnosed his friend with an imaginary 'type-B epileptic fit', and demanded they reopen the door to let him out. The crew couldn't believe their luck when they were offered a chance to get rid of that madman: after recovering their luggage from the hold directly on the runway (Pisa airport was rather casually managed back then) the two friends headed towards the terminal as the plane started rolling.

As soon as they were back on solid ground, Duccio calmed down – in fact he was absurdly euphoric, like someone who had literally just escaped from hell. Marco was furious, but in order to avoid another scene he kept his temper in check and withdrew into a sullen silence. Sullen but also increasingly sinister, because underneath the blistering anger and the shame (the shame that made him run away like a thief in the night for fear that news of Duccio's tantrum would spread beyond the plane where it had taken place), underneath all that, for the first time he realised how other people would interpret that incident. His friend had boarded a plane and had a panic attack, ruining a carefully planned weekend. That, and *only* that, was what had happened as far as Marco was concerned – but what about everyone else who knew Duccio Chilleri? What remarkable, terrifying feat had The Omen performed on that plane?

Marco pictured how any of his other friends would have reacted and he immediately felt a gripping sensation around his stomach that he just couldn't shift. That night – after depositing Duccio outside his house without even saying goodbye and making up a story for his parents – he tossed and turned in bed, thinking over and over again about their fellow passengers, abandoned to their fate on that plane. About the poor, unsuspecting boy scouts (just where did they think they were going?). About the Eastern European flight attendants with their heavy make-up, foolishly relieved to see him and Duccio get off the plane after that outrageous row (when actually, according to the eye of the storm theory, they should have formed a human chain to stop him from leaving).

As Marco Carrera lay in bed, tormented by these thoughts, sweating between his sheets and unable to fall asleep (and least of all to enjoy the fragrant smell of the star jasmine wafting in from the half-closed window), unbeknown to him the tragedy had already played out off the northern coast of Cyprus, and the Koper Aviopromet DC-9-30 that never made it to Larnaca had been swallowed by the Mediterranean. The people Marco was thinking about with a mix of pity and apprehension were all dead.

Still unaware of what had happened, Marco Carrera did eventually fall asleep – late and racked by anxiety, but he did – and among his many other last nights, that was his last night of innocence.

# Urania (2008)

To: Giacomo jackcarr62@yahoo.com
Sent: 17 October 2008 23:39
Subject: Urania novels
From: Marco Carrera

Dear Giacomo,

Today I'd like to talk to you about Dad's (almost) complete collection of Urania sci-fi novels. This collection, albeit incomplete, is worth a lot of money – remember how meticulous Dad was with these books, wrapping them one by one in that glossy paper? Because of that, they are still in astonishingly good condition after fifty or sixty years – but that's not what I want to talk to you about. The way I see it, these books should be yours for the reasons I'm about to explain, and seeing as they don't take up much space, I'd be happy to keep them for you if you don't want them, but I wouldn't even dream of selling them.

Anyway. The collection. It runs from n.1 to n.899, that is from 1952 to 1981, with only six missing volumes. Here are the missing ones, and why they are missing:

**n.20, *Pebble in the sky*, by Isaac Asimov (Urania – 20 July 1953)**

It's rather odd – don't you think? – that after regularly purchasing the first nineteen volumes, Dad (who at twenty-seven had just completed his master's) should miss this one, apparently one of the best novels by his favourite author. And he did, in fact, buy it, because on the bookshelf in his study where he always kept his Urania novels (it's listed as 'Sergesto modular bookshelf' in the inventory I sent you last month, and you must remember it because you had an identical one in your bedroom, where it still is in fact, together with your comics), on that bookshelf, I was saying, between volume n.19, *Prelude to Space* by Arthur C. Clarke, and n.21, *Terror on Earth*, by Jimmy Guieu, is a card dated 19 April 1970 that says 'lent to A.' 'A.', you'll agree with me, must be his friend Aldo Mansutti. Remember 'Aldino' as Dad called him? The one who died in that absurd motorbike accident Mum and Dad wouldn't stop talking about (clearly the reason our parents were so reluctant to let us have mopeds). I have a vivid recollection of us all going to Aldino's funeral, I was definitely in secondary school, probably year 6, or beginning of year 7 – and so it must have been precisely 1970. Here's what must have happened: Dad lent the book to Aldino, replacing it with a card on the shelf because he cared about his collection. Shortly afterwards, however, Aldino had died, and Dad obviously never thought of claiming it back from his wife (Titti, remember her? Titti Mansutti. I saw her a few days ago – she looks so old now – for some other business I'll tell you about.) What is more, by that point, i.e. in 1970, the collection was already incomplete, there were five more missing volumes: n.203, 204, 449, 450 and 451. Stay with me Giacomo, keep reading.

**n.203, *The Tide Went Out*, by Charles Eric Maine (Urania – 10 May 1959) and n.204, *Race Without End*, by Gordon R. Dickson (Urania – 24 May 1959)**

There were no cards replacing these volumes on the shelf, which means Dad hadn't lent them to a friend – this time he didn't buy them at all. And looking at the dates, I think I know why: Irene's infamous high chair accident. Remember that? They must have told us the story a thousand times: Irene fell off her high chair in the kitchen in the old house on Piazza Dalmazia, hit her head and ended up in a coma for two days at Meyer Hospital. Mum swore she'd give up smoking if Irene made it; Irene made it, Mum didn't quit smoking. Irene made a full recovery but still blamed all her future issues on that fall, etc. The two of us weren't around at the time, but it's fair to say that (at least until her death) Irene's fall had been the most dramatic event in our family. So dramatic – and that's what I was getting at – that it prevented Dad from buying his beloved Urania novels twice, i.e. for a period of 28 days. No one can confirm my hypothesis now, but as you may remember, what made the whole thing even more dramatic was the fact that Mum was pregnant with me. (Equally dramatic, perhaps, was the fact that Mum didn't manage to quit smoking even though she was expecting.)

Whenever I pictured the scene, I'd always imagine Irene falling off her high chair and fainting and Mum having to get on the ambulance with her and then sit by her bedside at the hospital – all while being heavily pregnant. But actually, if we assume she was only two or three months pregnant, everything adds up. I was born on 2 December, right? Which means I was conceived at the beginning of March. The two missing volumes are from May, and so Mum must indeed have been in her first trimester. Mum wasn't heavily pregnant then, and this does explain why Dad missed those two volumes: Irene was in intensive care, then being monitored in hospital, then just home from hospital. After about a month, once the danger had passed, he went back to regularly buying his novels (n.205, *The Dawning Light*, by Robert Randall – 7 June 1959) and kept at it without missing a single one for over seven years, until we get no fewer than three missing volumes in a row, namely:

**n.449, *The Genocides*, by Thomas M. Disch (Urania – 20 November 1966);**
**n.450, *There's Always a War* – a collection of short stories by Walter F. Moudy, Poul Anderson, Robert E. Margroff, Piers Anthony, Andrew J. Offutt (Urania – 4 December 1966);**
**n.451, *Of Godlike Power*, by Mack Reynolds (Urania – 18 December 1966)**

Here, the reason is obvious: the flood. Dad was busy rescuing cattle from the fields with the council's rubber dinghies and then rescuing books from the National Library together with the other 'Mud Angels'. But – you must be wondering – if he couldn't buy these three volumes because of the flood, then how was he able to buy n.448, *The Chrysalids*, by John Wyndham, published on 6 November 1966, when Florence was still literally under water? To explain this, my dear Giacomo, we need to get to the reason I think this collection should be yours. It's something I've discovered by complete chance, which is precisely what makes it seem so precious.

So, here's what happened. As I was browsing the volumes, all neatly stored on the Sergesto modular bookshelf, I came across a title I knew: *Starship Troopers* by Robert Anson

Heinlein. Heinlein is one of the few sci-fi authors I've read, and the title reminded me of a film I'd seen. So I picked it up and yes, it was indeed the book that inspired a mediocre nineties film also called *Starship Troopers*. But let's get to the point: while I was checking that reference I also saw, on the first page, the one immediately after the cover where you find the name of the author, the title and the publishing house – what do you call that again? Where authors sign their name, what do you call that? Title page? Let me check. Yes. A title page, according to Wikipedia, 'is the page at or near the front which displays its title, subtitle, author, publisher, and edition'. That's it. So, as I was saying, I saw something had been written in pencil on that page, in Dad's handwriting. A few lines, that I reproduce here in full: 'Good morning Ladies and Gentlemen! I'm about to introduce you to my new friend, Miss Giovanna Carrera . . . or perhaps Mr Giacomo Carrera . . . who knows . . . Ah here we go . . . Here comes the nurse . . . Can't quite see yet . . . Ah yes . . . Ladies and Gentlemen, say hello to Giacomo!'

Isn't that amazing? Mum had just given birth to you and there he was – young, excited, completely cut off from all the action, not even knowing if you were a boy or a girl, smoking his Murattis and scribbling nonsense on the title page of one of his Urania novels in a hospital corridor. So different from our experience as fathers: we knew the sex of our children months in advance, and saw them being born while wearing scrubs and propping up our wives . . .

And that's why I think you should be keeping this collection in your house on Chapel Hill, the house I've only ever seen from above on Google Earth.

And now let's get to the conundrum of how Dad managed to get his hands on the volume dated 6 November 1966 despite the flood. After reading Dad's lines I closed the book and paused for a while, ruminating (remember this term? Remember who used it all the time?), then I snapped out of my trance, and as I was putting down the book I noticed a red square on the cover, bottom left, displaying the price (150 lira), the volume number (276) and the date of publication: 25 February 1962. Now, as it happens, you were born on 12 February: so how could Dad be holding a book that wouldn't be published for another thirteen days? I was mystified for a moment, but then I had a brainwave. I remembered that when I played tennis, I had a subscription to *Match Ball* magazine – which was published fortnightly – and I would always get the latest issue several days before the date marked on the cover. For a while I thought that was a special treat for subscribers – some sort of preview – until one day I (rather brutally) discovered that the magazine was on newsagents' shelves several days before the date on the cover, too. Having picked up on that, I started noticing that the same was true of several other weeklies I'd find lying around the house, like *Panorama* and *L'Espresso* or even crossword magazines. It must have been a psychological trick to give out an impression of being hot off the press, so that readers wouldn't think they were reading old news if they picked up an issue dated four, five or even six days before. Even though it doesn't make much sense, I figured that's what must have happened with Dad's Urania novels too. It's quite likely that the date on the cover coincided, in fact, with the last of the fourteen days the volume would be on sale. This means that when Dad took Mum, in labour, to the hospital on 12 February 1962 (it was a Monday, I checked on my computer) the novel he brought with him had only just come out, dated 24 February. Dad might have even bought it at the hospital's newsstand after they took Mum to the labour ward.

That's why Dad owned the volume dated 6 November 1966, even though on that day, he had already spent forty-eight hours on a fire brigade rubber dinghy rescuing cattle adrift on hay bales: because that volume had been out for thirteen days already.

After those three missing volumes from 1966, Dad didn't skip a single one for fifteen years – which is truly impressive: from n.452 (*The Secret Service Book*, short stories by Asimov, Tucker, Van Vogt, Martino and Philip K. Dick), his collection carries on uninterrupted all the way to n.899, *Commune 2000 A.D.* by Mack Reynolds. Four hundred and forty-seven consecutive volumes Dad bought, wrapped in glossy paper, read and then neatly stored on his bookshelf as the price of those books went from 200 to 1,500 lira, and as the world, Italy, Florence and our family were being swept up by all manner of events.

I left the last volume in the collection for last, because it is the very symbol of things coming to an end. I'm looking at it right now. I see the white cover with a red circle in the middle, the bizarre illustration (a boy and a girl standing in a park, talking to an older man sat on a bench – all naked – plus other naked figures between the trees in the background). I see the title (*Commune 2000 A.D.*) and the author (Mack Reynolds). I see the date, too: 23 August 1981.

But 23 August 1981 is the day the world ended. That volume, however, had already been out for thirteen days, i.e. since the tenth, when the end of the world was still unimaginable. I bet Dad bought it before the mid-August bank holiday at the newsagents' in Castagneto Carducci where he got all his newspapers, and I bet he read it in a couple of days as he always did, on the beach – or in bed, lying on his right side, facing away from Mum (because the house in Bolgheri was always full in August, so they had to sleep in the same room). The next volume would have been available from Monday, 24 August (perhaps not in Castagneto, perhaps there it would have arrived on the Tuesday or the Wednesday), but Urania novels – like everything else – had suddenly become irrelevant to him. And this time there was no going back. Mack Reynolds' *Commune 2000 A.D.* is Dad's last sci-fi novel, the last one in his (almost) complete collection, which runs from n.1 to n.899. The last one of his life.

All right, Giacomo, I blamed you, and it was awful of me to blame you. But it's been thirty years, for fuck's sake. I apologise for blaming you, I apologise for making our family's life even more unbearable than it already was for so many days – days that kept piling up on top of each other, and yet were still too close to that wretched day. But it's been thirty years. We were boys, now we're men. We couldn't be strangers even if we wanted to. Siblings usually fall out over their inheritance once their parents have died – it would be nice if we made up over our inheritance, for a change. More than anything, it would be typical of our family for things to work the wrong way round.

Answer me,
Marco

# Gospodineeeee! (1974)

It was early on a Sunday morning and Piazza Savonarola had vanished. The trees had vanished, the sky had vanished, the cars had vanished. Nothing was there anymore. It was just like the film he'd watched with his mother over Christmas, the one where the old man gets lost in the fog outside his house: Marco Carrera was lost in the fog, right outside his house. Fog was an extremely rare phenomenon in Florence, especially fog like that. He could barely see his own feet.

It was early on a Sunday morning and it was an utterly senseless day. There were traffic restrictions in place ('austerity measures' they called it) which was a cruel twist of fate in and of itself: Marco had spent a year working side by side with his parents, getting along with his brother and sister, getting good grades in school – a whole year of common sense and level-headedness and patience, all so they'd buy him a Vespa. He'd barely tasted victory when, on the very day of his birthday, an emergency law was passed, preventing him from riding his Vespa on Sundays. Oil had become a commodity that needed to be rationed (just like that, overnight?), and therefore so had petrol. Marco Carrera couldn't make sense of what he heard on the news. In his view, before a commodity became so scarce you had to ration it, there should at least be some sort of intermediate phase where you begin to realise what is going on. Instead, everything had happened at once: there had been a war somewhere, OPEC countries had decided to limit oil exports and just like that, you were expected to shut everything down. In the space of a month, streetlights were switched off at night, TV shows cut short, central heating at home severely curtailed and all private vehicles banned on Sundays – including Vespas. Was it really that easy to bring his civilisation to its knees? And did it have to happen just as he turned fourteen and got his first taste of adult life? Just as he quit skiing so he could enjoy his Vespa on Sundays, even in winter? No more endless weekends spent at the Abetone ski resort training and racing non-stop down the slopes throughout winter and spring, only to see the locals (who, let's face it, were twice, three times faster) swoosh past him.

But no. Walking it was.

And that day, to top it all off, the fog.

It was early on a Sunday morning. Marco Carrera had barely taken a few steps and already he hesitated, a few yards from his house, unable to orientate himself. Where was he? On the pavement or in the middle of the street? Was his house to the left? To the right? There was no sound of traffic to help him get his bearings, either.

He was meant to be at the train station by eight thirty – Verdi, Pielleggero, the Sollima twins and him were to catch the train for Lucca together with their coach and one of their tennis club managers to compete in the final of the first regional indoor doubles championship (beginners' category). And that was another good reason to quit skiing: air domes were becoming popular, which meant tennis tournaments could be held all year round, and it made a lot more sense for Marco to focus on tennis instead of continuing to split his time between tennis and skiing. Despite his developmental issues, in fact, his tennis game was getting stronger – he had become more precise, more aggressive. This (coupled with the fact that his opponents tended to underestimate him because of his height) had enabled him to achieve some pretty astonishing results that year. Skiing, on the other hand, had no psychological or strategic dimension, no direct opponent: there was only gravity, and his four feet nine and seven stones were too big a handicap.

It was early on a Sunday morning then, the streetlights on the square were out and Marco could see nothing but fog all around him. The plan was to get to the bus stop on Via Giacomini (buses, at least, were still running), and then get off at Santa Maria Novella train station. This, however, had suddenly turned into a formidable challenge. Where had Via Giacomini gone? Normally, it would be on the opposite side of the square from his house, alongside the church. That said, where was his house? Where was the square? Where was the church?

The accident was sudden and frightening, like accidents often are. Everything happened at once: the bang, the crash, the jammed car horn, even the shouting: everything seemed to materialise at the same time, with no apparent chronology (after all, as good old Albert said, where there is no space there can be no time, either).

The shouting consisted of a single word that Marco had never heard before:

– *Gospodineeee!*

A single word he'd never heard before, set off like a flare in the fog. As if to say (ostensibly to him, Marco Carrera, since there was no one else around): 'Help! We're over here!'

But here, where?

– *Gospodineeee!*

And so Marco started walking in the direction of that sound. As he took the first tentative steps, he felt as if time had started flowing again, too. The jammed car horn had stopped.

Clanking noises. More incomprehensible words from a male voice – while a woman kept yelling *Gospidineeee!*

At that moment a woman emerged from the white wall of fog, frighteningly close. A Romani woman. Her face was covered in blood and twisted in a desperate grimace: *Gospidineeee!* The male voice felt very close now, but the source itself remained invisible. A figure did appear – an elderly Romani man, blood streaming from his forehead and down his neck – but he wasn't the one speaking. A Ford Taunus appeared beside him: the doors were open and a puff of smoke billowed out from the bonnet. Marco kept moving forward in that enormous bowl of milk, not knowing what to do, not knowing what he was looking for. The other car, perhaps? Was he looking for the other car? Did he have a premonition? Did he recognise the car horn?

– *Gospodineeee!*

There it was, the other car. Hurled against a lamppost, the nose all but obliterated. A Peugeot 504, by the looks of it – like his father's. Metallic grey, by the looks of it – like his father's. And was that another Romani man, younger and apparently unharmed, opening the door and dragging someone out of the car? Someone unconscious, or dead.

A girl, by the looks of it.

His sister Irene, by the looks of it.

– *Gospodineeee!*

Dad, can I borrow your car? No, Irene – don't start. But I have to go skiing, I have to go to the beach, I have to go to a party, how do I get there? Can't someone drive you? But it's just me here, who's going to drive me! Irene, you don't have your driving licence yet. But I have a provisional licence. With a provisional licence you can't drive unless there's someone with a licence in the car with you. But my friends all do. Well, you don't. Ah come on, I'll be careful, I promise. No. Are you afraid they'll stop me? Yes. But they won't! I said no. Well I'm taking the car anyway. Don't you dare . . .

How many times had Marco witnessed that endless diatribe in the past few weeks. And how (as always) he'd rooted for her, for his incredibly smart and incredibly tormented sister, his North Star, his role model! Angry, angsty, manic, with that bluish vein sticking out on her forehead that made her so look different – noble almost, rebellious, superior. Now she was lying there on the ground, in front of him, where the young man had carefully deposited her – he was trying to resuscitate her actually, breaking every basic first aid rule (not that anyone, there, would have known) but undoubtedly with the best intentions. She looked pale, seemingly unharmed, unconscious. Irene. Was she dead?

– *Gospodineeee!*

No, she wasn't dead, quite the opposite in fact, there was not a single scratch on her. She had just passed out, as Marco would find out in a minute. But the way he looked at her in that minute was exactly the same way he'd look at her corpse, seven years from then, at seven in the morning, in the morgue at Cecina Hospital: the same desperation, the same pity and rage and powerlessness and horror and tenderness. The way Marco, in some mysterious way, had always known he'd end up looking at her one day. Like that summer night when he was barely five, in Bolgheri, and he saw the most spectacular shooting star on the same beach where Irene would die, and everyone (his mother, his mother's friend, his mother's friend's daughters and Irene herself) asked him to make a wish, and without even knowing what that meant he said: 'I wish that Irene does not *suicide herself*.'

Irene, his idol. The sister who never wanted him around (never wanted anyone around for that matter, at least no one from her family). The sister who always left a trail of calamities in her wake: falls, accidents, broken bones, arguments, depression, drugs, psychotherapy. In short, at the age of eighteen she had already become a thorn in the side of her family, with the sole exception of Marco: he had always been immune from the general feeling of resigned pity that seemed to follow her around. He was the only one who always understood her and justified her and rooted for her and *loved* her despite her antics.

Several years after that morning, after all the other tragedies Irene would go on to inflict on him and his family – including, obviously, her own death – several years after he lost his parents, and several years after (beyond unspeakable) losing his own daughter – that's it, it's out now – several years after *everything*, one might say, Marco Carrera, now almost old and almost alone, almost about to die himself, would underline this phrase in a novel he was reading: 'with the darkness and confusion inside'. He was thinking of her, of Irene, who didn't die that time in the fog, nor on many other occasions when she could have died, but who did eventually die all the same – too young, too soon, for real.

It was early on a Sunday morning. *Gospodine*, in Serbo-Croatian, means 'Oh my God'.

# Second letter on hummingbirds (2005)

Marco Carrera
117/b Strada delle Fornaci
Villa Le Sabine
Castagneto Carducci (LI)
57022
Italy

Kastellorizo, 8 August 2005

Suppose I say summer,
write the word 'hummingbird',
put it in an envelope,
take it down the hill
to the box. When you open
my letter you will recall
those days and how much,
just how much, I love you.

~~Raymond Carver~~
Luisa

# A thread, a wizard, three cracks (1992–1995)

It should be common knowledge – and yet it isn't – that the course of every new relationship is set from the start, once and for all, every time; and that in order to know in advance how things will end, you only have to look at how they began. At the start of any human connection, in fact, there is always a moment of clarity where you can see it grow, stretch through time, evolve as it will evolve and end as it will end – all at once. It's easy to see because in fact the whole relationship is already captured in its own beginning, just as the shape of all things is already contained within their first manifestation. But it is only a moment, and then that prophetic vision disappears, or is erased from memory – and it is only because of this lost knowledge that relationships then go on to generate surprise, cause harm, bring us unforeseen pleasure or pain. We see it – at the beginning we really *do* see it, for a fleeting, unclouded moment – but then for the rest of our life it's gone. Just as when we get up to go to the bathroom at night, fumbling around in the dark in our bedroom, and we feel lost, and we switch on the light for a split second then switch it off straight away, and in that flash we see the way, but only for the time it takes to relieve ourselves and get back to bed. The following night we'll feel lost all over again.

When his daughter's disorder first manifested itself, around the time she was three, Marco Carrera experienced that flash of clarity. He saw everything, but that vision was so unbearable (it had to do with his sister Irene) that he immediately erased it from his memory and went on living as though it had never happened. Perhaps psychoanalysis might have helped him recover it, but besieged as he was by its disciples, Marco had developed an unconquerable aversion to its methods. Or so he said. A therapist, of course, would counter that his aversion was nothing more than a defence mechanism, a strategy he had adopted to justify erasing that vision. Nevertheless, the vision was immediately and permanently erased, never to resurface again, not even after things went the way they were meant to go – the way Marco Carrera knew they would, for a moment, at the beginning, and then never again.

The onset of the child's disorder coincided with the beginning of her relationship with her father, which up until that day had remained rather abstract. This was prompted by the child herself, following what was probably the first autonomous decision of her life. It was on a bright August Sunday – as father and daughter were having breakfast in the kitchen in Bolgheri and Marina was still dozing in bed – that Adele Carrera decided to announce there was a thread attached to her back. Despite her age, she was very clear in her description: there was a thread anchoring her to the nearest wall, at all times. For some reason, no one but her could see it, which in turn meant she always had to be with her back against the wall so people wouldn't trip over it or get tangled up. And what happens, asked Marco, when you can't be with your back against the wall? How do you manage then? Adele answered that in those situations she had to be very careful, and if anyone walked behind her back and got tangled in her thread, she had to walk around them to free them – and then she showed him how. Marco kept asking questions. This thread at the back – did everyone have it, or was it just her? Just her. And didn't she think that was odd? Yes, it was odd. Odd that she had it or that other people didn't? Odd that other people didn't. So how do you manage at home? – he asked – how do you manage with Mummy, with me? But Daddy, explained the child, you never walk behind my back. And so it was in that precise moment – faced with the revelation that he never walked behind his daughter's back – that Marco Carrera felt a shiver down his spine and his relationship with his daughter started in earnest. And it was also in that precise moment that he saw, that he knew, that he got scared – and therefore he immediately forgot that he saw, that he knew and that he got scared.

For the rest of the summer that thread remained their secret. Or rather, Marco immediately told Marina, but without saying anything to his daughter, who had asked him not to mention it to anyone. Marina, therefore, made an effort never to walk behind her daughter's back – on the beach, at home, in the garden – with mixed results, because she always remembered too late. On those occasions, she watched her daughter patiently and meticulously retrace her steps to disentangle the thread, and she was deeply moved. Then she watched Adele's grandparents, completely unaware of the thread, *regularly* walk behind her back (were they doing it on purpose?) and Adele backtrack with the same patience, the same meticulous determination – and she was deeply moved by that too. She observed the blossoming relationship between Adele and her father and admired his talent for never – *ever* – walking behind her back, and was again deeply moved. Marco saw how moved she was, which in turn moved him. It was a moving summer for them both. They weren't even remotely worried.

Adele was due to start preschool in September, so Marco convinced her to tell her mother about the thread before they left Bolgheri: the child then repeated what she had explained to Marco a few weeks before, in that same kitchen. Marina was moved. She also asked her daughter a few questions – practical questions, less sentimental than Marco's – and therefore more difficult for the child to answer: when did she realise she had the thread? What was it made of? Could it break? From Adele's (albeit confused) answers, Marco and Marina surmised that the idea of having a thread attached to her back came from watching fencing with them on TV: Giovanna Trillini and the Italian women's foil team at the Barcelona Olympics, the body cord attached to their white vests to record the hits – and then celebrations, gold medals, smiling female faces and ruffled hair suddenly emerging from those droid-like masks – all this, they surmised, had made a deep impression. They weren't worried.

They decided not to mention it to the preschool staff, at least not until there was an incident of some sort. There weren't any. It was a tiny school, crammed in a stuffy flat on Largo Chiarini, where it was easy to keep your back against the walls without being too conspicuous. Adele's problems were the same as all the other children's: separation anxiety, settling into a new routine. No one noticed the thread. Adele, after all, remained calm and patient when someone walked behind her back: little by little, she would trace back their movements to disentangle the thread without anyone ever noticing, children and adults alike. At home, Marco and Marina had turned the thread into a game: Marco pretended it was a skipping rope, Marina a washing line. For that whole year – a happy year – they didn't worry. The following year went off without a hitch too, except for a single incident when the school took the children to visit a farm in Maccarese and Adele refused to get off the bus. Usually, the child had no issues being outdoors and she always found a way to manage her thread, but that day she dug her heels and one of the teachers had to stay on the bus with her. When her mother picked her up in the afternoon and learnt what had happened, she immediately understood the reason behind what the staff called 'Adele's tantrum', but she was in a hurry and didn't think it made sense to explain the whole thread situation there and then. Once in the car, however, she asked her daughter if she had insisted on staying on the bus because of her thread, and the child answered that she did: there were too many animals in that place, and it was very dangerous to be around animals with that thread. She said this calmly and rationally, as if she was truly concerned about everyone's safety, and Marina was moved. That evening she told Marco, and he was moved too. Then they played with Adele and her thread. They weren't worried.

They moved house, and after the summer they enrolled Adele in a different school. Not that it was easier for them to get to – on the contrary: it was past Tor Marancia, on Via di Tor Carbone, between the Via Appia and the Via Ardeatina, practically in the countryside – but it came highly recommended and was situated in a big airy villa that had belonged to celebrated Italian actress Anna Magnani. That, at least, was Marina's pitch; Marco, for his part, saw it as nothing more than a hindrance (this idea that you always had to change, improve, expand, grow – all the time): it was in the sticks, it stank and it was much more expensive. Marina had prevailed only because she had committed to doing all the school runs, *every single one* – and that was the first real crack, the first observable wound on the (otherwise still intact) surface of their relationship. Because obviously Marina couldn't get Adele to school and pick her up every single day, which meant that from time to time Marco had to endure the forty-five-minute drive, and as a result they both ended up complaining: she blamed Marco for doing the bare minimum and not helping out enough, and he blamed

Marina for not keeping her side of the bargain. What is more, there were issues from the start. Adele didn't want to go to the new school, and when they picked her up they'd always find her crying alone in a corner. Marco saw this as proof that he was right, that moving her to a different school had been a mistake, that Adele was suffering for being needlessly uprooted, that she missed her old teachers and friends, etc. Marina, however, asked her in front of him if (by any chance) the reason she was unhappy had anything to do with the thread, and she said yes – without adding anything more.

Before they got round to requesting an appointment with the head teacher, she summoned them. Before she got round to explaining why they'd been summoned, they told her about the thread. The head teacher didn't take it well, she seemed shocked that such a serious matter had been kept from her. Marco and Marina tried to reassure her, but only succeeded in demonstrating to what point they'd been underestimating the situation for the past two years – which in turn earned them a stern rebuke. This, the headteacher explained, was a clear perception disorder, probably of an obsessive-hallucinatory nature, and it had to be treated, not encouraged. She had a degree in child psychology and she knew what she was talking about.

And so it was that a therapist made his first appearance in Marco Carrera's daughter's life: Dr Nocetti. He was some kind of ageless man-child: he sat slumped at his desk like an old man but his eyes were as lively as that of a child. He had thin, limp ash-grey hair and miraculously wrinkle-free skin. His glasses (that no one ever saw him wear) were constantly hanging from a chain around his neck. Marco could never quite follow his line of reasoning, even though it was clear that he was a very smart man – he just seemed to have lived in a different world, reading only books that Marco had never heard of, watching films he hadn't seen, listening to music he had never come across, and vice versa. In that context, it was impossible to build any kind of rapport with him beyond what was strictly necessary, which made things easier. Naturally, given Marco's aversion to therapists, trusting him with his daughter required a considerable leap of faith: faith in the head teacher who sent them there, faith in the diplomas hanging on the walls of Dr Nocetti's practice on Via dei Colli della Farnesina (another absurdly long drive), and above all faith in Marina, who had felt reassured by that extremely bizarre man from the start. Once he'd taken this leap of faith, however, the situation quickly normalised: they began taking Adele to his practice twice a week ('they' meaning Marina nearly all the time, Marco almost never) and stopped feeling like the foolish and inconsiderate parents the head teacher thought they were.

For the first two months, Adele's attitude towards the school remained unchanged, and getting her there every morning remained a struggle. On the other hand, she really enjoyed her bi-weekly visits to Manfrotto the Wizard, as Dr Nocetti was known by his little patients (what kind of name was that? How on earth did he come up with it?). When they asked her what she got up to with Manfrotto the Wizard in that room for fifty minutes, Adele simply answered 'we play'. She never said anything more than that. Until one day, just before Christmas, Marco and Marina were summoned to the practice on Via dei Colli della Farnesina, 'both of them,' he specified, 'and without the child'. Completely dismissing their previous theory and without revealing how he'd arrived at his conclusion, Dr Nocetti informed them that in his opinion the thread anchored Adele to her father (and not to the walls, as she claimed): a strong, exclusive bond she had purposely built with her dad, in all likelihood because she feared she might lose him somehow.

His interpretation sounded plausible enough (if slightly unexpected), so instead of objecting or requesting further explanations, Marco and Marina found themselves simultaneously asking him the same question: what now? Well – said Manfrotto the Wizard – Adele should be spending more time with her father, a lot more time, if possible. Ideally, he added, she should spend more time with her father than with her mother. A lot more time – he repeated – if possible. It was possible, of course – Marco enjoyed spending time with his daughter – but it would mean a complete restructuring of their roles. Admittedly, their family had been rather old-fashioned up to that point: the father was a much more peripheral figure than the mother in the child's life. Although that was not the kind of family Marco had been raised in (far from it), it was nonetheless a rather convenient set-up for him: fewer chores, a lot more time to devote to his various interests, and – because that's the nature of that antiquated family model – Marina would always end up doing the dishes. But, it went without saying, they'd do anything for Adele, even revolutionise their lives.

And revolutionise their lives they did. Marco resigned himself to the forty-five-minute drive to Tor Carbone twice a day – without complaining, because Adele's happiness was at stake now – and to all the other daily tasks that had previously been his wife's remit. He found himself spending a lot more time at home, drastically cutting back on his hobbies (photography, tennis, poker) but also on his job (ophthalmology): he'd given up going to conferences and even turned down a couple of career opportunities. And yet – much to his surprise – this didn't feel like a sacrifice: on the contrary, he found that he was much happier than before. Marina, however, didn't adjust to her new role anywhere near as well. Freed from those constraints, her life became suddenly empty: she found herself with a lot of time on her hands, and free time is bad news for people with rather unstable personalities. This, incidentally, is what generated the second crack in their relationship, because – as the old adage goes – idle hands are the devil's workshop (or at least they are in this story), although the damage would only become apparent further down the line.

What's relevant here is what happened to that thread – and the thread, as it happened, disappeared.

Marco (the kind of parent who had previously come home from work at 8 p.m.) was now Adele's primary caretaker, i.e. the one who put up with the daily odyssey through Rome's traffic to take her to school, or to see Manfrotto the Wizard, or to the paediatrician's; he was the one who bought her new clothes as needed, prepared her meals and gave her a bath before bed; as a result, he also got to make all the important decisions in all aspects of her life. It was his decision, for instance, to enrol her in the state primary near home (Vittorino da Feltre primary, in the Monti neighbourhood); there was little Marina could do about it, despite her preference for public school. Looking after his daughter meant he got to make the rules (now that was something!) and as he began to exercise that power, Marco had an epiphany: Adele was going to take fencing classes. He thought of it and then just went and did it, one of those short, milky January afternoons – a quick trial lesson and that was that: he signed her up and started taking her there twice a week, without consulting Marina, he simply informed her after the fact. After all, even if he turned out to be wrong about the thread, what harm could a bit of exercise do to the child? As it turned out, it worked: the thread disappeared almost immediately. Children in that class didn't actually use electric jackets, so Adele's imaginary thread didn't disappear because she finally got to use a real body cord. But they did use masks, and from the very first lessons Adele had to contend with a world of face gear and flexible swords and rapid thrusts and adrenaline rushes – the very world (as Marco and Marina had thought back then) the thread had originated from. Fencing, a sport Marco knew nothing about, ended up solving his daughter's problem in that drastic manner children's problems often get resolved – when they do in fact get resolved at all. Just like that. Without saying a word, from one day to the next Adele stopped walking around people when they walked behind her back. She stopped talking about the thread at home. She stopped dragging her heels to go to school, and at school she stopped crying alone in a corner. Just like that.

To Marco Carrera's great surprise, however, Manfrotto the Wizard did not alter his theory one bit: he still thought fencing had nothing to do with it, and in his opinion the thread had disappeared because it had been made superfluous by Marco's now constant presence in Adele's life. And despite previously subscribing to the fencing theory, Marina agreed: it was mere coincidence that the thread had disappeared when Adele had started taking those classes. In the end, the thread problem was solved, and to everyone's great relief it was solved just in time (i.e. before she started primary school, where the issue could have become a lot more serious). This was undoubtedly a success, but – crucially – the moral price of that success was paid exclusively by Marco. The whole matter, in fact, was archived under one single label: the thread had appeared because he didn't spend enough time with his daughter (i.e. it was *his* fault) and it disappeared not because he'd introduced her to the magical world of fencing (i.e. *thanks* to him), but thanks to Dr Nocetti's intuition. All right, Marco Carrera thought, it wasn't the truth, but it was an acceptable version, a tolerable sacrifice. At the end of the day, so very few people were involved (his wife, Dr Nocetti, the head teacher and himself) that it wouldn't make sense to keep arguing about it. So he didn't object and thanked Manfrotto the Wizard. To keep the peace. For his daughter's sake. Without complaining.

This generated the third crack.

# Top-notch (2008)

To: Giacomo jackcarr62@yahoo.com
Sent: 12 December 2008 23:31
Subject: Top-notch
From: Marco Carrera

Today's email, dear Giacomo, is to tell you how I managed to rehome Dad's model railways. It wasn't easy, but it may well turn out to be my finest work. The architectural models were no bother at all in comparison: the Indiano Bridge (given to Dad by the architects after their design won the national competition) I donated to the School of Engineering, and they immediately placed it in the main lecture hall. The one of Villa Mansutti in Punta Ala I gave to Titti, Aldino's widow, who is still alive – and sharp, too. I hadn't seen her in thirty, maybe forty years – the villa was sold a long time ago, but she was happy to have the model, and was quite touched, actually. The Brunelleschi dome (the large one, not the small one Dad had already given away) – anyway, the large one, that I'm sure you remember because you once got a right bollocking for using it as a fort for your toy soldiers – that one I donated to the Florence Institute of Engineers: it blew them all away, and in exchange for that, I asked them to stop sending payment reminders for Dad's annual subscription fee. The infamous Bolgheri house extension (the one without planning permission) I'm keeping for myself, even though it's the least impressive. And then, well – there's the dolls' house on the waterfall that he'd made for Irene (a perfect reproduction of Wright's Fallingwater) which I haven't touched: I've left it in Irene's room, we'll make a call when we sell the house. Anyway, those were the easy ones.

The three model railways were a lot trickier. One you haven't even seen because Dad built it after you left: minimalist, incredibly ingenious, three and a half metres long and only sixty centimetres wide, you can run up to eleven trains on it at the same time, as if by magic. (The magic is actually a rather mundane trick: it's built on two levels, the one 'above ground' and an invisible one, hidden in the base, so when the trains get to the end of the tracks, they enter a tunnel, turn around and a set of points gets them down to the lower level, where they run in the opposite direction without anyone seeing them; then once they get to the other side they climb up from another tunnel, and having turned around again they re-emerge onto the tracks – like that film where Stan Laurel carries a ladder on his shoulders, and you see the ladder going on and on and on, and in the end he reappears carrying the other end of the ladder too.) In short, a masterpiece, I couldn't just get rid of it. And the same goes for the other two, both of which you should be able to remember: the huge one from the sixties and the one going uphill (the Piteccio hairpin turn on the Porrettana railway outside Pistoia). Except you can't really sell a house with all that scaffolding taking up an entire room. So I set out to find a way to donate them to someone who could appreciate their value.

I remembered that before he got really ill, Dad mentioned a colossal model built in the basement of the Railway Workers

Club (you know the tennis club near Le Cascine? Right next door.) So I turn up – and it must be something like forty years, Giacomo, since I'd last set foot in there. It's changed a lot, obviously, and it took me a long time to even find someone who knew what I was talking about. The thing is, the model railway builders that meet in that basement are very elusive, they don't meet on set days at a set time, the basement is locked when they're not around and the other club members know nothing about what goes on in there. I had to stalk him for a month, but in the end, on a Saturday morning, I managed to track down the president of the model railway builders' association – one Beppe – as he played rummy with other members. As soon as I mentioned Dad's name, he got up and took me to the basement – and I have to say Dad was right, the model railway they built in that room really is impressive. Beppe switched it on it just for me, and I'm telling you, it's crazy: it's an urban rail segment the size of the whole room, complete with buildings, roads, cars, people – all in scale. Anyway, I explained the situation and he agreed with me that Dad's models couldn't be destroyed – agreed in principle that is, because he had never seen them. He talked about Dad with great respect, it must be said, even though it was clear that Dad had kept him at arm's length (as was his habit): he barely talked about his model railways and then again only in technical terms, which means our Beppe had no idea what exactly we were talking about. We arranged for him to come see them as soon as possible, which was one month later – don't ask me why. When he finally saw them, he was blown away, especially by the Porrettana railway – by all of them really – and told me they'd take the lot. By 'they' he meant the model railway builders' association of which he was president. The one you've never seen is, apparently, perfect for their school – because they even have a school where they teach kids the art of building model railways, how about that.

Our Beppe was over the moon; it was only a matter of finding a big enough van to transport them: he took my number, left me his, and then vanished for another two months. I tried to call him a couple of times but the number was no longer in use. I even went back to the club asking for him – God forbid something had happened, you know – but no one knew anything. Until, two weeks ago, he called and told me he had finally found the van. We agreed a date, and last week he turned up with 'the boys' as he calls them (all comfortably over fifty) to pick up Dad's creations. I mean, Giacomo, you have no idea the respect these 'boys' had for Dad: there were six of them, Beppe included, hat in hand (they all wear hats, those old-fashioned fedora ones, don't ask me why), spellbound and on the brink of tears, looking at fifty years' worth of Dad's work – 'The Engineer' they all called him. One of them muttered that it was a great honour for him to be there, and to inherit Dad's creations: it was the (now retired) owner of the shop where Dad bought his model trains and discussed technical details. He confessed that seeing The Engineer's work had always been one of his greatest wishes, but Dad was rather intimidating and therefore he'd never asked. Once again I realised Dad never really got close with anyone, and in return no one ever tried to get close with him: despite sharing the same all-consuming passion and despite thinking highly of each other, for decades Dad and 'the boys' had lived in two parallel universes, their paths crossing but a handful of times. And this is Florence, you know, not Tokyo.

Anyway. After the initial pleasantries, they got down to work: they applied purpose-built protective braces to each model railway, then they bubble-wrapped them and carried them out on their shoulders. The very large one didn't fit through the doors, so they had to lower it down from the big window with a rope: an hour and a half that took them. At the end they thanked me (they were all a bit emotional), and drove off in their van, Beppe in the driving seat, two sitting next to him and the other three at the back, clutching the large model rail that was sticking out by about a metre and would not otherwise have survived the journey. Out of respect for Dad's discretion, I am sure I will never see them again. Except – and this is just to reiterate how secretive they can be – yesterday (Sunday) I went to the usual deli to pick up the usual roast chicken, and one of the guys at the counter (the old one, with a large rubbery face and rotten teeth, I've known him for years) came over to me and whispered in my ear: 'I hear the boys have been to see you.' I didn't understand what he meant, so he winked and lowered his voice even more, as if it were a secret the other customers could not, under any circumstances, be made privy to: 'Your dad's model railways: I hear they're top-notch.' That's exactly what he said, 'top-notch'.

I mean, see how things are around here?

No, maybe you don't – my bad for not explaining things properly. My bad.

Merry Christmas
Marco

# Fatalities (1979)

No survivors. That was the brutal outcome of the 'Larnaca tragedy' (as it became known) or, in less sensationalist terms, '94 fatalities' as was recorded in the Civil Aviation Authority report.

Because the plane had taken off from Pisa airport, said fatalities were mostly Italian, and naturally the Italian media had a field day when the story broke. Soon, however, other, more newsworthy 'fatalities' (in the sense of events randomly determined by fate) emerged. First, only a few hours later, there was another plane crash, the biggest in US history (an American Airlines DC-10 malfunctioned as it was taking off from Chicago airport: 271 dead); impossible to ignore, and impossible for journalists to resist the temptation to conflate the two tragedies into one big horror story, muddling everything. The two accidents, in fact, had nothing in common except for the make of the aircraft (and even so, the planes were two different models.) But then, only three days later, the entire country was gripped by news of the capture of Valerio Morucci and Adriana Faranda, the two most wanted Red Brigades terrorists in Italy. Another five days later, an early general election took place, followed by European elections the week after. There was simply no contest: reporters had very little time to scratch beneath the surface of the Larnaca tragedy, which meant they never got as far as Marco Carrera and The Omen leaving the plane just before take-off. Quite simply, the story died. There was a lot of talk of lives being 'cut short' – especially the very young lives of the Boy Scouts heading to their international convention in Ljubljana – but there wasn't enough time to get much further than that. There wasn't even enough time, actually, for decent coverage of the funerals after the bodies were sent back to Italy (or to announce that the black box had been retrieved from the bottom of the sea) because after only two days the Larnaca tragedy began to slip to the back of newspapers reports, where column inches tend to shrink rather ruthlessly.

What kind of life would Marco have lived if the press had found out he had survived the crash? If he'd become a public figure? Or even if the police had found out? As it turned out, Marco's biggest source of anxiety on learning about the disaster (reporters stalking him outside his house, being summoned by detectives) never materialised. And while it was clear why the press lost interest so quickly, it was much harder to fathom why the inquiry ordered by the Civil Aviation Authority never got to him and Duccio. If anything, in those dark days of extreme left terrorism, a couple of twenty-somethings fleeing the scene two hours before the plane was swallowed by the sea should have raised suspicions (at least until the black box proved the crash was caused by structural failure). But no. Nothing happened. Just another Italian mystery – a small mystery compared to others, but a turning point in the lives of the two friends.

Finding themselves so unexpectedly excised from an event they assumed they'd be involved in (because, to all intents and purposes, they *had* been involved), neither of them mentioned it to anyone. And after two, three, four, five days, it seemed odd to start telling people how they'd got off that plane at the very last minute – no one would believe them.

There was another reason for their silence, of course: what would happen to The Omen if people knew he had been on that plane? How could Duccio Chilleri ever so much as come near another human being in their hometown of Florence without them running away, screaming in terror, fearing for their lives? It would validate all the rumours that for years had circulated about him, and the fact that Marco Carrera was still alive would be taken as scientific proof of the 'eye of the storm' theory. The two friends couldn't even talk about it between themselves; they tried a few times, but a cloud of gloom weighed on them, making them too uncomfortable to broach the subject.

As a matter of fact, Marco did have a chance to talk to someone about it, because thanks to what he considered her 'supernatural' powers of intuition, his sister Irene had understood everything. Tell me the truth: that's the plane you and your friend were meant to be on, the one that crashed? – she asked him abruptly after a few days, walking into his room without knocking while he was lying on his bed listening to David Crosby's 'Laughing'. How she found out was a mystery to him, seeing as he'd told his family he was off to Barcelona to see the sights, and most definitely not to Ljubljana via Larnaca to gamble. It didn't even cross his mind that she might have spied on him like she spied on all family members, all the time – that she might have eavesdropped on his phone calls with Duccio, or listened to them from the phone in the kitchen while he spoke to his friend in his bedroom – in short, that she might have been aware of the whole scheme from the very beginning. Shocked, he thought his sister really must be psychic, and he panicked. He panicked and denied everything. Irene insisted: Why won't you tell me? You'll feel better if you do. Marco denied everything again, but decided he'd come clean if pressed a third time. Except – by a twist of fate – Irene did not press him a third time: she walked out of the room as abruptly as she'd entered it and left him sitting there like a lemon, unable to even get up from his bed to flip the record over ('Laughing' – the last track on the LP – had ended and the needle was scratching ominously against the groove).

Scrrt. Scrrt. Scrrt.

What would have happened if he'd answered Irene's questions, or if she'd asked another one? And above all, what would have happened to Duccio?

Because maybe, just *maybe*, if he'd opened up to Irene about that crazy experience, he might not have needed to discuss it ever again, with anyone else. If he'd confessed to his incredibly smart sister that he'd begun to suspect the universe really was governed by mysterious forces and his childhood friend really did possess supernatural powers, maybe his doubts would have been laid to rest. In the days that followed, Marco waited in vain for his sister to resume their conversation, but Irene never did. He waited to be found out, summoned, questioned by the press and the authorities, so that the whole thing would become public knowledge whether he wanted it or not – but no one came. He tried to talk about it with his friend at least, but he couldn't find the right words and his friend wasn't even his friend anymore. In the end, he tried to carry that burden all by himself, but failed at that too. He did, eventually, talk about it – and did so carelessly and deviously. The day before he left for the holidays, he contrived to casually bump into two old friends he barely saw anymore, except there was nothing casual about it. After dinner, he deliberately went to the bar on Piazza del Carmine where he knew they usually hung out – some sort of perverse euphoria had got hold of him, like an ex-junkie who decides to start using again. Two old friends he had nothing in common with except the good old days: their old antics, their old flings, and the adventures of The Omen. Having failed, repeatedly, to do the right thing, he did the wrong one, the most spectacularly wrong thing he could have done.

He left them speechless – positively shocked, in fact. He told them what in two months he hadn't revealed to anyone, and he told them as if he'd always been one of *them*, on their side, as if he hadn't always fought that toxic mix of cynicism and superstition that marked Duccio out as a jinx. He faithfully reported the terrible words Duccio had aimed at those poor sods ('You're all dead! You're dead already and you want to kill me too!'). He described, with extreme compassion, how lethally relieved the unwitting flight attendants looked when they got them off the plane. He spoke as someone who'd undergone a profound, world-shattering conversion, like someone who'd received a sign from God. It wasn't like him, and in fairness it's not what he intended to do, or at least not what he'd set out to do. And yet, as he unburdened himself to his old acquaintances, Marco did precisely that: he doomed the friend who saved his life to a fate he'd fought and rejected for years – a fate Duccio Chilleri would never be able to escape for the rest of his days.

The following morning, dirty and light-hearted like never before, he went to the beach to fall in love with Luisa Lattes.

# The wrong kind of hope (2010)

WEDNESDAY, 20 MAY

Good evening. Is this still Dr Carrera's number by any chance? Apologies for the inconvenience.
**20:44**

Yes, this is still my number. Who is this?
**20:44**

Hello, Dr Carrera. Carradori here, your (I imagine ex by now) wife's former therapist. Hopefully I'm not bothering you, getting in touch after all this time, but should that not be the case, please just say so and delete this message. Otherwise, could you kindly let me know a convenient time for me to call you? Tomorrow or whenever suits: I need to talk to you.
**20:45**

You can call me tomorrow around 9:30, but on one condition.
**20:49**

Yes?
20:49

That you take that 'hopefully' back straight away.
20:50

I'm only teasing, mind you.
20:50

My apologies. I meant 'I hope'. Speak tomorrow. Thanks.
20:54

Speak tomorrow.
20:54

# How it all went (2010)

– Hello?
– Good morning, Dr Carrera, it's Carradori.
– Good morning.
– Is this a good time?
– Yes. How are you?
– I'm fine, thank you. And you?
– I'm good, thanks.
– Great. I'm glad.
– I've been meaning to ask, Dr Carradori – you didn't take it personally yesterday, did you, that 'hopefully' thing? Because I was joking, but it's so hard to tell with these text messages . . .
– No, not at all. I was ashamed, that much I can tell you, because I don't usually make this kind of mistake . . .
– But of course, happens to the best of us. I thought about it and my reply came across as rather rude, I'm afraid, considering we barely know each other.
– Don't worry, no offence taken, I promise.
– That's settled then. What can I do for you?
– Well, to cut a long story short, you could tell me how it all went. Unless you have any objections to that?
– How what went?

– Your life. Yours and your wife's and your daughter's. All these years.

– No kidding.

– Yes. But perhaps it's easier if I tell you about my life first. Would that be OK?

– OK . . .

– Because a few months after we . . . after our encounter shall we say, ten years ago, I quit my job. Done. A clean cut. Technically we call it 'burnout'. Let's just say, to make things easier, that I couldn't slot back into the system I'd left behind when I came to see you.

– It was my fault, then.

– It was *thanks* to you. You know, I can't even imagine being a therapist anymore . . . I wasn't free. Psychotherapy is a trap.

– Tell me about it. So what do you do now?

– Disaster relief psychology. I've joined a WHO programme that offers counselling to communities hit by natural disasters and the like.

– Blimey.

– I've spent very little time in Italy in the past few years.

– Lucky you.

– I've just come back from Haiti, for instance. And I'm going back in two weeks.

– Pretty nasty, that earthquake.

– The worst natural disaster in modern history, believe me. Something people like us cannot even imagine.

– I can imagine. I mean, I can't . . .

– It's a real job, Dr Carrera, a *useful* job. People who lost everything – children, old people who have no one left in this world: and yet they must go on living, because that's their lot. Helping them make sense of their lives is the most useful thing I have ever done.

– I believe you.
– But I confess that on several occasions throughout these years, despite the enormous volume of work, the difficulties, the sacrifices and the frustration (because sadly, in many places around the world counsellors are shunned, especially by those who need them most) – anyway, despite living a very full life, so to speak, throughout these years I often found myself thinking of . . . you.
– Really? Why?
– Well, to begin with, because as I said, to a certain extent you are the reason I stepped away from my job. That is to say, if I hadn't come to you that day, if I hadn't decided to break the rules I'd always followed until that moment, my life wouldn't have changed. And God only knows how much it did need to change. But above all, I thought many times that I never knew what had become of you, your daughter, your wife . . . your ex-wife, am I right? Are you divorced? I don't even know that.
– Oh yes. Quite divorced.
– You see, Dr Carrera, now that I don't operate within the boundaries of my old profession anymore, this is unacceptable to me. I need to know what happened in your lives, seeing as I chose to meddle instead of simply observing, as I was supposed to do. What happened to you all?
– She didn't kill me, as you can see.
– That's something, I guess.
– Nor I her.
– Good. So what did happen?
– Well, quite a few things happened . . . For starters, everything she did behind my back came out, and we split up. Better late than never. Then she accused me of terrible things to cover up the fact she had run away to Germany with that guy – you definitely know more about him than I do.

– And the child?
– The child (who, incidentally, is twenty-one now) she took with her. But it didn't work out, so to speak, and the following year Adele came back to Italy to live with me.
– Thank God. That's what I kept suggesting she should do, you know, when she . . . Well, when she was planning to do what I came to tell you. I insisted she should leave the child here and go live her life with that man without dragging her into it. And what about the other child? The one she was expecting when she stopped coming to see me, what happened to him?
– To *her* – it was another girl. Greta. She was born in Munich. But it was her, in fact, that messed it all up for Marina. That said, Adele more than played her part in that, too . . .
– What do you mean?
– I mean she decided to get her thread back. You remember the issue with the thread on her back when she was little? Did Marina tell you about that?
– Yes, of course.
– Well, we'd got rid of it, thanks to a colleague of yours, before she started primary school. But when she moved to Germany the thread came back, and Adele refused to leave the house. So I brought her back to Italy.
– And the thread disappeared again.
– Of course. For years I put it down to her fascination with fencing, but your colleague was right: it was nothing to do with fencing. It was to do with me.
– I see. And how is she doing now?
– Adele?
– Yes.
– She's doing fine. She's well enough, I guess.
– And your ex-wife?
– Not so well. She is still in Munich, but she split up from that

other man too. She can't work, she's in and out of mental institutions. She needs pretty serious medical treatment.

– How serious?

– I don't know, to be honest. Serious enough. I know that at some point she started seeing Adele only once a year – she'd spend two weeks with her in the summer in some sort of mental institution in Austria. But she hasn't seen her at all for a few years.

– Ah. The worst has happened, then.

– I'd say so, yes. She's like a ghost. You know, for all the horrible things she did to me, I can't hold it against her now – she's literally in pieces.

– And how did you manage with Adele, all by yourself? Did you stay in Rome? Did you move?

– Dr Carradori, I'm not sure I can give you a detailed account of the past ten years over the phone . . .

– You're right. Tell me just one thing then: was it very painful?

– I'd say so, yes. Painful enough.

– And is it all over now? I mean are you over the worst of it, at least? The two of you, at least?

– Dr Carradori . . .

– Just tell me if you're living a normal life, the two of you. Just tell me this one thing.

– Well, yes. We live an almost normal life.

– You made it.

– I don't know that you can say that for sure, but yes – we're still standing.

– Thank you, Dr Carrera.

– For what?

– For telling me this. Really. And I'm sorry for intruding.

– Intruding! Nonsense! I was glad to hear from you. It's just that I can't tell you everything like that, over the phone.

– Indeed. I won't bother you anymore, I promise. I was mostly worried about you and your daughter, really, because I knew your wife was a lost cause. Unfortunately.

– Indeed.

– Can I ask you one last thing, Dr Carrera? It's nothing to do with any of this, but it's been bugging me since we met, ten years ago . . .

– By all means.

– It's such a silly thing . . .

– Do tell.

– Your name is Marco, right? Marco Carrera. And you were born in 1959, like me – right?

– Yes.

– In Florence.

– Yes.

– And you played tennis as a kid.

– Yes.

– Played in any tournaments?

– Yes.

– What about the Rovereto tournament, ever played in that one? Around 1973, 1974?

– Of course I did. It was one of the big ones.

– Aha! It *was* you. Rovereto, 1973 or 74, can't remember which year. First round. Marco Carrera beats Daniele Carradori, 6–0 6–1.

– Well I never . . .

– And I always thought you let me win that one game so I wouldn't lose 6–0 6–0. You don't remember, do you?

– In all honesty, I don't.

– I'm not surprised. You were in a different league, really. And you know what? With tennis too, I ended up quitting because of you.

– Seriously?

– Yes. After being thrashed like that, at the first round, knowing

I'd won that one game because my opponent let me have it . . . I realised I wasn't cut out for tennis. At least not at that level. And so I stopped training, stopped trying so hard, stopped playing in tournaments. And that was a relief, too.

– I see.

– It appears you have a knack for freeing me from life's various traps.

– That I will always be proud of. Professional tennis really is a deadly trap. I got out two years after you did, in the same way, losing 6–0 6–0 in the first round of the Avvenire Tournament. My opponent didn't even let me have that one game.

– Ah!

– And do you know who my opponent was? Do you know who freed me from that trap?

– Who?

– Ivan Lendl.

– No!

– And he was a year younger to boot. Thin as a rake, and he had just one uniform – the one he wore when he played against me. I think the Ambrosiano Tennis Club gave him some spares. He went on to win the tournament.

– Unbelievable.

– I know.

– Well, that can be my claim to fame as a professional tennis player then. Just one degree of separation between me and Lendl. Thank you for telling me.

– My pleasure. And so now you're going back to Haiti.

– In two weeks, yes. Some jobs can't be put on hold for longer than two weeks.

– Good luck, then.

– Good luck to you too. And thanks again.

– You're welcome. Do get in touch when you're back.

– I will if you ask me.
– I just did.
– Then I will.
– Goodbye.
– Goodbye.

# You weren't there (2005)

Luisa Lattes
21 Rue La Pérouse
75016 Paris
France

Florence, 13 April 2005

Dear Luisa,

I've just woken up from an extremely vivid dream, of which you were the protagonist. All I can do is tell you about it.

We were kids, in a place like Bolgheri – except it wasn't Bolgheri, it didn't look like Bolgheri at all in fact, but we all felt at home there. I say 'we all' because there were quite a few people in my dream, but I was always alone, from beginning to end.

It was by the sea, but again, there was no sea, it looked more like autumn somewhere in America: a long, breathtaking road flanked by trees with orange leaves, and the ground underneath was carpeted with flower petals. I was running down this sloping road, alone – I mean running but not as in jogging, I was wearing a suede jacket. To my right, villas and gardens; to my left, trees, and behind them the sea (but you couldn't see it or even sense it, and so it wasn't actually there). Your house was at the end of the road, at the bottom of the slope – you had invited a lot of people over to a pool party, except there was no pool. They were the sort of people you used to hang out with when we met: young scions of well-to-do Florentine families, twenty-something socialites – except it wasn't actually them. I, for sure, wasn't invited. My brother Giacomo was, though, and he walked through the gate with a beach towel over his shoulder, looking at me with pity. But above all, Luisa, *you* were there – because you were everywhere, because that entire place was you, and you were everything right from the start of the road, up there, from the orange trees and the absurd blanket of petals we trod on, and your voice was telling me to meet you in the evening, after the party I wasn't invited to, 'at quarter to eight'. And yet, Luisa – like Bolgheri, like the sea, like the pool – you weren't there. And I was torn, ripped in two: on the one hand I was disappointed that I wasn't invited to the pool party, on the other I was relieved to know there was no pool, and in all likelihood no party either. On the one hand I adored you, because you were everywhere and made that place wonderful, on the other I was disappointed by your absence, because you weren't there. I was caught between the absurd hope of getting my dose of you at quarter to eight, and the sadness I felt seeing Giacomo and the others walk into your garden without being able to join them. Your voice, Luisa, held it all together – including me, including my life, like some sort of voice-over that was somehow painting all that beauty, but you weren't there. You weren't there. You weren't there.

I woke up with a start five minutes ago and I immediately began writing this letter to you, because there is no other way to tell you how I feel. And I'm still torn, Luisa, even now that I'm awake, I'm still ripped in two: on the one hand I'm happy there is a place in the world where you'll receive this letter, on the other I'm sad because that place is not here, where I woke up, where I'm writing to you, where I live and will live, every day.

Kisses
Marco

# Except (1988–1999)

How do you begin telling the story of a great love when you know it ended in disaster? And how do you tell the story so that the one who gets duped (because it was all a lie from the beginning) doesn't look like an idiot? And yet: we must tell how Marco and Marina met, and fell in love, and got together, and got married – but make sure you don't fall too hard, because at some point this will stop being a love story.

This is how things went. Or rather, this is how everyone – except for one person, one woman to be precise – thought things went.

It all started with a former flight attendant from bankrupt Yugoslavian airline Koper Aviopromet appearing on Italy's main morning show *Unomattina* (she was Slovenian but naturalised Italian and had since gone on to join Lufthansa's ticket desk at Rome's Leonardo da Vinci airport). It was the spring of 1988, and the young woman, called Marina Molitor, was in the TV studio to share her tragic story: it should have been her – and not her colleague Tina Dolenc – on board the DC-9-30 that crashed into the Mediterranean nine years before, in what became known as the 'Larnaca tragedy'. They had swapped shifts at the last minute so that Marina could donate her bone marrow to her elder sister Mateja, who suffered from leukaemia, at the

Forlanini Hospital in Rome. This act of generosity (donating bone barrow isn't exactly a walk in the park, even less so back in those days) was meant to save her sister but ended up saving Marina instead, and claiming not one, but two lives: that of the aforementioned colleague who died in the plane crash, and that of the sister herself, who after a few months passed away all the same due to transplant rejection. The young woman cried as she told her story.

Except . . .

As chance would have it, that morning Marco Carrera wasn't at the eye hospital on Piazzale degli Eroi where he'd started working the year before, after completing his training and securing a job. Instead, he was in his flat on Piazza Gian Lorenzo Bernini in the San Saba neighbourhood: splayed on his sofa, running a temperature of 38.5°C, groggy from the antibiotics and dozing in front of the TV. As chance would have it, said TV (which was almost always off, especially in the morning) was showing *Unomattina*, and Marco Carrera emerged from his stupor just as Marina Molitor was on screen: and just like that, in a matter of seconds, she became an unavoidable, inescapable part of his life. They'd both lost an elder sister and they'd both escaped the same plane crash: on the strength of these astonishing coincidences alone, Marco Carrera fell in love with that weeping young woman on the spot (her touching beauty didn't hurt either).

The following day, drugged up to the eyeballs, he tracked her down at the Lufthansa ticket desk where she'd said she worked (that part was true) – and there, before his dazed eyes, stood Marina Molitor in the flesh. Cue an instant discombobulation of their already discombobulated lives, a staggering array of additional synergies uncovered in a single afternoon – and of course, irresistible physical attraction. From then onwards, time swallowed them whole and in the space of twelve months they moved in together, got pregnant and had a daughter – all in one fell swoop.

Except . . .

The little flat on Piazza Bernini (their love nest), then the one on Piazza Nicoloso da Recco with a balcony looking out over Rome. Cocooned deeper and deeper in their own little bubble. Winter weekends in bed, playing with the baby, or making love when the baby slept. Spring weekends at Lake Bracciano, at the beach in Fregene, at the Monster Park in Bomarzo, or in town – picnics at Villa Pamphili, Villa Ada, Villa Borghese. City breaks too, on the hugely discounted flights Marina had access to – Prague, Vienna, Berlin. Their little life. Two salaries paying for small luxuries like the porter's wife cleaning the house and preparing meals, and a babysitter. Christmases in Florence with what was left of Marco's family. Holidays in Koper with Marina's mother, a policeman's widow who treated Marco like a saviour, a hero, a gift from God (which should have rung some alarm bells, but it didn't). And meanwhile Adele was growing up and starting to look like both of them – she had Marina's colouring and eyes, Marco's curls and nose. Then she started to talk, and to walk, and then to grow a thread behind her back, and so the problems began. Problems – it must be said – tackled with equanimity, strength of character, faith in a brighter future and a willingness to make sacrifices so that their relationship would come out of it stronger (because there's no obstacle you can't overcome together, and there's nothing like solving a crisis as a couple to strengthen family bonds).

Except . . .

Except it was all a lie, from the start. There is often an element of deceit when people get together and then start a family, but in this case it was deceit on an unimaginable, pathological scale, and disaster was unavoidable. Neither of them was innocent, to be fair. Incidentally, it was precisely the thread on Adele's back –

and the remedy recommended by Dr Nocetti – that burst their little bubble. The very role reversal that cured Adele (her father looking after her and her mother looking after herself) produced the cracks that would go on to destroy everything. And even if it hadn't been that specific incident, something else would have inevitably come up – because their relationship had no foundations and the future Marco thought he was building was simply not there.

Neither of them was innocent. Not Marco, who so desperately wanted to be happy that for years he systematically underestimated every sign, every clue – everything. And not only did he merrily run towards a cliff, oblivious to Marina's actions: he was also foolish enough to believe that his own highly destructive behaviour (which started one day, in Paris, with a phone call he shouldn't have made to someone he shouldn't have met) would have no consequences. It was while he was in Paris for a conference, in fact, that Marco Carrera found himself thinking of Luisa. Not that he had never thought of her in those years: he thought of her practically every day, but those were vague, resigned musings on what could have been but never was, feeble fantasies worn out by her absence and made feebler still every time she reappeared at the beach in Bolgheri, in August, accompanied by her husband and children (one at first, then two). She was so far away now from the girl Marco had adored in the most tragic period of his life, and she kept getting further and further out of reach each year. That afternoon in Paris, however, under an impossibly bright sky, Marco thought of her as something close and attainable and during a break in the conference programme he called her from the Lutetia Hotel, where he was staying. He tried one of his superstitious rituals that never worked: if that's not her number anymore, or if she doesn't pick up, or if she does pick up but can't meet me, I will never call her again. It didn't work. That was still her number, she picked up in a flash and in half an hour she was at the hotel bar where he'd suggested they meet – beautiful, exhilarating – as if she'd just emerged, unscathed, straight out of Marco's past. He hadn't seen her since the summer, but they hadn't really talked since they'd stopped writing to each other, which was before Marina had even entered the picture. (It all happened because of a run-in with the Italian authorities while Marco was attempting to join Luisa in Paris: during a passport check at the border he was mistaken for a namesake of his – a terrorist on the run, a member of the Armed Communist Proletariat group – dragged out of the Palatino Express at one a.m., held for a day in a police station in Bardonecchia, taken to Rome in a dedicated police van escorted by four Carabinieri, locked up in Regina Coeli prison, interrogated without a lawyer by two public prosecutors who were like some sort of yin/yang opposites – one tall one short, one from the north one from the south, one old one young, one blond one dark – and finally unceremoniously kicked out, just like that, with never so much as an apology. That episode persuaded them both that every attempt they made at being together would forever be frustrated by a cruel twist of fate, and they gave up.) But when a love story doesn't end – or, in this case, never truly begins – it keeps haunting the lovers with words left unspoken, things left undone, lips left unkissed. It is true of every love story but especially true for Marco and Luisa, because that afternoon, with that walk on Rue D'Assas and that innocent conversation, they started seeing each other again, which in their case meant writing to each other, often, passionately, like nineteenth-century lovers, like they'd been doing ten years before. And that was far from innocent, because now that they were both married and had children, they had to lie. And little did it matter that the series of events they triggered that afternoon in the Lutetia Hotel stopped just short of fulfilling their desires and changing the course of their lives: that was just masochism on their part.

Whatever innocence was left between them – if it was ever there – was now gone for good. They started seeing each other again all year round because Marco made sure to only attend conferences within a 250-mile radius of Paris (Bruges, St Étienne, Lyon, Leuven), so that Luisa could join him; how she managed that, what she told her husband, was never mentioned. They went from staying at two different hotels to booking different rooms in the same hotel until, inevitably, they ended up spending the night in the same room in Lyon, on 24 June 1998: and while France was beating Denmark in the World Cup final at the local Stade de Gerland, the two of them were eating a club sandwich and watching an old Jean Renoir film in room 554 of the Hôtel Collège at No.5 Place Saint Paul. After the film, as the French were out in force honking and shouting outside their windows, celebrating their first World Cup victory, Marco and Luisa's impossible love story culminated in the ultimate act of masochism: a *vow of chastity*. A pact sealed with unhealthy enthusiasm as they listened to Sinéad O'Connor's 'Sacrifice' on Luisa's Walkman, an earphone each. And because of that sacrifice – they thought – no harm was done: no one was being cheated on, nothing was being destroyed. They had never made love and swore they never would. They had only kissed once (*that* night, seventeen years before, while Irene was drowning) and swore they would never do it again. At the tender age of thirty-nine and thirty-two, respectively, Marco and Luisa actually slept in the same bed without giving in to what they'd both fantasised about for years, without kissing, without cuddling, without even touching, without doing anything at all. Idiots, the pair of them.

For her part, Luisa was fully aware that her marriage was doomed, and she knew that every step she took (including rekindling her old relationship with Marco Carrera and stoking it with that childish display of abstinence) was a step away from it. Marco, however, really did believe that his great love stories could coexist, that they didn't have to be mutually exclusive. He really did believe that it was enough *not to consummate* his relationship with Luisa to preserve the one with Marina, and that's how colossally naïve he was – naïve to a fault. To believe, as he did, that something so huge, with a conspicuous trail of evidence (hidden letters begging to be found, credit card statements just waiting to be checked, suspicious emails filed under 'College of Physicians', and only partially deleted messages with a habit of resurfacing like bloated corpses in a pond at the touch of a key) – to believe that such a monumental pile of evidence would slip under the radar of a woman like Marina Molitor really was a foolish mistake. Marco Carrera made that mistake, and he kept going day after day until it all came crashing down, safe in the knowledge that the only threat to his family's happiness was his love for Luisa Lattes, and that he had it under control.

As for Marina, the story gets easier. Simply insert a 'not' before anything she'd said about herself, and that'll do: she had *not* swapped shifts with a colleague on the plane that crashed (she was off that day); she had *not* donated her bone marrow to her sister (they weren't compatible); she had *not* fallen in love with Marco (she was simply overwhelmed by the consequences of her own lies); she had *not* been at all happy to get pregnant (she was just proud she could give her beloved mother a granddaughter); she had *not* been at all happy with Marco, never (quite the opposite in fact: she'd harboured a silent, dull resentment against him for years); she had *not* been faithful to him, even before that fateful affair, and so on. Quite simply, she was *not* the person she fought so hard to be. It was a constant struggle. Every day, Marina got out of bed and started fighting. Every day. With herself. With her instincts. Every single day. For years. The bubble that gave her husband the illusion of happiness granted her protection from the monster that had always threatened to devour her. Throughout the years, that bubble and that monster had been called many different things, depending on her therapist's background at the time. Dr Carradori, for instance, called the bubble 'narrative' and the monster 'counter-narrative'. The battle between narrative and counter-narrative had started early: as a child she would announce to her school teacher (or her Sunday school teacher, or to a friend's mother) that her own mother and sister had died, and she was alone in the world. Bereavement was her narrative. Depression, self-destructive behaviour, aggression and addiction (to various substances, to sex) were her counter-narrative. Therefore, after her troublesome teens (during which she nevertheless managed to be crowned Miss Koper in 1977 and become Koper Aviopromet's youngest flight attendant in 1978) the only peaceful years Marina ever knew in her entire life were those that followed her sister's death – because she really did suffer from leukaemia, and did actually die from it. Since bereavement was Marina's narrative, those were her only good years. (Let that sink in: her only good years were those spent mourning her sister.)

But grief fades away spontaneously even when you try hard to keep it alive, and after a few years the monster regained control of her life. Drugs, again. Sex, again. She was suspended from Lufthansa (where she now worked) for disciplinary issues. A casual encounter with a writer for the *Unomattina* morning show provided the perfect opportunity: the story she told in front of the cameras was touching and credible, and the double tragedy she recounted during her TV appearance became her new narrative. That's all Marina wanted, to take shelter in grief. That story, however, catapulted her into another narrative altogether, a more robust, more articulated one – an unpredictable one, too, because she had never conceived of it before: marriage. Since we mentioned that no one was innocent in this story, it must be said that Marina's mother knew all too well about her disorder, but she happened to be a member of the Slovenian lower middle class, and like lower-middle-class mothers the world over she believed that marrying her daughter off to a doctor was a cure for all evils, and therefore she never said a word to Marco Carrera. It didn't even cross her mind. She saw him as a saviour, and worshipped him. And seeing her mother worship Marco gave Marina the strength to get out of bed every day and fight to make her happy.

Except . . .

Except one day, Marina's mother died – died before her time, at the age of sixty-six, of liver cancer. Perfect, one might think: fresh grief for Marina, actual, real grief that would keep her going for a while, if not forever. But no: that death, the death of the only person she had ever loved, devastated her. She didn't grieve, she was positively enraged. Her mother's cowardly departure seemed an insult to all the sacrifices she had made for her. How dare she die! And how could Marina's obedience possibly survive her? How could she go on when the narrative she struggled to live by every day (the miserable marriage she had kept alive to keep others happy) was, in essence, all but dictated by her now-deceased mother? Still very beautiful, Marina was pursued by a number of suitors – at work especially, but also at the school gates when she picked up Adele, or at the gym she'd joined when Marco started doing the school runs because of Adele's thread. What was the point of being *virtuous* now that her mother was six feet under, being eaten by worms?

She started screwing around again. Quickies in deserted notary offices or hotel rooms, but also (because her narrative was heterosexual, but her counter-narrative was bi) rather sublime lunch breaks with Biagia, her beautician, a petite, ultra-tattooed, rough-looking girl from the Mandrione council estates: a great source of orgasms. Marina was seeking the thrill of debauchery, of living on the edge, which to her was the only proper way to live, free from all the bloody bubbles. Being a mother was what held her back: she was uneasy about that shimmering chaos infiltrating her neat world of kisses on the forehead and little girls with strings on their backs like puppets. Therefore, she set out to build yet another narrative – to take cover, to stay in control. An affair. A stable affair, with the highest-ranking suitor (just like her mother would have wanted): a tanned, silver-haired Lufthansa captain with 25,000 flight hours under his belt, a wife and two teenage daughters in Munich, a house in Rome and one on the Austrian Alps, and a highly infectious passion for bondage. They'd meet in the afternoon in his house on via del Boschetto, once, maximum twice a week, depending on his schedule. And they had fun – quite a lot of fun. Marina would tell Dr Carradori everything with shameless candour, and for that reason he truly believed he could stop her from drifting away completely. Sometimes he'd scold her, sometimes he'd surprise her by quietly listening to the obscenities she told him, but he always, always believed her: he was convinced he had established a genuine connection with this woman whose every word was meant to deceive. He believed that their connection was the only possible narrative Marina could be safely encouraged to cultivate (and hopefully sustain in the long term). After all, their apparently precarious balance seemed to work: a year, then two, then two and a half.

Except . . .

Except it was too easy. Marco didn't suspect a thing, he was too easily deceived – and when a woman like Marina begins wondering why, it won't be long before she finds an answer. She started looking and immediately found the letters: the idiot had hid them under the lid of the box where he kept his sister's ashes (which Marco had managed to obtain at the morgue in the Trespiano graveyard in Florence, where an attendant by the name of Adeleno was known to open the sealed urn from the crematorium and, for the price of 50,000 lira, illegally distribute the ashes to those relatives who asked for them). She didn't even miss a shot – hit the bullseye straight away. And then came the emails, the credit card statements, the hotel bills, all of it. That's why he didn't suspect anything: that piece of shit had been having an affair with that whore right under her nose. For years, Christ. For years. They used a poste restante address, like nineteenth-century star-crossed lovers. In Bolgheri they'd play it cool, barely speak to each other all summer, keep a low profile; but the rest of the year they spoke all right, the little lovebirds. Thinking of you, dreaming of you, here's a song that reminds me of you, here's a poem – yuck. They'd been in love for eighteen years, in short, and thought they could get away with it because they didn't have sex. Bastard. Bastards! And to think she'd been feeling guilty . . .

Now, you can't even begin to compare Marina's lies to Marco's, we're talking a different order of magnitude altogether. And yet, finding out about that affair (who cares if the bastards didn't actually fuck, it was still cheating) plunged her into previously unattained depths of viciousness, making her a very dangerous person indeed. Marina found herself hurled out of yet another narrative, and the safety net provided by Dr Carradori couldn't hold her anymore, and so Marina did the terrible things she did, which was second only to what she very nearly managed to do. She was a wild creature, wild and untameable: abandoning all narratives once and for all felt to her like coming home after an entire life lived in exile, and the shockwaves produced by that homecoming didn't spare anyone within range of her pain. Because one thing is for certain: Marina suffered. She suffered terribly for her mother's death and she suffered when she found out about Marco's affair. She suffered a lot doing what she did afterwards, suffered even more when she couldn't do it the way she wanted, and then suffered – dreadfully, unspeakably – once it was all done, when she found herself alone in the middle of the void her fury had generated.

Except, once again, Marco would only understand this many years later, when it all became clear to him, when it was no use to him anymore. He would realise that it had been his fault. All she did was make up a tragic story, but he was the one who had swooped in, proclaiming they were made for each other. But they weren't made for each other. No one is made for anyone else, in all fairness, and people like Marina Molitor weren't even made for themselves. She was only looking for shelter, for a narrative that would keep her going a little longer, while he was looking for happiness – no less. She had always lied to him, and that is wrong, of course it is, because lies are like a cancer that spreads and takes root and blends with the very substance it corrupts. But he had done something worse: he had believed her.

# Let's stop at that (2001)

Luisa Lattes
21 Rue La Pérouse
75016 Paris
France

Florence, 7 September 2001

Tell me, Luisa, did you change your mind because they offered you a job at the Sorbonne or because I am too rigid, too dogmatic? Is it because 'you love me but you just can't do it' or because 'every man looks for a woman that matches his symptoms'? I don't know if you've realised, but – assuming we were, in fact, together – you've left me, and you did it in two separate languages, for two separate reasons: a double whammy. You've left me twice, in short, and that feels rather excessive.

Why can't we just say that after this wild year we spent together, breaking all the rules we'd set for ourselves, after going straight to the heart of the matter – and the heart of the matter was *us*, Luisa, you and me, together, you and me HAPPY together – after all this, when it was time to return to the fold, so to speak, we got lost? We got lost because of those practicalities that you and I never had to face in twenty years. We were very good at *not* being together and when we finally had a chance to be together, we failed. Why can't we just say that?

Me last year: a wretch, a survivor. I roamed around Europe like the proverbial wandering Jew just to spend a weekend with my daughter. Rome, Florence, Paris, Munich – it was all the same to me, because I had nothing left to lose. Mine was desperation pure and simple: and that desperation gave me incredible strength, a kind of savage strength, as you could see, because it is towards you that I directed that strength.

You: caged, trapped. All you could do was lie – to yourself, to your husband, to your children – and lying kept you in that cage. But for a whole year, you saved my life. Those Mondays we spent together in Paris, that August in Bolgheri: they literally saved my life. And as you saved my life, you stopped lying, you left your husband, you did everything you never had the strength to do. You broke free of the cage.

I have never been as happy as I was with you when I was a wretch. Had you told me then what you said to me last night, I would have gone straight to Mulinelli to top myself, just like Irene, I swear. But that didn't even cross your mind, no – you told me the most beautiful things anyone had ever said to me, and you knew perfectly well that you had never been loved and would never again be loved like I loved you in those wretched days. Because they were wretched days, Luisa, wonderful and wretched. And now it's over. Why can't we just say that?

I still love you, Luisa, I have always loved you, and the idea of losing you again is breaking my heart: but I understand what happened, what is happening, I understand and there's nothing I can do about it. I can accept your decision, I really can: I have my daughter back now and I have to accept everything. But I beg you, let's stop at that. Don't tell me you're leaving me because of who I am, like you tried to do the other night, even if it's the truth. I beg you, Luisa, let's stop at that, don't be so honest. Don't destroy everything just because you don't want to spend your life with me anymore. We only talked about it, in those happy days when we were unhappy: but you didn't promise anything, you mustn't feel guilty. You're free now and you can open any door, you can stay or leave, change your mind as many times as you like without ruining anything. Say that you can't turn down that job offer. Say that your children wouldn't be happy in Florence. Or that I couldn't possibly move to Paris. That's more than enough – no need to destroy me.

The words you whispered to me only a few months ago are the most beautiful thing that ever came my way: let me have them.

Remember you're a good person, Luisa. Stop before you finish me off.

Yours,
Marco

# On growth and form (1973–1974)

One night, in the house on Piazza Savonarola, Marco, Irene and Giacomo Carrera heard their parents fight. They never argued so openly: usually they did it in private, whispering so the children wouldn't hear, which meant only Irene was aware of their rows, because Irene spied on them. For the boys it was a first. They were arguing about Marco, but the two brothers didn't know that: only Irene knew because she had been following the argument from the beginning, while Marco and Giacomo had only appeared by their mother's bedroom door when the screaming began.

The fact was, Marco hadn't been growing like other children: ever since his first year, his development curve had been stuck towards the bottom, and from the age of three it was off the growth charts altogether. He had always been a beautiful boy and perfectly proportioned, which according to his mother was a sign that nature was singling him out, setting him apart from other children to highlight the precious qualities it had bestowed on him. He was tiny for his age, yes, but bright and graceful, and even – as unusual as that may sound when it comes to children – *manly*: in her opinion, this clearly indicated he was quite simply on a completely different development pattern (as also evidenced by the fact that his adult teeth had come out very late). There was nothing to worry about. As soon as his growth deficit had become apparent, Letizia had coined the most reassuring of nicknames for her child: he was 'the hummingbird'. Marco didn't just share his diminutive size with that precious little bird, but had been blessed with the same beauty and agility: physical agility, yes (which was indeed impressive, and came in rather handy in sports), but also a supposed mental agility, which allegedly manifested itself at school and in social interactions. For years Letizia kept repeating the same mantra: there was nothing to worry about, absolutely nothing, nothing at all.

His father, however, had been worrying from the start. While Marco was still a child, Probo had tried his best to believe his wife's reassuring theory, but when Marco entered puberty and his body continued to show no sign of developing normally, he felt guilty. How could they let nature simply run its course? That was a serious condition, never mind all that hummingbird nonsense. He began to look up scientific papers, at first without involving the child directly; but when Marco turned fourteen, Probo couldn't bear it any longer and he decided to drag him into his quest. A series of specialist consultations, medical examinations and diagnostic checks ensued, which determined that Marco suffered from a form of height-related hypoevolutism (so far, so obvious), caused by an insufficient production of growth hormones. Unfortunately, there was no established cure at the time, only experimental treatments, which tended to target only serious forms of hypoevolutism, i.e. nanism. Only one out of the many specialists they consulted said he could help them – a paediatric endocrinologist from Milan named Dr Vavassori who had been running a programme for a few years with (he claimed) very encouraging results.

Hence the fight.

Probo told Letizia he planned to enrol Marco in that

programme, Letizia replied it was madness, Probo retorted that letting things run their course for all those years had been madness, Letizia reiterated her theory of harmonious growth and hummingbirds – and up until that point they'd been whispering as usual, and as usual only Irene had heard them. The fight entered a completely new phase when Letizia mentioned a book – *the* book even – fetishised by contemporary architects (or at least the ones she hung out with, that is the *most* brilliant, *most* cosmopolitan architects, since the book had never been translated into Italian and so had to be read in English): *On Growth and Form*, by D'Arcy Wentworth Thompson. At that, a sharp, feral cry – so out of place in that large, usually quiet house – pierced the walls, reaching the two brothers who had been watching TV in the living room: 'YOU CAN STICK THAT FUCKING THOMPSON UP YOUR ARSE, DO YOU HEAR ME?!!?'

From then on, the quarrel continued like an academic dispute, albeit one packed with insults and a lot of shouting: Marco and Giacomo didn't understand what was going on, and Irene – smirking – wouldn't explain anything. Letizia called Probo a poor sod, Probo countered that she kept quoting that fucking book but she'd never even read it, same as those other arseholes of her professor friends who kept name-dropping it; at which point Letizia felt she had to try and sum up the chapter called 'Magnitude' (where it is *mathematically* proven that in nature, growth and form are indissolubly linked by an intrinsic law of harmony) in such words that even an imbecile like him could comprehend; and then Probo called her a fraud, because she only ever quoted from that chapter – the first one, as it happened – because it was the only one she'd read; and so forth. The quarrel dragged on and ended up very far from where it had begun: Letizia kept invoking concepts that a failed engineer like him couldn't even begin to fathom, such as Jung's mandalas and

Steiner's art therapy; Probo, for his part, reiterated his invite to stick said mandalas and art therapy and Jung and Steiner in the orifice hitherto reserved for *On Growth and Form*. And further still: Letizia was fed up, fed up to the back teeth, she couldn't cope anymore. And what the fuck was she fed up with? With having to put up with a wanker like him. Oh well did she have any idea just how bloody sick and tired he was of her bullshit. Oh fuck off! *You* fuck off!

Marco and Giacomo were genuinely worried: it sounded like their parents were one step away from getting a divorce. Instead of wasting time worrying, Irene took action: 'What the fuck's got into you?' she shouted, banging on their door, 'Shut up!' Her brothers immediately fled to the living room, but Irene stood her ground, ready to face them. She was eighteen now: the way she saw it, no one was entitled to leave the house before she did – so divorce was out of the question. Her mother peeked out from behind the door and apologised, followed by her father. Irene looked at them with contempt and said that luckily Marco hadn't understood what they were fighting about: and with that (and we can only say this in hindsight, but we can still say it) the fate of at least three members of that family was sealed – if not four members, if not all five of them actually, but definitely Marco's fate and that of his parents.

Probo and Letizia – shocked to be reprimanded by their own daughter – felt so guilty, so mortified and selfish that they immediately mended the tear in the web of hypocrisy they'd been spinning around their family for years. There was something unwavering, actually, in their relationship – unwavering and unchangeable – that they themselves couldn't articulate: Letizia couldn't explain it to her therapist during their turbulent sessions that so often focused on her inability to leave Probo, and Probo couldn't explain it to himself during his long, solitary days at his drafting machine – steady-handed, sharp-eyed, his smoker's nose hissing as his mind wandered off to encompass his own endless suffering. Why did they stay together? Why, if they'd both wholeheartedly voted in favour of divorce at the referendum only a few months before? Why, if they couldn't stand each other anymore? *Why*? Fear, perhaps – they were definitely afraid, but not of the same thing, and so fear, too, drove them apart. There was something else, something unintelligible and unspeakable that kept them together, a single, mysterious anchor point that bound them to the promise they'd made almost twenty years before, *when the violets blossomed*, as in a recent song by Fabrizio de André (recent compared to the quarrel, not to the promise, which preceded it by several years, even though it was exactly the same: '*We will never, ever, ever break up*'). After all, even that song drove them apart, just like everything else, and like everything else that drove them apart, it seemed to generate fault lines through the whole family too: Letizia and Marco liked it (but listened to it on separate record players, unbeknown to each other), Giacomo and Irene didn't (Giacomo was too young and Irene found it sickening), while Probo was unaware of its existence altogether. And yet they stayed together, the family didn't break up, the knot kept loosening without ever coming undone. *Canzone dell'amore perduto* was the title of that song – 'Song for a lost love'– but their love never seemed to lose its way beyond recall. '*Per un amore nuovo*' (for some new love) went the last line – but there would never be any new love for them.

Irene's intervention during her parents' quarrel was what kept them together. At the same time – as we said – it set the course of their lives, as well as Marco's. From then onwards common sense and compassion prevailed, and their children's (supposed) happiness took precedence over theirs. Not that it would ever work out between them, Letizia and Probo were smart enough to realise that: misery is no different when one is miserable by choice, and if at some point misery becomes the only real product of a marriage, then that is what is passed on to the children. They were also smart enough to know that unhappiness hadn't somehow swooped down on them out of the blue: looking back with a modicum of honesty, they both had to acknowledge that there had never been even a hint of happiness. They had *always* been miserable, even before they'd met – sadness was like a substance they'd produced autonomously, like human bodies produce cholesterol. The only fleeting happiness they ever experienced they experienced together, at the beginning of their relationship, when they fell in love and got married and had children. That evening, they immediately stopped fighting – and they stayed together, irritating each other, hurting each other and fighting under their breath for the rest of their days.

As for Marco, they tried to come to an understanding. Letizia worked hard to give up on what her therapist called 'the hummingbird myth' (her boy staying small, his grace and beauty inaccessible to any woman other than her, etc.) and accept Probo's view that they had to try everything that was scientifically feasible to help him grow. This also meant sacrificing the high-minded beliefs about growth and form she derived from D'Arcy Wentworth Thompson's opus (which, whatever Probo thought, she had read in full). For his part, Probo made sure not to consider this a personal victory (which would have made him even lonelier) but rather an unexpected opportunity to share something important with his wife again, whom he still loved despite everything. He therefore took Letizia to Milan to meet Dr Vavassori so she could see for herself that he was someone they could trust and requested that she independently verify the effectiveness of the planned treatment, promising she would have a say in the final decision. Therefore, Letizia embarked on the same solitary quest Probo had undertaken in the previous months and came to the conclusion that the treatment developed by the specialist in Milan really was the only existing option for Marco. It wasn't like walking together, but at least, for the first time in a very long time, they were walking down the same path.

# First letter on hummingbirds (2005)

Marco Carrera
44 Via Folco Portinari
Florence
50122

Paris, 21 January 2005

Marco, how are you?
You won't think I'm crazy will you – or a hypocrite, or worse – for writing to you like this, out of the blue? It's just that I miss you. I miss you. All it took is one summer – just one – without seeing you in Bolgheri to leave me gasping for breath. I've realised that even just catching a glimpse of you on the beach (like I've always done, every August, for twenty-five years), even just a quick chat with you is essential to me. Writing to you is essential to me. I held out for three years, now I can't hold out anymore: up to you if you want to answer or not. Know that I will understand if you don't, because I was the one who walked away on you. I haven't forgotten about that. But that's not why I'm writing to you, Marco. I'm writing because last week a friend came to visit for a couple of days on her way to New York, and she had a copy of an Italian newspaper

from a few weeks back because it had an article on an Aztec art exhibition at the Guggenheim she was interested in. And it's a beautiful article, about sacred animals and human sacrifices and how the Aztecs believed the end of the world was nigh, and unavoidable, but that we could postpone it by making an offering of human blood to the gods. And as I read on, I came across this passage that made my heart burst, because it is about you:

> Unlike Hinduism, Islam and Christianity, where the afterlife (be it reincarnation, heaven or hell) depends on how a person has lived, the Aztecs believed that – except for kings, who were gods – life beyond death was determined by how and when a person died. The worst fate was reserved for those who died of old age or from an illness: their souls would fall all the way down to the ninth and lowest circle of hell, the dark and dusty Mictlan, where they would remain until the end of time. Those who drowned or were struck by lightning would go, in turn, to Tlaoclan – the kingdom of Tlaoc, god of rain – where they would live surrounded by abundant food and riches. Women who died in childbirth – that is, giving birth to future warriors – would lie with the sun for four years, but then turn into terrifying spirits and forever roam the world at night. Lastly, the warriors who died in battle and the human sacrifices would join the sun in his daily battle against darkness. But after four years they would turn into hummingbirds or butterflies.
>
> And now that the whole Aztec civilisation has sunk into Mictlan, we're still wondering what sort of people these were, whose highest aspiration after a heroic death was to turn into a hummingbird.

I'm sorry, Marco. I messed up.
I'm sorry.

Luisa

# 未来人 (2010)

Miraijin, which means 'Man of the Future' in Japanese, was born on 20 October 2010. That is, for those who care about these things – and Adele Carrera did care – on 20.10.2010. That name and that date had been set ever since Adele told her father she was pregnant.

'This baby will be the New Man, Dad,' she said. 'It will be the Man of the Future. And it will be born on a special day.'

'I get all that,' answered Marco Carrera 'but who's the father?' Adele wouldn't say.

'But I mean, but why, how come, how do you think you'll . . .' She still wouldn't say.

Adele was an honest, wholesome girl – which was a miracle considering what she'd been through – but she could be stubborn too, inflexible even, once she'd made a decision. And in this case, she had made a decision: there was no father, end of. Marco Carrera knew there was no point insisting, fighting, pressuring her: for the umpteenth time, life had thrown him a curveball – and he'd learnt that the thing to do with curveballs was to simply acknowledge them. It wasn't easy, though. He'd raised his daughter to be free, to always make up her own mind about things, and therefore he'd always assumed she'd fly the nest early – he was prepared for that. Instead, he found out she had no intention of going: she wanted to stay with him. She told him loud and clear, with embarrassing candour: I have no intention of leaving you, Dad – you've been a fantastic father to me, you still are, and if you are a fantastic father to me then you can be a father for Miraijin too, the Man of the Future.

But wait, but that's got nothing to do with it, but that's different, who . . .

She still wouldn't say who the father was.

Marco's feelings for his daughter were complex: he loved her of course, more than anything else – and since she'd gone back to live with him, he had sacrificed practically everything to look after her. But he pitied her as well, knowing that her mother was in such a state, and he felt guilty for not being able to give her the normal life every child should be entitled to. And he also worried about her, about her emotional stability – although the thread that had reappeared in Munich during their *annus horribilis* disappeared for good as soon as she'd moved back to Florence, and was never so much as glimpsed in the following nine years. Marco powered through those years barely catching his breath, and he emerged from that time light-hearted and optimistic – which, come to think of it, was rather remarkable seeing as in less than a decade he'd lost Luisa, given up on his academic career, seen his parents fall ill and then die one after the other, got Luisa back, severed all ties with his brother, and lost Luisa again. That had been one formidable chunk of time, during which Marco had constantly kept his head down – waking up at the crack of dawn, working like a dog, doing the shopping, cooking, taking care of a million daily chores, looking after his daughter, his mother, his father and the whole menagerie around him. Marco had *kept together* a small, fragile world that without him would have unravelled in a heartbeat, and in this he found new strength and self-confidence. But he had also steeled himself to see that world unravel all the same, because everything comes to an end and he knew that (Venice, for instance, would be submerged by water in a thousand years), and everything changes – he knew that, too (in about thirteen thousand years, due to a phenomenon called 'axial precession', the North Pole would no longer be marked by the North Star but by Vega). That said, things can come to an end and change in many different ways, and his task was to shepherd people and things towards a *dignified* ending, towards the *right* kind of change. And this he did for nine years.

Not a single day in those years had gone to waste, not a single euro, not a single sacrifice. Despite his packed schedule, he'd managed to carve out moments of unadulterated peace and enjoyment. Undeterred by the tragic memories, every summer he'd take Adele to Bolgheri – where nothing had changed in forty years – so she could fall in love with the sea as he had done. He took her skiing in winter, not racing (and losing) like he did as a kid, but simply letting her enjoy the thrill of gravity in the woods and teaching her how to do it safely. They went hiking in those woods too, in the summer (which he never did as a kid), looking for wildlife to photograph, hoping to capture that fleeting moment when they bother to return your gaze before dismissing you as unworthy of their consideration, and refocusing their attention on the things that really matter: moss growing on a stone, holes in the ground, fallen leaves.

Adele repaid his efforts by growing up healthy and full of life, getting good grades in the same schools he'd attended, avoiding the usual scrapes kids her age got into, and keeping fit. Not playing your average sports though; she lost interest in fencing and discovered a real talent for non-competitive disciplines that channelled her father's elemental fascination with the sea and the mountains, distilling it into a real philosophy of life: surfing and free climbing. As a result, from a very young age Adele joined one of those communities you never leave, because they are spiritual communities that misfits from all over the world flock to (and Adele remained a misfit, that's for sure): forever looking for beaches and walls and waves and spectacular leaps, but above all looking to escape the trappings of middle-class life, which have a tendency to make people miserable. While she was still too young to travel alone, Marco would discreetly accompany her to extreme, stunning locations – Capo Mannu, La Graviere, the Verdon Gorge. He'd wander around all day by himself, photographing wildlife or watching his daughter's gang grapple with waves or ascents. Sometimes he'd join them for dinner, more often he'd dine alone in a restaurant recommended by his Guide Bleu and wait for his daughter to come back to the B&B where they were staying – and Adele always came back, of her own accord, always sober, conscious of the caution a sixteen-year-old should exercise while enjoying her freedom. Then, around the time she turned eighteen, Adele started hanging out with her tribe on her own – and Marco learnt to wait anxiously for her return, and to feel lonely, and to be grateful when she eventually came back to study and work for months on end. She had started a degree in sports science (as chance would have it, her department was directly opposite Marco's hospital and they would often have lunch together) while also working part-time at the gym where she trained, teaching an aerobics class for middle-aged ladies and a beginners' climbing class. She didn't earn much, but still more than Marco did at her age from his gambling escapades with Duccio – and at any rate enough to pay for clothes, petrol for her Renault Twingo, and the inevitable (but in her case probably necessary) therapist. She was a strong girl, stronger than he'd hoped, and very beautiful too, a straightforward, touching kind of beauty like her mother's, but mitigated by a few graceful imperfections.

That's why Marco expected to see her fly the nest early, so much so that he'd planned ahead for her departure: he'd set aside enough money to support her for a few years, so she'd have the leisure to follow her passion and keep studying without worrying about anything else. He also expected her to leave Florence one day, or Italy even, or Europe altogether, and eventually settle in some paradise in the arse end of nowhere (he even toyed with the idea of quitting everything himself and joining her in that unspecified location one day). He expected her to get pregnant very young too – as was indeed the case – and he'd resolved not to look too upset when she'd tell him, perhaps as she clutched the arm of one of those impossibly fit guys in her tribe. And yet – as is always the case when you think you've planned for every eventuality – Adele's move caught him unprepared. 'This baby will be the Man of the Future, Dad.' 'I get all that, but who's the father?' She wouldn't say. The Man of the Future was going to have no father, and Adele was going to be a fearless, unapologetic single mother, content and full of life. As for providing a 'father figure', that was going to be Marco's job, since he was so good at it.

On the one hand, that was the most powerful declaration of love Marco had ever received, and he felt overwhelmed with gratitude and joy. On the other, there was something deeply unsettling about that plan: without even bringing Adele's thread into it, it was clear that his relationship with her risked becoming overly complicated. Wasn't it too morbid? Wasn't it *unhealthy*? What if the reason Adele didn't want her child to have a father was because of the damage caused by him and Marina? Or maybe she was going through some other personal trauma he knew nothing about (just like Irene) – had she been callously abandoned by the baby's biological father? Or did he simply refuse to face up to his responsibilities? And did Adele then try to dissimulate by pretending it was her decision to go it alone? What if Adele had inherited her mother's tendency to escape reality and take refuge in her own bubble of deceit? And what if he, Marco Carrera, was once again made responsible for watching over that bubble? And what if he failed again? And if it was indeed a bubble, how long before it burst? And at any rate, what sort of New Man would this be, raised by a twenty-one-year-old mother and a fifty-one-year-old grandfather?

A few years down the line all these questions would be answered at once, and with no possibility of appeal. But for the time being it was up to Marco Carrera to meet his daughter's expectations, and he couldn't give her a half-baked answer: he followed his heart and embraced the idea fully, ending up believing in this Man of the Future malarkey himself. After all, he thought, why not? This New Man was bound to crop up sooner or later, in some place or other. He remembered a line from a poem by St John of the Cross that Luisa quoted in one of their many farewell letters: 'to go where you know not / you must go through what you know not'. Marco Carrera didn't know where he was going, and he had no idea what he'd have to go through, but for the sake of his daughter he decided to get there and go through it.

From then on, things got easier: timings and requirements were dictated by biology week after week, and all Marco Carrera had to do was keep the right distance between himself and what was happening inside his daughter's body. His experience with pregnancies was limited to Marina's, so he used that as a starting point to work out the part he had to play. Accompanying Adele to antenatal appointments: yes. To antenatal classes: no. Putting his hand on the bump to feel the baby kick: yes. Banning all surfing and climbing outings: yes. Indulging all her pregnancy-related whims: no. Relieving her of all chores: yes. Amniocentesis: no (Adele was against it). Finding out the baby's sex from the scan: no (as above). No to choosing a name using his 'tennis scoreboard method' (that's how they'd picked Adele's name. Lara was the runner-up – which Marco would have preferred actually, seeing as he'd specialised in ophthalmology because of *Doctor Zhivago*, even though he'd never told anyone): the baby's name had already been decided from the start. Yes to a water birth, and specifically a water birth at Santa Maria Annunziata Hospital, with the assistance of a midwife called Norma – both chosen by Adele, both non-negotiable. And consequently no to Marco's hospital, which also had birthing pools, and where he could have offered his daughter a few small comforts.

Yes, also, to understanding the meaning and origin of the name Miraijin, on which point Adele could fully satisfy her father's curiosity. For starters, it was made up of three Japanese characters or *kanji*: 未 来 (Romanised as *mirai*, meaning 'future' or 'future life', which in turn consist of 未 'not yet' and 来 'arrived') and 人 (*jin,* meaning 'man' 'person'). Man of the Future. Those same three characters are pronounced *wèilái rén* in Mandarin, *mei lai jan* in Cantonese and *mirae in* in Korean: the meaning remains the same. Adele had come across that name in a Japanese manga saga called *Miraijin Chaos* by the great Osamu Tezuka. That man (considered the 'god of manga') was his daughter's idol and he had never even heard of him: an unpardonable omission, quickly remedied by Adele's passionate account of his impressive life. *(Here goes, in case you're interested: 手塚 治虫 a.k.a. Osamu Tezuka, born in Toyonaka City, Osaka prefecture, in 1928. Direct descendant of the legendary samurai of the Sengoku period Hattori Hanzo. Disney fan from a tender age, he watches his favourite films dozens of times –* Bambi *almost eighty times. He starts drawing comics aged seven, signing them with the pseudonym Osamushi, a species of beetle belonging to the Adephaga suborder, which he identifies with due to the similarity with his own name. His characters already exhibit the trait that will revolutionise the entire manga genre, namely disproportionately large eyes. Still very young, he develops a rare and painful condition which causes his arms to swell – he is successfully treated by a doctor, which inspires him to become a doctor himself. In 1944, aged sixteen, he works in a factory to support Japan's economy during the Second World War. At the age of seventeen, while radiation devastates the survivors of Hiroshima and Nagasaki, he publishes his first comics and begins his medicine studies after securing a place at Osaka University. Success comes at eighteen, especially with* Shin Takarajima, The New Treasure Island, *inspired by Robert Louis Stevenson's novel – meanwhile, he pursues his medicine studies. In 1949, aged twenty-one, he publishes his first acclaimed masterpiece, a sci-fi trilogy entitled* Zenseiki ('Lost World'), Metoroporisu ('Metropolis') *and* Kitarubeki Sekai ('Next World'). *At the age of twenty-three he graduates from Osaka University, while the robot-child who would become his most famous character – Astro Boy – makes his first appearance in the* Ambassador Atom *saga. From then on, he begins to serialise his work, a first step towards his momentous arrival on the animation scene, while continuing his medicine studies with a master's and then a PhD. In 1959, at the age of thirty-one, he marries Etsuko Okada, a girl from his native Osaka prefecture, but is terribly late to the ceremony because he is busy working on some boards urgently required by his editor. At the age of thirty-two Osamu and his wife move to the Tokyo suburbs and build a large house-studio where they are also joined by his elderly parents, bringing the whole family under one roof. At the age of thirty-three, in 1961 – the year his first child, Makoto, was born – he completes his PhD at the University of Nara, the ancient capital of Japan on Honshu island, with a thesis on spermatogenesis. In the same year, he starts building an annexe which will house the first incarnation of his animation studios, Mushi Productions. Between the age of thirty-five and forty, his daughters Rumiko and Chiiko are born, and true to Tezuka's famous motto that 'a good story can save poor animation, whereas good animation cannot save a poor story' his little independent studios produce the first animated black-and-white manga saga for TV –* Astro Boy *– on a shoestring. His popularity extends outside Japan and earns him the respect and friendship of many other masters: Walt Disney, whom he meets at New York's 1964 World's Fair, wants to hire him for a sci-fi project that was subsequently abandoned; Stanley Kubrik offers him the role of art director on* 2001: A Space Odyssey *in 1965, which Tezuka reluctantly turns down due to his inability to quit Mushi Productions and relocate to Britain for a year; Moebius – whom he met at a festival in France – becomes fascinated by his work and visits him in Japan the following year; but above all Brazilian cartoonist Mauricio de Souza, who will become an intimate friend of his and will be greatly influenced by his style in the following years, to the point of including some of Tezuka's characters – Astro Boy, the Sapphire Princess and Kimba – in the prequel to his most popular saga,* Monica's Gang. *Miraijin's saga – published in three volumes in 1978 – clearly anticipates the plot of* Face/Off, *directed by John Woo almost twenty years later. It's the story of a boy who is murdered by a friend in order to take his place on a space programme he'd failed to join – the boy, however, is resuscitated by a mysterious girl. Meanwhile, the murderer has become very powerful and manages to capture the boy before he can reclaim his rightful place, exiling him on the obscure planet of Chaos. The boy suffers terribly, but after many a heroic battle he manages to escape the planet, defeat his evil friend and become the Man of the Future. Beetle collector, amateur entomologist, Superman, baseball and classical music fan, Osamu Tezuka dedicates his last creations to Beethoven, Mozart and Tchaikovsky. He dies of stomach cancer three months after his sixtieth birthday, in February 1989. According to the relatives who were present, his last words – to the nurse who was putting away his sketch pad – were: 'Please, let me work.')*

Marco Carrera liked this man, and he liked the photo of him that Adele kept in her diary – cheerful smile, thick-rimmed glasses ('difficult glasses' as Marco called them), black flat cap. It reassured him that a man like Tezuka had something to do with Adele's choice to have a child and he sensed, in terms of age and sensibility, a strong connection with his own father, with old Probo and his enthusiastic collection of sci-fi novels. And yet, as much as he admired him, Marco still couldn't be persuaded to read his comics: they were in English, for starters, and on top of that he had never liked manga, a point on which he had no intention of changing his mind.

Japanese culture in general had a lot to do with this New Man who would soon join them. Marco realised this when Adele's surfing and climbing friends started visiting her at home, seeing as she couldn't join their outings anymore, and sometimes stayed for dinner. Marco had never seen them like that before (indoors, in civilian clothes); they all seemed rather normal and sensible after all, which reassured him: they didn't exclusively exist in the daring world of athletic feats and extreme nature, but fit in even in the boring world of ophthalmologists and lasagne. They were polite and respectful. They really loved Adele. And they all loved Japan. One in particular stood out for his charisma and knowledge: Gigio Dithmar von Schmidveiller, nicknamed Smidge. Blond and very handsome, his manners as aristocratic as his name, Smidge was an incredible climber (if slightly less impressive a surfer) but indeed so short, delicate and slight to deserve that almost derogatory moniker – which of course reminded Marco of his own, still in use among some of his childhood friends.

Smidge could talk for hours on end about samurais, shogunates, Murakami's books, Kurosawa's films, martial arts, manga, robotics, Shintoism, sushi and tea ceremonies, and he always sounded like he knew a lot more than he was saying. He had a beautiful voice and spoke elegantly – it was a pleasure to listen to him. His degree was in engineering, not Japanese studies, which meant that all that knowledge of Japanese culture he'd accumulated out of sheer passion (and like all passions, it was contagious). He once said something that helped Marco shed some light on his daughter's choice: to run a thread through the eye of a needle, in the West you push the thread through from the chest outward, while in Japan they do the opposite: the thread comes in from the outside towards your chest. The difference, said Smidge, was all in there: Western civilisation = inside-out; Japan = outside-in. It was clear that this obsession with Japan shared by the whole gang had originated from Smidge, which, in Marco's eyes (still desperate for clues despite accepting his daughter's choice) made him a godfather of sorts, another male role model – beside Marco himself and Osamu Tezuka – for this fatherless grandchild of his. Truth be told, Marco initially suspected that the child might be the fruit of Smidge's very loins, seeing as his girlfriend (Miriam) was the alpha female in the group, older than Adele and very good friends with her, which would have explained Adele's obstinate refusal to reveal the father's identity. However, observing Smidge's spontaneous and unaffected behaviour around Adele, he eventually concluded that couldn't be the case. He had his suspicions about other members of the group too – that Ivan perhaps, with his shiny earring, or the impossibly handsome one who worked as a props manager on film sets and came to see her less often, Giovanni – but those leads went cold fast for the same reason, that is, the natural way they (all of them, boys and girls) behaved around Adele. No, the father wasn't one of them. That said, they must have known something, because the 'misdemeanour' (as Probo would have called it) had taken place the previous January during a surfing trip to Faro and Sagres in the southern Portugal region of the Algarve, where surfing tribes from all over Europe convened each year to take advantage of the ideal conditions afforded by the enormous Atlantic storm waves and the sheltered coves of Cabo de Sao Vicente. But even if they did know, the father's identity was as irrelevant to them as it was to Adele. They never spoke about it: to them, as to Adele, it made complete sense that a twenty-one-year-old girl should raise a child without a father. Marco Carrera tried his best to embrace this philosophy, even though it ran counter to his beliefs. He kept reciting that line by John of the Cross to himself and even quoted it once, over dinner, as the whole gang was debating how to make the world a better place: 'to go where you know not / you must go through what you know not'. He made an excellent impression, because that line fit in well with their way of life, but Marco kept thinking things were not as straightforward as that.

The days flew by, and in the end there was only one decision left to make: sitting on the edge of the birthing pool, legs in, holding Adele throughout labour and birth – yes or no? Adele had no doubts: yes. She had obviously discussed this with her therapist, she explained, proving she was fully aware that Marco might find the prospect embarrassing. Once again, as with all pivotal moments in his relationships with women, Marco felt crushed by the weight of the countless conversations about *him* that had taken place without *him*, in order to make a decision that would affect *him*. And once again, he caved. And so it was that at 11 a.m. on 20 October (a fairly unremarkable day according to Wikipedia, on which few notable figures were born except for Arthur Rimbaud and Italian Renaissance sculptor Andrea della Robbia, and yet – according to Adele – a day positively brimming with karmic energy in 2010 ) – on 20 October 2010 then, Adele's forecast turned out to be correct and Marco Carrera found himself immersed in lukewarm water with his daughter and Norma the midwife.

It all happened much faster than Marco – mindful of Marina's excruciatingly long labour twenty-one years before – had expected. Judging from Adele's few, feeble moans, and from her fluid movements to encourage the contractions, it was also much less painful. He felt no awkwardness as he held her and propped her up, none of that powerlessness he remembered experiencing as Marina, screaming and farting, gave birth to Adele. On the contrary, Marco felt like an active participant, he felt useful, and was horrified to have ever considered not being there. As Adele had always firmly believed, everything was very *natural* – in the most literal sense of the word, i.e. in its Latin etymology of 'pertaining to the ability to procreate'. And when the baby had been pushed out and the midwife held it under water for another ten, twenty, thirty seconds, Marco felt no anxiety, no impatience. Not because he knew that babies were immersed in liquid in the womb and the breathing reflex was only triggered once they left a liquid environment, but because he himself was immersed in that liquid, and in those moments his own decaying body was being permeated by the same feeling of relief as Adele's trim and athletic limbs and Miraijin's soft, brand new flesh. That water held them together, and spoke to them, and reassured them: that water knew. Those thirty seconds were the most enlightened in his entire life. That murky broth they swam in was the only happy family he'd ever known.

As the baby was taken out of the water and handed over to Adele, Marco Carrera found himself reassessing his entire life through the lens of this formidable experience. Amazed to feel so elated where he'd only expected fighting and screaming and filth, he wondered why water births were still so uncommon, why they didn't *all* go for it. He sat there speechless, etching in his memory the moment Miraijin drew her first calm breath, uttered her first cry, opened her (almond-shaped) eyes for the first time – and he didn't even realise it was a girl. He found out shortly afterwards from Adele's first words, as they were all still in the pool and she held the baby tight against her chest, with a look of fulfilment on her face that every father should see in his children at least once: 'See, Dad? We're off to a very good start. The Man of the Future is a woman.'

# A whole life (1998)

Marco Carrera
Poste restante
4 Via Marmorata
Roma Ostiense 00153

Paris, 22 October 1998

Dear Marco,

I've just realised I'll never escape Giorgio Manganelli.

I was finally clearing my books, notes and all the other material I kept on my desk for years after finishing my PhD. I don't know why but I started reading some photocopied poems stuffed inside my copy of Manganelli's *Centuria*, which I must have leafed through and read dozens of times while I was working on my thesis. Three sheets of paper, three photocopied poems – which I certainly didn't use for my thesis because they had nothing to do with it – sitting there, forgotten and rediscovered yesterday when I decided to evict Manganelli from my desk. I immediately recalled the day I first read them in one of my lecturer's books – the sudden, violent urge to photocopy them: not the other poems, just those three. It must have been

1991 maybe, or 1992 – you and I had lost touch and hadn't written to each other in a long time. I'd just got back to Paris from Bolgheri, it was September and like every September I was under your spell, stupefied by the days we'd just spent in that cursed place, days spent with you and yet without you. I read those poems and I wanted to have them, because they were about us. I photocopied them and stashed them in the book I thought I'd never part with. Then one day I forgot about them, and one day I stopped reading that book too, even though it was still there, cluttering my desk for no apparent reason. Yesterday I'd finally resolved to part from the book altogether and put it away on the bookcase with the others, hoping to get over my fixation with Manganelli (which rather hampers your academic career here at the Sorbonne). And so just as I was going to break free once and for all, those three poems re-emerged and took me back where it all began.

Here's one:

We've got a whole life
NOT to spend together.
On God's shelves
Undone things gather dust:
Heaven's flies sully
Our caresses,
Our feelings
Perched like stuffed owls.
'Unsold goods' – will shout the brass angel –
Ten cases of unlived lives.
And we'll have a death to die, too:
Casual, unnecessary death
Indifferent, without you.

It sounds like a made-up story, I know. But you know me, and you know I can't make up stories, because I have no imagination. It's true, Marco, just as it's true that at the bottom of the third poem, in blue ink (and I even remember exactly when I did it, and why, and what I'd just drunk, and the weather outside, but I don't want to bore you) I transcribed this quote – also by Manganelli, my jailer now:

'You know, then, that this is the definition of our love – that I never be where you are, nor you where I am?'

Hugs (via post it's allowed)
Luisa

# Mulinelli (1974)

Irene Carrera chose the Mulinelli beach that August evening, and of all the family members Marco (who was almost fifteen but looked twelve because of his hormonal imbalance) was the only one to realise.

Irene's turbulent disposition manifested itself in an endless succession of tantrums, acts of rebellion, gloomy silences and misleading moments of recovery during which she was given to occasional outbursts of optimism, only to plunge again into sadness and rage. At the age of sixteen, seventeen – even eighteen – she was still acting up to get attention, and as a result her family's alert threshold was rather high: everyone was used to her extreme behaviour. In Florence, she was being treated by a very competent therapist – Dr Zeichen – who, like all therapists, was off in August. He did leave a phone number Irene could call if need be, but it was a foreign number, with a strange area code – a very long, *intimidating* one. To begin with, Irene was determined to get through the summer and enjoy it, even: there had been grandiose plans of a post-A levels trip to Greece with two friends (later abandoned because one of them failed her exams), followed by a much touted (but never arranged) replacement trip to Ireland, and then a quick jaunt on the Versilia riviera where many of her friends were apparently having a great time – but all her plans fell through, as they did every year after all. As a result, by mid-August Irene found herself trapped in the same place she'd spent all her summers, that house in Bolgheri she really thought she could escape now that she had turned eighteen, passed her driving test and graduated from school with straight As. Instead, all it took was a friend bailing on her for her plans to evaporate, which brought home again just how devastatingly limited her friendship circle was (one of the consequences – but also one of the causes – of her depression). There she was, like every summer, with her hyperactive younger brothers running riot, her father cooking or reading, her mother reading or sunbathing, the boat trips on the old sea-worn dinghy, her local friends cramming the intolerable local clubs and Dr Zeichen buried under that foreign area code. The customary array of frustrations was compounded, that year, by her anxiety about the treatment her unwitting younger brother was due to start in the autumn (treatment which – despite their truce – her parents kept discussing every single evening, as Irene eavesdropped on them).

One of those August evenings then, when the weather had already turned and a south-westerly wind swept the coast, Irene got up after a frugal dinner consisting mostly of leftovers and announced that a storm was brewing, so she was off to the beach to secure the dinghy to the shed. She said that as if it was a normal thing for her to do, but it wasn't: if anything, Probo – not Irene – was the one constantly fussing over the dinghy and worrying about keeping it safe. Probo, however, barely noticed: 'good on you' he replied, then retreated to his room. But Marco immediately saw that Irene was going to top herself in the sea – on that small, lethal stretch of beach by their shed they called 'Mulinelli', where the water eddied around in a whirlpool and the currents pulled you down even when there were no waves. Since the Carreras had started holidaying in Bolgheri, four people had already drowned there – all four of them, rumour had it, had been suicides. Irene walked out of the house with an old hemp rope coiled around her shoulder, and Marco watched, dismayed, as neither his mother (who was doing the dishes) nor Giacomo (who was helping her) did anything to stop her. He was terrified but he knew that it was up to him to save his sister: it was between the two of them, he thought, and that thought immediately gave him strength. He made for the French window in the kitchen and slipped out without saying a word.

The sky was overcast, heavy with rain, the air hot and sticky. The sea roared in the murky twilight. Marco ran out of the garden and down the path that led to the bottom of the dunes, and in the fading light he caught a glimpse of Irene's white top. He sped up to keep up with her, but Irene had spotted him and – without even turning – shouted at him to go back home. Marco didn't listen: she'd seen him anyway, so he ran even faster. If she hadn't decided to drown herself, at that point Irene would have waited for him, glad to have her brother with her as she secured the boat to the shed. But she wasn't glad. She turned to face him and told him again to go back home, her tone more menacing this time. Again Marco didn't listen, and ran even faster. She paused, waiting for him to catch up and when he finally did, panting by her side and not knowing what to do, she put her hands on his shoulders, spun him round like a bowling pin and landed a good kick in his buttocks, which took him by surprise and sent him flying to the ground. 'Go away!' she shouted, and set off again – she was running now. Marco got back up and ran after her. Even though he was much smaller than her (he'd always been much smaller than everyone, for that matter) he felt strangely energised – enough to stop her from jumping into the sea. Of course, if there had been someone around he'd have asked for help, just to be safe, but the place was completely deserted and they'd almost got to the dunes, and Marco was ready to pounce on his sister, pin her down if necessary, and hold her down on the sand until she gave up. He was agile, quick, he could fight: Irene had caught him by surprise with that kick, but that wouldn't happen again.

By the dunes, where the sea roared even louder, Irene stopped again and turned to face him. Marco stopped too, a few steps behind. They were both panting. Irene looked at her brother with a savage grin that frightened him, then started cracking the rope she carried like a whip. Walking backwards, she kept cracking the whip at Marco, who kept following her without losing sight of the rope darting back and forth a few inches from his nose. His eyes were locked on that rope whisking through the air like a snake, so they wouldn't stray onto Irene's face and see that devilish grin again.

They got to the beach. Irene stopped lashing the air with the rope and stood next to the boat – which was indeed dangerously close to the shore and at the mercy of the rising tide that could easily carry it away. The whirlpools that gave the beach its name were out there, foaming in the dark sea that kept swelling and swelling, stoked by the wind. Irene stopped to look at them, strained like a pointer dog. Marco stood there catching his breath, ready to pounce on her and anchor her to this world. But Irene stepped aside and hugged – literally – the prow, gently stroking the sea-worn plywood like she would stroke a horse. Marco – his muscles still poised, ready to spring – kept looking at her from behind as she secured the rope to the prow with a bowline knot and then tied the other end around her hips. He let her hoist the boat up to the shed, walking backwards, without rubber rollers, without a trailer, in spurts, by brute force: he didn't step in, didn't help her. Once the dinghy was safe, Irene unhooked the rope from around her hips and tied it to the shed with another bowline knot, then turned towards Marco: this time, as the darkness set in, he looked her in the eye – looked closely – and the devilish grin was gone.

They walked back home together, trying to sync their steps so they could hug – a rather unusual hug, Marco clinging to her waist and Irene with an arm wrapped around his shoulders. Every now and again she'd scratch between the two nerves down the back of his neck with her thumb – ever so gently, light as a feather.

# Weltschmerz & Co. (2009)

To: Giacomo jackcarr62@yahoo.com
Sent: 12 December 2009 19:14
Subject: Universal pain
From: Marco Carrera

Dear Giacomo,

Something's come up and I need to tell you, because you are the only other person left in this world who might be interested in it, or at any rate who had something to do with it.

I went to the house in Piazza Savonarola to check that everything was in order. Don't ask me why I do it. Every now and again I go and check. The house is slowly falling apart – it should be emptied, tidied up, rented at least, seeing as selling it is out of the question during this economic crisis: every once in a while I pop in to see if there are any leaks, or damages, or other issues – to make sure it doesn't fall apart all in one go, in short. It's all I can manage for now. I cancelled the gas contract – the water one is still running though, otherwise we couldn't clean the house even if we wanted to. Not that I go there to clean up, far from it (who would I clean it for?) – I just want to check. To make sure it doesn't fall apart all in one go. I wonder if you can understand why I do it, since you refused to ever set foot in that house again. Maybe not. But that's not what I wanted to talk to you about.

Anyway, yesterday I went over to the house. And at some point, I don't know why, I felt the urge to go to Irene's room. I knew nothing had been touched, because I'd gone in many times while I still lived there and even later, when I'd come visit from Rome during the holidays. I knew Mum and Dad had always kept it intact, clean, the bed made – ready, as it were, for Irene to come back any moment. I'd open the door, walk in, and look around: the bed, the blue duvet, the tidy desk, the messy bookcase, the pretty lamp and the ugly lamp, the guitar on its stand, the records and the record player, the wardrobe with the Jacques Mayol poster, the Lydia Lunch poster, the dolls' house on the waterfall that Dad built especially for her – that masterpiece. I'd walk in, look around, and leave. I'd do it more often back then, to be honest: now I barely even check her room because I'm certain there can never be any problems in that room again, ever. That room is at peace, if you see what I mean. Yesterday morning, however, I don't know why, I went in. And I didn't just look around: I sat on the bed, spoiling the immaculate blue duvet. I switched on the pretty lamp. I sat at her desk. Now, if in all these years (these many, many years) you'd asked me what was on Irene's desk, in that room at peace with itself, I'd have answered you 'nothing'. Or rather: the pretty lamp, the National Geographic world map under its glass plate, the framed *Rocky Horror Show* poster that Irene never hung on the wall – nothing, in short. But there was something, actually, it had always been there, it still is. A book. One of those old books, well preserved, no images on the cover, wrapped in a glossy protective sheet like Dad's sci-fi novels.

Maybe it's because it's almost the same colour as the desk, but I'd never noticed it. A collection of poems. *Molte Stagioni* (Many Seasons) by Giacomo Prampolini – an author I'd never heard of. I picked it up and felt the urge to stroke that glossy protective sheet. Then I opened it on a random page. It wasn't random, actually: I opened it where it – the book – wanted to be opened, that is on page 25. Lodged in it was a folded notebook sheet that fell on the desk. Before opening it, I read the poem on that page. This poem:

Abandoned by you
I'll break, you know this;
You're counting on it, and I know you're thinking:
I'll be steadier by then.
Certainties are what our love is made of!
And yet . . . yet
Every misfortune that befalls you
Will be born of me;
And I will suffer what you suffer
With no hope of a smile.
At dawn indifferent poplars
Sway in the wind;
Men and women walk by, first
And eternal image of time

I don't know, Giacomo, that seems to me the saddest poem that was ever written. Then I picked up the sheet of paper that had fallen out and opened it. It was Irene's handwriting – fountain pen, blue ink. I read it:

*June 1981*
*Weltschmerz & Co.*
*Weltschmertz – Universal Pain.*

*Being tired of the world. Jean Paul. Tolkien. Elves.*
*Giacomo Prampolini, 'Many Seasons'.*
*Anomie – Emile Durkenheim, 'Suicide' (1897)*
*Dhukha – Sanskrit. Suffering. Literal translation: hard to bear.*

*The bhagava was in Shravasti and said: 'Bhikkhu, I will tell you all about how dhukha arises and also how dhukha ceases. Listen, pay full attention to my words, I will speak.'*

*'Very well, oh venerable one,' answered the bhikkhu. And the bhagava shared his wisdom:*

*'How, bhikkhu, does dhukha arise? From the eye and the visible objects visual awareness arises; and when these three meet, contact arises. From contact comes sensation, from sensations comes coveting. This, bhikkhu, is the origin of dhukha.*

*From the ear and from sound auditory awareness arises; from the nose and from smell olfactory awareness arises; from the mind and the objects of cognition mental awareness arises; when these three meet, contact arises; from contact comes sensation; from sensations comes coveting. This, oh bhikkhu, is the origin of dhukha.*

*And how, bhikkhu, does dhukha cease? From the eye and the visible objects visual awareness arises; and when these three meet, contact arises. From contact comes sensation, from sensations comes coveting. Only by completely eliminating coveting through the path of arhat can one eliminate attachment; by eliminating attachment, bhava ('becoming') will cease; when bhava ceases, rebirth ceases; when rebirth ceases, growing old and dying cease; and therefore suffering, physical pain, mental unrest and agony cease. This is how all this mass of dhukha ceases. This, bhikkhu, is how dhukha ceases.'*

She was more miserable than we imagined, Giacomo. I took the book home and read it all in one sitting. The one on p.25 is by far the best poem, and the saddest. And then – I almost missed it – hidden in the fold of the dust jacket, written upside down to make it even harder to spot, I found this sentence written so small, in pencil, perhaps so that no one would read it:

> *One should always be very careful when letting off steam, Lorenzo. Always.*

Lorenzo?

Who the fuck is this Lorenzo?

We knew nothing about her, Giacomo. She knew everything about all of us, but we knew nothing about her.

Virtual hugs
Marco

# Gloomy Sunday (1981)

Time: Sunday, 23 August 1981
Place: Bolgheri, or rather, that stretch of coast south of Marina di Bibbona known by some as Renaione, by others as Palone, and by the Carreras generically as 'Bolgheri' – meaning not so much the nearby village wrapped around the Gherardesca castle, but the pine grove and beach immediately below (both of which, incidentally, are still almost entirely owned by the Gherardesca family). It was on that rugged stretch of coast that, in the early 1960s, Probo and Letizia Carrera managed to purchase an old derelict farm building right behind the dunes, together with an adjacent strip of the pine grove. That place was meant to be the very symbol of the happiness that – with two small children and a third on the way – they thought they could spread around them. The renovation works were overseen by both (Letizia handled its form, Probo its growth), so that throughout the years the old farm building was constantly extended and renovated – with or without planning permission – turning into an elegant holiday home on the Tuscan coast. Meanwhile, however, Letizia and Probo's happiness had run out, and the stubborn commitment to spending every summer holiday in that house with the whole family had begun to resemble an exercise in self-harm.

Another place worth mentioning with regards to that same Sunday is a beach restaurant in San Vincenzo, which had opened just the year before and would shortly gain an excellent reputation.

Yet another is the gulf of Baratti, about which there is very little to say, other than it's one of the wonders of the world.

Back in Bolgheri, the Carreras are all in the house. The ragù Probo had cooked four days before has finally run out after being reheated and consumed multiple times, to the point that it seemed to regenerate itself like Odin's wild boar, killed and eaten every night by the Norse gods. It's Sunday, so Ivana (the lady who comes in every day from Bibbona to clean the house and cook their meals) is off, which means there's nothing for dinner. Normally, Probo or Marco would handle such an emergency, but tonight they are both preoccupied with more urgent commitments. Probo and Letizia are about to go out for dinner to a restaurant in San Vincenzo called Il Gambero Rosso, to celebrate the fiftieth birthday of his friend Aldino Mansutti's widow. It may be her birthday, but it's Probo's evening, really: that new restaurant on the beachfront was his idea, and he was the one who convinced Titti Mansutti it was worth the forty-five-minute drive from Punta Ala. It might be her birthday, but the booking is in his name, and the bill will be his to pay too. The void he leaves at home is the last thing on his mind.

Marco, for his part, is about to embark on an adventure that will change his life: he has asked Luisa Lattes out (he's been in love with the girl next door for the past two years) and she said yes. It's not your average date though, for three reasons: (1) Luisa is only fifteen, while Marco is twenty-two, which means he fell in love with her when she was thirteen; (2) his family and Luisa's have been embroiled in a feud for years, and both are persuaded they are the victim in the eternal farce that are neighbour disputes. It all started a few years back when Luisa's father (a very large, arrogant, diehard conservative lawyer, who the following year would go as far as uprooting his entire family to Paris 'for fear of the Communists') accused Marco's mother of having poisoned his beloved pointer (the dog, incidentally, did keep everyone awake at night and was indeed a pain in the arse).

The blood feud mostly concerned Letizia and the lawyer: Mrs Lattes and Probo, of a similar disposition, had always stayed out of it, passively enduring their respective spouses' tirades. As for the children, they had first made friends (as is only natural in a desolate place like that, where your neighbours are often the only people you'll see on a daily basis) and then more or less secretly fallen in love with each other. Irene had broken the embargo four years before by dating Luisa's elder brother, Carlo. A basic lad, so to speak – sporty, blond hair, devoted to his parents – someone Irene would have most likely despised, had the feud not turned him into a forbidden fruit of sorts. As a result, Irene spent a whole summer smooching him under the livid gaze of their warring parents, only to unceremoniously dump him in September, once they were back in Florence and no one was watching anymore. More recently (two years ago, as we said) Luisa's transformation knocked Marco sideways: she'd grown up all of a sudden, unsettlingly so. Not on paper perhaps – she was still only thirteen – but she certainly looked very different from the previous summer; and she'd grown in other respects too: Marco caught her sitting on the beach, her back against the shed, engrossed in no less than *Dr Zhivago*, i.e. his favourite book. He'd spent the following two years simply waiting for Luisa to get to an age when his love wouldn't be considered unhealthy, but that summer it became clear to him that if he'd waited another year to make his move, he'd lose any right he thought he could claim over her (like some sort of 'finders keepers' rule, so to speak, same as his father with that fancy restaurant, or Irene with Nick Drake's music). But aside from all that, what makes their date truly scandalous is reason (3) something Marco – unlike Luisa – is not aware of: that very same morning, having come back from his post-A levels trip to Portugal with his girlfriend, Giacomo (his impulsive, muscly, narky, generous younger brother, so different from him, so handsome, elegant, tanned, but also fragile and touchy, insecure even) Giacomo then, after an equally lengthy, secret and tormented journey (even more secret and tormented actually, considering he'd been in a relationship for two years) Giacomo, in short, had also asked Luisa out. And Luisa – who'd made her choice years before, as a child, that is, before either of them – turned him down. And even though Marco hadn't been parading his date with Luisa around the house, Giacomo, still sore from her rejection, feared the worst: he'd seen them, thick as thieves, on the beach. As a result, he's really not in the mood for food either.

Irene, meanwhile, is at the end of her tether. And it shows. It really shows. You can see it in her sunken eyes, her shattered gaze, the blueish vein pulsating on her forehead, her dishevelled hair caked in seawater that she won't even bother tying up in a ponytail as she shuffles around the house like a ghost, headphones constantly on. And above all, it's in the music playing in those headphones, if anyone had bothered to check: 'Gloomy Sunday', a.k.a. the Hungarian suicide song – which, according to several urban legends, was singlehandedly responsible, due to its overwhelming sadness, for scores of people taking their own lives in 1930s Budapest. The version Irene was listening to was the rasping, acidic, off-key, desperate version recently released by her idol Lydia Lunch, a cover which, crucially, didn't include the line that had been added to the original to soften the blow ('dreaming, I was only dreaming'). Irene had recorded the song on a deadly loop on both sides of the only tape that, for days, had been playing in her red Walkman (a Christmas present from her brothers).

No one saw it. Not even Letizia – who doesn't want to go out for dinner with her husband, and who, therefore, could use her daughter's condition as an excuse to stay home and cook Irene some spaghetti, ask her if she feels like having a chat, perhaps earning a wholehearted 'fuck off' in reply – which under the circumstances may well rescue Irene from herself. But Letizia can't see the stampeding herd of elephants in the room, about to trample all over her family. She is dissatisfied, listless – as always. As always, she has a slight headache. She doesn't feel like doing what she is about to do, but she will do it – as always.

No one is thinking about food tonight at the Carreras', no one is thinking about Irene, and little by little the house empties. Marco is the first to leave: he has to create a diversion because of the feud between the two families. He says goodbye and leaves, completely absorbed by the ploy he's concocted with Luisa. She'll be leaving too, soon, on her bike, saying she's off to her friend Floriana's (who is in on their little ploy, like Juliet's nurse). Instead of stopping at her friend's house, however, Luisa will keep going until Casa Rossa, where she'll find Marco waiting for her. She'll leave her bike there and get in his VW Beetle. He's already decided where he's going to take her: to the most beautiful place in the world. For the first time, at the age of twenty-two, Marco is about to be happy and he knows it. They haven't even talked about it, but he knows that Luisa loves him back. He knows – more or less – what will happen, and there's room for nothing else in his head.

Probo and Letizia leave too. They're all dressed up and in a cheerful mood – Probo for real, Letizia faking it – but only at the start, because to her great surprise, once in the car she'll find that her husband's cheerful mood is contagious. Rather than actual cheerfulness (which, for Letizia, would be a stretch) what she begins to feel is some sort of healing, a sisterly tenderness for her husband – he's so excited, so focused on his evening, Probo who is never the centre of attention (least of all, for many years now, hers). And tonight won't be 'his' evening either, because the birthday girl is this wiry widow who always wears rather outrageous jewellery, and as always the conversation will revolve around her husband Aldino, a childhood friend of Probo's who was killed eleven years earlier in that absurd accident. (An accident incorrectly referred to as a 'motorbike accident', but only because he was riding his brand new Guzzi V7 Special on the Strada Statale Aurelia when, immediately after crossing the bridge on the river Arno by the San Leonardo church between Pisa and Livorno, he was flattened by a tank carrying 170 litres of water. The tank had come loose from its hook on the Bell Model 206 Jet Ranger helicopter supplied by the nearby US military base of Camp Darby to help the local fire brigade put out a blaze on the Pisan hills, which was threatening the town of Fauglia.)

That night, as they're driving to Il Gambero Rosso on that very same Strada Statale Aurelia, only fifty or so kilometres south from where the accident took place, Probo decides to share with Letizia his own methodology for processing grief – which, as it happens, is directly linked to Aldino's accident, so distant and yet still so vivid in his mind. As they drive in the twilight, he tells her something he'd never told her before: how he'd gone to great lengths to mathematically demonstrate the absurdity of that cruel and unacceptable death, which – as illogical as it may sound – enabled him to come to terms with it. Letizia is moved. He'd taken it upon himself, he says, to calculate the probability of that accident. He'd got hold of all the data gathered by the subsequent inquiry: helicopter route and speed, flight altitude, tank weight, wind speed as well as the speed the motorbike was travelling at the time of the impact. After a series of laborious calculations, the results pointed to the exact opposite of what he was trying to demonstrate: namely that far from being extremely unlikely, the accident was the inescapable consequence of a fixed interplay of factors: there was no way out for Aldino. Then – he continues – he'd changed tack and tried to approach the problem like she would have done, i.e. in a simple and creative manner. Letizia is moved, again. All it took was a single, simple calculation: how far did the helicopter travel in one second? An easy calculation, considering all the data he'd already gathered: 43 metres. Every second, the helicopter travelled 43 metres. And what about Aldino? How fast did he travel, in metres per second? 23.5. Therefore, Probo explains, if the hook had broken a second later, the tank would have ended up 43 metres further east, that is right on the San Leonardo church (he'd checked), and Aldino would have been 23 metres further down the road anyway. So, not only he'd still be alive, but he might not even have noticed anything and happily carried on, on his way to Punta Ala. This, assuming the hook had broken one second later. And what if – he continues – it had broken just *one tenth of a second* later? In real life, Probo says, a tenth of a second is nothing, it's an abstraction, the blink of an eye – but if that day the hook had broken a tenth of a second later, the tank would have fallen four metres and thirty centimetres beyond the spot where it actually fell, and Aldino would have been almost two and a half metres further down the road. That is to say, he would have noticed all right, and it would have given him a good fright, but again, nothing would have happened to him. What about one twentieth of a second – i.e. five hundredths of a second later? Still nothing: the tank would have fallen two metres and fifteen centimetres away, Aldino would have been one metre twenty-five further down the road – the closest of close shaves, but again, he'd be alive. What about three hundredths of a second? The tank would have fallen one metre thirty away, Aldino would have only been seventy centimetres further and boom – man down. Therefore, he concludes, Aldino's death had been a matter of three hundredths of a second.

At this point, Probo interrupts his narration to ask if Letizia is still with him. Yes, she answers, because it's true, she is still with him, paying him real attention for once – attention tinged with tenderness as we said, because to her, Probo's story is nothing short of his self-portrait. Meanwhile, they've arrived at the square by the restaurant: without saying a word, Probo parks the car. Lights off. Engine off. Window down. He lights a cigarette.

He'd come to that conclusion – Probo continues – by imagining how she would have approached the issue: a single calculation leading to a simple, devastating result, rather than ten calculations leading to a complicated and insignificant result. Spoken like a true architect, says Letizia. No – retorts Probo – spoken like Letizia Calabrò. This completely new outlook on Aldino's death – he says – had stayed with him for years, and he'd decided to share it with her that evening. There was no need to calculate the probability of that helicopter hook breaking in the precise moment Aldino found himself in the exact spot where the tank would fall, to know that it was close to zero. One in a million? One in a billion? It doesn't matter. Definitely much lower than that of being struck by lightning while running for cover, Probo says, like poor Cecchi that time in France: but that had happened during an electric storm, lightning striking the ground everywhere, and Cecchi was, precisely, on the ground. No – he carries on, smoking and staring at an indefinite spot before him – the context that led to his friend's death was much more exceptional and complex, and the accident that caused it belongs in the category of *almost* impossible events, those that simply defy calculation. These events (whose likelihood of actually taking place is infinitely close to zero) number in the order of millions – says Probo – but seeing as they're talking about Aldino's death, only one other such event immediately springs to mind, and one he'd never be able to ignore: the possibility of him killing his friend.

Probo smiles. He takes a long drag from his cigarette. Night has fallen now, and in the darkness his face is lit up red by the cigarette ember. Without saying a word, he stares at what he can make out of his wife's face.

How do you mean? she asks.

Theirs – Probo replies – had been the perfect friendship, as she knows. Intense, emotional, full of adventure – and yet, he and Aldino had had at least two memorable fights, which were never mentioned again by either of them because they'd ended quickly and without consequences. One of these fights had happened in their twenties when they were students: Probo can't quite remember the reason, something to do with a party, maybe even a girl, maybe he was in the wrong. The one Probo remembers well (and the one he'd gone back to after Aldino's death) was the second one, which happened many years later once they'd both graduated and married and had children. What made it so memorable, Probo says, is the fact that they were both *armed* – because they were out hunting, just the two of them, in Titti's father's estate in Vallombrosa. Aldino had shot a partridge that should have been Probo's, and he'd shot it from behind Probo's back, the barrel of his shotgun appearing over Probo's shoulder without warning and giving him the fright of his life, because he was taking aim and was not at all prepared for those loud bangs a few inches from his ear. Aldino was in the wrong – what he'd done was selfish and dangerous – but Probo's reaction was over the top, hysterical even. Enraged, he'd shouted out all manner of abuse at him (some of which was completely undeserved) and then stormed off, still shaking with anger and fear, leaving Aldino alone as the dog deposited the bloody partridge between his feet. So – Probo asks his wife – isn't it possible that during that outburst, for three hundredths of a second, he might have felt the urge to kill Aldino? He was holding a loaded shotgun and pouring out all his rage and indignation over Aldino as if he was the most despicable of men: doesn't Letizia think that for such an infinitesimal (and therefore undetectable) moment, during that outburst, Probo could have had an impulse to raise his shotgun and shoot him in the face?

Silence. Letizia doesn't know what to say. Yellow headlights approach, slicing through the darkness: it's Titti Mansutti's Citroën DS. Letizia remains silent. Yes – says Probo – of course he did. And since Aldino's fate was to die in one of the universe's most unlikely chain of events in the space of three hundredths of a second, then it's as if Probo had killed him that morning, really. It's the exact same thing. He flicks his cigarette, opens the door and gets out. Letizia follows him. The Citroën stops, Titti and her two daughters get out. They all hug and walk into the restaurant.

At that moment, twenty kilometres up north, Irene is leaving the house to go to the beach. Giacomo sees her leave and he's relieved, because he's decided to do something but didn't dare do it while Irene was around, because she always hears everything that one, always finds out about everything, and what she doesn't hear or find out she guesses somehow. Now that she's gone, he can go ahead. He needs to check something. He picks up the receiver and dials the Lattes' number. Next door, just forty metres away behind the hedge, the phone rings once. Twice. Hello? (It's the mother). Good evening (puts on a fake voice), may I speak to Luisa, please? I'm sorry, Luisa is out: who shall I say has called? Giacomo sits motionless on the sofa, the receiver on his lap. Hello? (voice from the receiver).

Hello? Giacomo hangs up. She told him she was staying in. Irene, meanwhile, has already crossed the garden and is shuffling down the path like a ghost, towards the dunes. Beyond the dunes is the beach. Beyond the beach are the whirlpools.

Meanwhile, Marco and Luisa are eating hot focaccia bread outside a shed among the pine trees in Baratti. Restless as two people who are about to rip each other's clothes off, they eat, share a beer and don't speak much. Is yours tasty? Very. Mine too. Shall we get another one? They've both been waiting for this moment for a long time, and now they both know it will happen, out there, soon, on the beach. Marco's been waiting for two years, Luisa for five, maybe ten – forever actually, as far as she's concerned. *Marco Carrera*: Luisa can't remember a time, throughout her life, when that name didn't make her heart skip a beat. Like when she was very little, before their families fell out, and Marco chased her around the beach, or when he and Irene taught her and her brother to sail on their dinghy; and even later when the name Carrera had become anathema to her family, but he kept smiling at her on the beach and being kind to her as if nothing had happened; or when Irene and her brother got together and kissed in front of everyone, and Luisa was only ten, and she was happy because it meant that love conquered all, and so one day she and Marco could do the same . . . Outside that shed, her eyes locked on Marco slowly chewing on his focaccia, Luisa calls to mind all the times she'd fantasised about this moment – that is, her entire life. The untamed beauty of Baratti, the towering pine trees with their broad crowns, the flat sea reflecting the town's lights, the infinite tenderness of that moonless August evening – it all feels conjured up to celebrate her (and Marco's) only real wish finally coming true.

Meanwhile, over at Il Gambero Rosso, Letizia is sitting opposite Probo and still looking at him fondly, with increasing fondness, in fact; fondness so intense it's beginning to feel like attraction. Now how is that possible? Letizia being *physically* attracted to her husband? How long since they'd had sex? Years. Was it the story about his friend's death – Probo, always so logical, square, *boring*? Or is it the restaurant where they're having dinner, full of perfect smells and perfect sounds, and beautiful dishes, and contented people – is that what's making him attractive? Letizia doesn't usually care much for food, but everything she tries tonight tastes incredible: saffron seafood soup, shrimp and tarragon sweet rice, wild salmon and spring onion gratin, orecchiette with shallots, seabass en croute, fresh fish from San Vincenzo . . .

That dinner is beyond time and space, it's *forward-looking* – as she describes every person or thing that truly fascinates her ('forward-looking', 'so forward-looking', 'truly forward-looking'). And what Letizia considers 'forward-looking' may or may not turn out to be so, meaning that it may indeed catch on (like that restaurant and that cuisine) or not (like radical architecture). Either way, that remains the only real requirement in her personal aesthetic framework: if it's not forward-looking, it can't be beautiful.

And in the end, Letizia is indeed attracted to Probo again: she finds him charming and alluring as she did a quarter of a century ago, which would have been completely unthinkable only a few hours before. Now, however, it feels natural: they're husband and wife, they chose each other twenty-five years ago, they wanted each other and still do. After dinner, a very sober and very grateful Titti heads back to Punta Ala in her Citroën, but the restaurant is still there (as is the bottle of Grattamacco white wine), and even though Il Gambero Rosso doesn't have any rooms, there's always the beach, quiet and wild, where they can wander – or rather stagger in a drunken embrace – looking for the darkest spot . . .

And so, on this special night – with the exception of Giacomo, who'd collapsed on the sofa knocked out by a powerful combination of rum and Nutella – four out of five members of the Carrera family are lying on different beaches along the same coast, lapped by the same sea and basking in a variety of blissful states. In San Vincenzo, Letizia and Probo are still dizzy from their escapade, which they know full well will never be repeated again: a unique kind of bliss. Over in Baratti, Marco's bliss is that of lips swollen with kisses, the certainty (misguided, sadly, ever so misguided) that those kisses will be repeated again and again. And finally, in Bolgheri, Irene is the most peaceful and blissful of them all: her mind switched off – untroubled at last, her limp, hollow body tossed and tumbled by the waves, regurgitated by the whirlpools onto the shore where, at low tide, it will be found.

# Here they come (2012)

To: Luisa
Sent: 24 November 2012 00:39
Subject: Help
From: Marco Carrera

Luisa,

What does it mean to have read a book, I wonder? You just have to stand in a square and look around: lots of people talking on their mobile phones. What have they got to say to each other, I wonder? And how did they manage before, when there were no mobile phones? Stripy toothpaste – how do the stripes come out so neat, I wonder? I tried to set a beautiful melody as my alarm ringtone instead of the default one but waking up is still awful. The time machine exists.

Adele . . .

Some people are against daylight saving time, Japan for instance doesn't observe it. It's very windy today, lots of things flying around. You get bored in waiting rooms.

She's dead.

Three years ago, when I moved back here, there was a crane on the street behind my house. In the end I think I've figured out what it is that kids just can't stand when their parents divorce.

Adele is dead.

I read that in Piedmont they're planning on culling four hundred deer because they cause accidents when they cross the road. I read that 80 per cent of real estate in Italy is inherited from the father's side. I read about an engineer in Milan who every weekend sets up a little stall in a park and listens to people for free. I read that Bill Gates and his wife strictly limited the time their daughter spent in front of a computer throughout her childhood.

Mine, instead, is dead – you see? My Adele is dead and I can't follow her because of the little one.

When I was sixteen I was obsessed with Joni Mitchell.

Help me, Luisa. I can't go on this time.

I've been hit by a grenade.

It's just one grenade after the other now.

Here they come.

Evil – you know – is there something like a fast track for evil, or does it just hit people at random, I wonder?

Here they come.

The mists of oblivion.

# Shakul & Co. (2012)

And in the end it came. The phone call all parents fear like hell – because it *is* hell, the gates of hell. It's dreaded by all but comes only for a few wretched, fated, doomed parents – god-forsaken, extremely unlucky – but it is dreaded by all, especially when it comes in the middle of the night (not the case here, but still). Dreaded the most when it wakes you up with a start in the middle of the night (rrrriiing): we are all familiar with it, even if we've never received one, because we all got a phone call in the middle of the night at least once, a call that woke us up with a start (rriiinng) and froze the blood in our veins, and the clock said it was three forty in the morning, or four seventeen, and we all immediately thought *this is it*, and we hesitated to pick up as the phone kept ringing (rrrriiing) and we prayed – even those of us who don't believe in God – prayed it wasn't that, prayed that our car would be on fire instead, or the building next door, but we know it's never going to be our car or the building next door anyway (rrrriiing), and so we all hesitated and prayed the victim was someone else at least, oh please Father, God Almighty have mercy, I have never prayed to Thee because I'm an idiot (rrrriiing) and I neglected Thee and broke Thy laws and sinned against Thee and took Thy name in vain, arrogant idiot that I am, and I am not worthy of speaking Thy name and I deserve nothing and will most certainly end up in hell (rrrriiing) and yet I beg Thee, Father, here, now, on this earth, from the bottom of my heart, down on my knees, bowing down, lying down, I beg Thee, let this not be that phone call (rrrriiing) that one phone call, please take me instead, now, straight away, but it's obviously not me you've decided to take, I'll have to stay here in this vale of tears, and so I beg Thee – take my mother, yes, which would break my heart but take her, or my father, or my brother; and please take everything I own, and my good health, make me an orphan (rrrriiing) a beggar, an invalid, but please God Almighty, I beg Thee, I implore Thee, don't make me a . . . And here we all stopped because the word we needed doesn't exist – English, Italian, French, German, Spanish, Portuguese: we all stopped because that word doesn't exist in any of these languages. It does, however, exist for us Hebrew, Arabic, Ancient and Modern Greek speakers, for many of us who speak an African language, and for the very few remaining Sanskrit speakers – but what difference does it make? In the end, it's just that some of us have a name for that particular type of hell and others don't (rrrriiing), and yet we all prayed, terrified, instead of picking up the phone that kept ringing in the middle of the night, and in the end we did pick it up and maybe there was no answer (more likely in fact than our car being on fire) 'Hello?' 'Hello?' – no answer – yes that does happen quite often, a prank call maybe, a cruel prank to make us think the time had come for us to get that call, in the middle of the night, to terrify us to the point of reciting the most heart-wrenching prayer ever conceived.

Our friend Marco would have prayed too, but he didn't, because the phone call – *that* phone call – did come for him, but it didn't come at night, it came on a Sunday afternoon in autumn, in the broken light that filters through the windows at four thirty-five, his granddaughter asleep on his lap as he sat on the sofa watching Hal Hashsby's *Being There*, and therefore content and at peace – fulfilled even – free from the angst that had gripped him years before when Adele went away for the weekend with her friends, who seemed to be decent people, responsible, reliable; and therefore he let her go with them, he always let her go ever since she was a teenager because she was really gifted, and of course he would tag along at the beginning, but after a while he'd stopped because it was embarrassing (he was always the only parent there, which was almost worse than not letting her go). And so at some point he began waiting for her at home, waiting anxiously of course whether it was morning, afternoon or night, racked by doubt (am I doing the right thing? Adele really loves these sports, but they're so dangerous, I mean it's not tennis, but then again Adele never liked tennis, the only thing she liked as a child was fencing, which already implied a *weapon*, a symbol of blood, death, danger). He could have said no to waves and ascents, no to those attempts to defy gravity – it was his prerogative as a parent – but he could also say yes, and he did, and so he let her go, and endured the resulting anxiety without complaining, and dreaded (without complaining) that phone call in the middle of the night every single time he went to bed and Adele was out. He dreaded that call before he fell asleep, and then when he woke up to go to the loo, and then again before he got back to sleep, or as he took his drops to get back to sleep – Klonopin, Xanax, Valium. Yet, nothing had ever happened in all those years, not even the smallest accident, by day or night, not a scratch, not a twisted ankle, nothing at all, except, well . . . except for the fact that one day she'd come back pregnant from one of those stunts – but that was a different story altogether. She was pregnant at twenty and the father was nowhere to be found: he'd accepted everything without complaining, without giving away his inner turmoil (am I doing the right thing?), because after all Adele was a good girl, conscientious, reliable. *She'd made it* somehow – and that was a real miracle actually, considering what she'd gone through as a child – traumatised, dragged from Italy to Germany and back to Italy again, Rome then Munich then Florence; with a clinically insane mother (let's face it) and an idiot of a father who wasn't able to protect her, pain pouring on her from all sides. She could have grown up dysfunctional as a matter of principle but had grown up surprisingly stable instead, she'd only resorted to dysfunctional behaviour to alert her parents to a danger they couldn't yet see (hence the thread behind her back), and she'd got better once her parents understood (so the thread vanished). When the situation got completely out of hand she resurrected the thread again, wrapping the whole of Munich into an inescapable web, thus signalling a way out to her inadequate parents (her clinically insane mother, the father who wasn't able to protect her): in short, she had always been the one who'd steered her wretched family not towards a happy ending as such – because you can't really call that a happy ending – but towards the lesser evil. And that much at least our friend Marco had understood, in the end: he'd realised his daughter possessed a powerful, intuitive kind of wisdom, and he strove to give her some stability (because that's all she needed in the end, a little – albeit painful – stability). A predictable, comforting routine made of regular visits to her mother at the care home, of Adele's indescribable love for her little sister – love she wisely put on hold until they'd be older and able to express it fully – a painful, complex stability then, but stability nonetheless, a new stability Adele could finally lean on, wrapping up that thread for good and becoming a so-called 'model student', and then a model single mother, who studied and worked and chased waves and climbed rock walls. And when she chased waves or climbed walls, Marco would stay at home with the little one, Miraijin, his granddaughter, and that's how things were supposed to be: Adele would go and recharge her wisdom in the wild and he'd be waiting at home with the little one, giving her stability, keeping his anxiety in check.

He'd been doing that for years and it did seem like he'd done the right thing to let her go, to accept everything, to persevere – it really did seem like the risk was paying off, until that phone call came, eventually, and he found out he really was one of those wretched, godforsaken people. And so it came, the phone call dreaded by all parents but received only by a few doomed, unfortunate ones, parents who, from then on, would only have a name in certain languages (like Hebrew for instance: *shakul*, from the verb *shakal*, meaning, precisely, 'to lose a child'; or Arabic: *thaakil*, same root as *shakul*; or Sanskrit *vilomah*, literally 'contrary to the natural order of things'; or many of the African diaspora languages; and Modern Greek: *charokammenos*, 'burnt by death' – said of all those who are devasted by grief, but almost exclusively used to describe a parent who has lost a child. And at any rate, on the topic of losing one's child, Fabrizio de André (one of Marco's idols) had already said everything there was to say: 'You know, I lost two children / madam that's rather careless of you': because come to think of it, it doesn't make sense to speak of 'losing' someone when they die, shifting the focus away from them and onto ourselves (*I* have lost my daughter, i.e. *I* have let her pass away, *I* have let her die, it's all about *me me me*). And yet . . . It's obscene when it's someone else doing the dying, but when *your* child dies, it does make sense in a way, because somewhere there is always a parent who feels responsible, guilty of not doing their duty: they didn't prevent, avoid, avert, protect, foresee. *They* let it happen, let them die, and therefore *they* lost their son or their daughter.

And so it came, that phone call, for our friend Marco, the phone call that obliterated his life, and it came on a Sunday afternoon, in autumn, and his life that had already been obliterated many times before was obliterated again, back to zero. Except life is the opposite of zero, and in fact Miraijin was asleep on his lap, and as he tried to breathe – because he was struggling to do even that, seeing as he'd been *shakul* for just a few seconds (that's not exactly how they'd put it, they were tactful, but he'd understood all the same), he'd been *thaakil, vilomah, charokammenos* for just a few seconds, and his lungs were sealed, and air was a blistering string down his throat, and his stomach a black hole, and his head a drum, and that's as close to zero as life can get – in that moment, Miraijin (who'd turned two the month before) softly woke up and smiled at him, and by doing so, by simply waking up and smiling at him, she said don't even think about it, Grandpa, she said. I mean it, she said. Grandpa, I'm here and you must go on.

# Weighed up (2009)

To: Giacomo jackcarr62@yahoo.com
Sent: 12 April 2009 23:19
Subject: Letizia's photos
From: Marco Carrera

Dear Giacomo,

I managed to sort out Mum's photo archive! It was a stroke of luck, but that's done too – now we can really sell that house.

It was a lot harder for me to take care of Mum's things than Dad's, for several reasons, and truth be told I didn't take care of it at all: those thousands of photos – so beautiful really – embarrassed me and sometimes hurt me. Looking at those portraits of architects and artists Mum collaborated with, I couldn't help but wonder which one of them had been her lover, and anyway my heart ached to see all those people, all that talent, that whole world around her where there was never any room for Dad, not even a tiny corner. It's true that Dad's world – with his sci-fi novels and his scale models – cut Mum out too, but there was no one else there: it was a solitary world for a solitary man. In Mum's work, however, there was a whole galaxy of men, women, art, talent, architecture, objects, lips, cigarettes, smiles, chats, clothes, shoes, music, landscapes: and Mum, taking the photo, is at the centre of it all, and it all whirls around her, and everything's in there, everything except Dad. This held me back. I was jealous, I think, or something like that. But – see how things go – even without handling it myself I managed to find a place for that archive, too. The Dami Tamburini Foundation. That won't ring a bell, I know, it didn't for me either until, by mere coincidence, I came across this Luigi Dami Tamburini, from Siena, who inherited a huge family fortune comprising several real estate properties, plots of land, a lake (!), a dam (!) but above all a small, ballsy business bank complete with its own foundation, which collects twentieth-century iconography.

This is how it happened: a friend of mine invited me to take part in a charity doubles tournament at the Cascine Tennis Club, organised by Pitti Immagine during the Pitti Uomo fashion week, and hence full of celebrities and assorted sycophants who can barely get the ball across the net (whereas I play regularly again now, and I'm in good shape, and I'm good, and so they needed me to raise the average). The teams weren't set: different partners were drawn ahead of every new round from the teams that hadn't been eliminated. I got to the semi-finals fairly easily, and that's when I came across this Luigi Dami Tamburini – as a partner, I mean. And he wasn't that bad, honestly – too many faults though – and anyway, despite his countless double faults we won. We ended up playing together again in the final, and that was a fierce battle: our opponents' game was strong, but I played very well, there were fewer double faults from Dami Tamburini, and in the end we won the final too.

Dami Tamburini was over the moon: he thanked God for ending up with me as a partner twice in a row, and to show his gratitude he invited me for dinner at his villa in Vico Alto, near Siena – once, and then once more – and during those dinners he took an interest in my life and told me about his. (Incidentally, I asked around and found out he's a gambler, and that twice a month that very same villa where we had dinner turns into a gambling den – but I told him nothing about my past.) He talked to me about his foundation too, which collects twentieth-century art: private photo archives, posters, postcards, billboards and the like. So I told him about Mum's archive – you never know. He said he didn't personally run the foundation but picked up his mobile and called the president, who gave me an appointment for the following day. So I took him to the house on Piazza Savonarola and showed him Mum's archive. While I showed it to him (all jumbled up as Mum had left it) I also inspected it carefully for the first time and I realised how precious it was: there are hundreds of wonderful portraits, Giacomo – architects, designers, artists – all in black and white, with a section entirely dedicated to female architects, which I bet you is the most exhaustive in the country. There are also beautiful sequences I'd never seen, documenting the creation of plastic objects (lamps, chairs, side tables) from design all the way to production; there are shots from practically every radical architecture showcase and exhibition in the sixties and seventies, and even several visual poetry events. There is an electrifying section dedicated to the flood of 1966 and the 'Mud Angels', that I also didn't know existed – and in one of those photos, Giacomo, just the one, Dad makes an appearance among those legions of angels: he's under a street lamp outside the National Library, wearing wellies and a cagoule, smiling, a cigarette stuck between his lips. The only trace of his presence in the piles of prints and negatives that Mum accumulated throughout her life. It really is a miracle that we were ever born.

The president of the foundation seemed impressed by the material (but I think it was all a show, I think Dami Tamburini had ordered him to take everything regardless of its quality and just be done with it) and when we got to planning how the archive would be transferred to the foundation, he offered me twenty-thousand euros. But I don't want any money, I said, which threw him. Don't even mention it, I said, this is a donation, it's you who are doing me a favour, really. At which point this man looked at me, I mean really looked at me, and weighed me up. I don't know if that's ever happened to you, being weighed up like that: it had never happened to me before, but that day, in the living room of our house in Piazza Savonarola I am certain that man was weighing me up – that is, he was wondering if I was being honest or not, if I was the greedy type, if he could bring me in on his little scheme or not. I don't have any proof of that, of course, but as he looked at me I just 'knew' that man was a crook who regularly embezzled the foundation money – I knew it with bizarre, vivid certainty. In the end he must have concluded it wasn't worth the risk of me exposing him, and he 'accepted' my donation. He was clearly disappointed though, and I'm sure that if he'd known from the beginning that I planned on giving away the archive, he wouldn't even have bothered to come to the house.

And so, my dear Giacomo, in the end what remains of Mum's journey on earth won't be 'lost in time like tears in rain' either. The Letizia Calabrò archive now belongs to the Dami Tamburini Foundation, and the house on Piazza Savonarola is officially on the market, even though my estate agent (my old school mate Ampio Perugini, remember him?

The one with the red birthmark around his eye? You were scared of him) he tells me that these days the real estate market has all but collapsed. What can I say – let's hope for the best. I'm not going to sell it off cheap, that's for sure. If we can get a fair price then fine, otherwise I'll wait.

I'm nothing if not patient, right?

Looking forward to your answer.

Virtual hugs,

Marco

# Via Crucis (2003–2005)

Probo Carrera fell ill shortly after announcing his intention of relocating to London. The cancer was already there when he made the announcement, but he didn't know yet – or maybe he did know without knowing, he sensed it somehow, which would partially account for his bizarre behaviour. That was indeed a remarkable plan for someone like him: leaving Florence, leaving the house on Piazza Savonarola, his workshop, his scale models, his model railways, and moving into a yet unspecified studio flat to be purchased in Marylebone, where – it transpired – he'd left a piece of his heart during a study holiday he'd spent there in the fifties, together with his friend Aldino. Twenty glorious days hosted by an aristocratic family (friends of the Mansuttis) who owned an entire mansion on Cavendish Square. Who knew? No one. He'd only been back to London twice since: ten years later for a romantic getaway with Letizia, just one block away at the Langham Hotel (when they were still happy and in love), and then with the whole family another ten years down the line (Easter 1972, when they were already unhappy). That last trip he had organised for the Florence College of Engineers, of which he was a board member at the time: the only input he'd provided to the travel agency was their budget and the mandatory location of the hotel (Marylebone). As a result, Probo, Letizia and the three kids ended up squeezed into two minuscule rooms in a minuscule hotel on Chiltern Street – which didn't go down well with Letizia herself, nor indeed with several others in the group. Probo, however, was thrilled: he was in Marylebone, and the simple fact of being there made him feel good. Who knew? No one.

Had he been a more talkative type instead of the extremely reserved man that he was, prone to unfathomable silences, in all those years he might have let slip that Marylebone was the most beautiful and reassuring place he'd ever known, the only place that could still tickle his fancy after the paralysis that followed Irene's death. But he'd never mentioned it to anyone, and therefore his announcement caught everyone by surprise that warm autumn Sunday in 2003, after an exquisite lunch he'd prepared for Letizia, Marco and Adele. During said lunch, Letizia had been complaining about Giacomo never coming to see them anymore – not even for Christmas – and Probo had remained quiet, as always when his wife complained about something. But then, once lunch was over and everyone was just waiting for a chance to break up the party, he'd dropped the bomb: he was moving to a studio flat in Marylebone. They were all astonished, especially Letizia – astonished and even slightly jealous, because the more Probo described his plan, the more it sounded like *she* should have thought of it: Georgian England, the last Adam Style houses in London, antiquarian bookshops, bakeries, the house where Turner died, the one where Dickens lived, the one where Elizabeth Barrett lived before she eloped (to Florence, as it happens) with Robert Browning, the Wallace Collection, the Langham Hotel itself, the legendary plane trees of Manchester Square, the house where the prophet Johanna Southcott lived . . . What on earth are you on about – asked Letizia, bewildered – what plane trees, what prophet? And Probo, with a sly smile, smoking his Capri, told the story of this crazy eighteenth-century lady who'd proclaimed herself the Woman of the Apocalypse described by John in the Book of Revelations. She died in 1814 at the age of sixty-four, a few weeks after her prophecy (according to which she would give birth to the new Messiah) had failed to come true. She did not give birth to the new Messiah. Instead, she fell gravely ill and eventually died just before Christmas – and even so, her followers waited for her corpse to begin decomposing before declaring her dead, in case she decided to resurrect herself. Her most famous prophecy stated that the world would end in 2004, and since there were only a few months left, Probo declared his intention of ending his days right there, in Marylebone. Nothing in his demeanour indicated he might be joking, nor did he specify if Letizia was included in his plans, or if him relocating to London had to be interpreted as a de facto separation – now that they were both in their seventies. He had even started looking into studio flats in the area (prices – rather high, actually – were nonetheless described as 'approachable').

Later that afternoon Letizia phoned Marco: had his father gone mad? Had he lost his mind? Despite being perplexed himself, Marco reassured her that it was clearly a joke: he'd checked and all the things Probo had mentioned about Marylebone (houses, plane trees and prophets) were straight out of the 'Marylebone' entry on Wikipedia. But Letizia – once so quick to embrace new things – didn't know what Wikipedia was. Unlike Probo, she didn't 'get' the internet – and that was astonishing news indeed. It was proof that, as they grew old, Letizia and Probo were swapping roles: now she was the one who couldn't keep up with progress, while Probo was perfectly at ease in it. It was a historic turning point, one that Marco attempted to explain to his daughter: Nonno Probo using the internet and planning to move to London, Nonna Letizia confused, left behind – a true paradigm shift. Adele, however, didn't know her grandparents as they had been *before*, and could not grasp the significance of that change. As for Giacomo, he had permanently moved to the US and – much to Letizia's chagrin – no longer showed any interest in family affairs.

Whether he was joking or not, Probo's grandiose plans were wiped out three weeks later, on a rainy November afternoon. Hidden traces of blood had been detected in his stool during a routine check and he was referred for a colonoscopy and a biopsy – and now the biopsy results were in: adenocarcinoma. Farewell London. Farewell Marylebone. It was indeed the end of the world, but not as Joanna Southcott had intended. Instead, Probo began his very own *via Crucis*: the pride and joy of modern medicine, which does away with the archaic practice of issuing patients with a death sentence immediately after the diagnosis, condemning them instead to a sluggish, lengthy (at times extremely so) journey towards oblivion. A veritable Way of Sorrows, punctuated by its own Stations of the Cross. A problem is detected. Biopsy. Biopsy results. Specialist consultations. Hesitating between operation and treatment. Choosing either operation or treatment. Encouraging results following the operation or the first rounds of treatment. Finding out that, even if you've chosen the operation, at some point the treatment becomes necessary. Side effects from the treatment. A new treatment protocol. Finding out that, even if you've chosen the treatment, at some point the operation becomes necessary. And it goes on, and on and on . . .

Marco took it upon himself, from the beginning, to look after his father – not much of a bother, he thought, compared with what Probo was going through – and he did so rather enthusiastically: getting Adele back had been a miracle that gave him new strength and determination. They removed part of Probo's intestines, but shortly afterwards previously undetected metastases emerged, attacking his liver and one of his lungs. The doctors recommended a cycle of intense chemotherapy during the winter, followed by a rest period in spring and summer, after which the treatment would resume in autumn. If Probo's body and morale held out – said the oncologist – he might have several years before him still, and an acceptable quality of life. Marco, therefore, had to take him to his chemo sessions, check for side effects, check he took all his drugs, take him to CT scans, arrange for a nurse to come take blood samples at home, etc. Considering he was also working and looking after Adele, that wasn't an easy time for Marco – but he was up to it. The question was – what about Probo?

Probo responded reasonably well and the metastases began shrinking with the very first blasts of chemo. As for his morale, that was harder to gauge because Probo talked so little. At any rate, he didn't look dejected. Letizia, however, was in a state of shock – she couldn't accept the situation, and therefore she couldn't look after her husband the way she felt she had to, which resulted in a dangerous tendency to wallow in her misery. Although he was no expert in such matters, Marco began to suspect that his mother's long-serving therapist (old, but stubbornly refusing to retire) might be losing her marbles. It was Adele who helped Letizia turn a corner by introducing her to a new mathematical puzzle called sudoku, which her surfing and climbing friends had discovered in the UK. She immediately took to it, thus corroborating the extraordinary hypothesis that she was gradually 'Probifying herself' (sudoku, in fact, seemed to be a much more fitting pastime for a sedentary engineer like him, rather than a restless architect like her).

Probo, for his part, didn't take an interest in sudoku and never mentioned Marylebone again, but frail and debilitated by chemo as he was, he started planning a new model railway:

the first section of the 1884 Circumvesuviana railway between Naples and Baiano, which he meticulously researched and accurately reproduced, only to abandon it when the treatment was paused for the summer. He felt his strength coming back (the oncologist's plan was working) and so he went and bought a used pilot boat in Marina di Cecina and started fishing. Off he went. Out at sea. Every day. Just like that. He hadn't been fishing since his friend Aldino Mansutti died – that is, over thirty years earlier – but such was his life now. And he was good at it. He'd catch garfish first, which he then used as live bait for bluefish: when he caught a big one, he'd have his photo taken holding his prey and the picture would then end up on the wall in Omero's shed (the line handler who'd sold him the pilot boat). Looking at those photos you really couldn't tell he was ill. Even without moving to London, this still resulted in a de facto separation from Letizia because it implied relocating to Bolgheri from mid-May until the end of September, and that house made her sick, especially if she had to be there alone (going fishing with Probo was out of the question). Once again, because of this bizarre conformist turn her life seemed to have taken, Letizia felt inadequate and guilty for not being able to look after her invalid husband – a task that was admirably fulfilled by Lucia (the daughter of their old Bolgheri housekeeper Ivana, who had taken over from her mother).

Marco shuttled back and forth: Florence–Bolgheri (to spend the day with his father); Bolgheri–Florence (to take his mother out for dinner at the Indian restaurant by the football stadium or to the cinema with Adele); Florence–Seravezza (where Adele went climbing with her older friends on the Apuan Alps); some weekends even Florence–Seravezza–Bolgheri, somehow managing to drop Adele off, drive down to Bolgheri to have dinner with Probo at Il Gambero Rosso and go fishing with him the following morning, then pick up Adele in the afternoon and finally take Letizia out for dinner on Sunday evening. It was complicated, but still better than what he had to do in the winter. And then August came and the entire family gathered in Bolgheri, as if by divine command.

Summoned by Letizia, even Giacomo came from North Carolina, together with his wife Violet and their daughters Amanda and Emily, and for two weeks the house was full again. Of all the Stations of the Cross, this was the most painful: playing happy family was ridiculous enough when everyone was in good health, but it was excruciating now that it was clear the only reason they were all there was Probo's illness – which, incidentally, was never mentioned, because while he'd changed his habits, his attitude had remained the same, and he never talked about himself. For Marco, the pain was compounded by the fact that Luisa hadn't set foot in Bolgheri all summer – and that had only happened once before, when she'd been pregnant with her second child and she'd stayed in Paris because the pregnancy was considered high-risk. The fact she'd stayed away again that summer – just as he was bearing that particular cross – he interpreted as definitive proof that he'd lost her for good. He was wrong, but at the time it seemed dishearteningly obvious to him.

In October, Probo resumed his chemo, but after a few weeks things took a sudden turn for the worse. During the summer Letizia had begun to lose weight and suffer from a slight fever. Her GP wasn't alarmed – he thought it could be diverticulitis – but in November, when Letizia went to see her gynaecologist for a routine check, it turned out that she had a very advanced tumour in her uterus. The doctor, a friend of the family, phoned Marco to give him the news even before he told Letizia, because he was rather upset himself. Marco left his practice and ran to his colleague's where he personally informed his mother of the situation, while the gynaecologist and his assistant sat there in silence, dismayed. Then he drove her home. 'I'm dead', Letizia kept repeating the whole journey, and she kept repeating it even at home, to Marco who stroked her hair as he sat on the sofa next to her, and to Probo who looked at her and couldn't understand what was going on. 'I'm dead.'

And so began the second *via Crucis* – a more abrupt, more desperate, far speedier one. From the very first examination, the same oncologist who the previous year had given Probo good chances of surviving wouldn't give Letizia any. To Marco, his sincerity was almost obscene: as Letizia and Probo (who had insisted on being present) sat there in front of him, he didn't leave any room for hope, none at all. Just the naked, devasting truth. Only Letizia wasn't shocked by his words, because she had already been in shock for quite some time and had drawn her conclusions (I'm dead) since the beginning.

Despite the oncologist essentially declaring it a waste of time, she was put through a round of chemo – and unlike her proud, radical younger self, forever fighting against superfluous things, Letizia submitted to it. Therefore, just before Christmas, Marco found out how it felt to accompany both his parents to the same hospital (but to two separate rooms) for chemotherapy, which reminded him of a book by David Leavitt he'd read many years before with Marina, when they were in love and she was pregnant with Adele. Of that book Marco remembered close to nothing, not even the title (it was a collection of short stories, just that) – and yet that bittersweet memory came back to him, simply by association with his own radical experience of accompanying both parents to the hospital. Giacomo came from the US to help out, and since it was the Christmas holidays the whole family came along. In those situations, in order to preserve the sanctity of Irene's room, Giacomo's daughters would always stay at Marco's, sharing a room with Adele. They were a little older than her, not much to look at and American through and through: it was as if Giacomo had done everything in his power to avoid passing on to them anything that could be traced back to his origins – including his beauty, which in his forties was still dazzling. It was enough to see them struggle with a plate of spaghetti or the most basic of Italian words to realise just how hard Giacomo had tried to distance himself from his previous life. He'd been living in the US for over twenty years, fifteen of them as a naturalised American citizen, ten spent teaching rational mechanics at university and – as forever lamented by Letizia – five without setting foot in Florence, not even for Christmas: was it any surprise that he'd forgotten his roots?

On the contrary, what was surprising was his decision to stay behind even after Violet and the girls had gone back home. Given how serious the situation was, he couldn't leave his brother to deal with it alone – especially because both Probo and Letizia had made clear their wish to remain in the house rather than ending their days in a hospital, which added to the workload. And so, for the first time in years, Giacomo exposed himself to his old family without the protection provided by the new one he'd built in the US. He tried to do what Marco did, because he seemed so at ease in that hellish situation: he accompanied his parents to the hospital with him, looked after them while Marco searched for a new nurse – a day nurse, on top of the night nurse, because the side effects were significant for both of them this time. He wanted to do *more* than him even – because Marco had his job and Adele to think about too, and couldn't be with Probo and Letizia all the time, while Giacomo spent his entire time with them, or rather at their disposal. He never left the house on Piazza Savonarola other than to meet their needs – buying food, stocking up on drugs. He spent his evenings preparing herbal infusions or watching TV with Probo, or helping Letizia with her sudoku. He had lived in Florence for twenty years, but it didn't even cross his mind to try and contact any of his old friends. One thing Marco was sorry to notice was that he didn't even make an effort to build a rapport with Adele, like he'd expected – like he would have done with a niece he never saw. Giacomo's entire existence, in short, was absorbed in nursing his dying parents: gritting his teeth, holding his breath, as if at war. Even when they finally found a day nurse, he continued to administer drugs, give injections, measure blood pressure – to the point that the nurse believed he was the one with a degree in medicine. At the same time, he was afraid of making fatal mistakes and constantly consulted his brother, who *did* have a medical degree. What do I know – Marco would answer – I'm an ophthalmologist. The old demon that pushed Giacomo to compete with his brother had been waiting for him in that house, all those years, and had resumed his torture.

He slept in his old bedroom – although 'slept' is an overstatement, because the slightest noise coming from his parents' bedroom would have him up and at their bedside in a flash, at all hours, faster than the night nurse. One night, around three, he phoned Marco – he was scared that a bout of diarrhoea might kill Letizia. Marco reassured him and told him to trust the nurse, but then ended up getting dressed and heading over to Piazza Savonarola himself. Once the emergency had been averted, as they sat in the large living room, unchanged since their childhood, the two brothers really did come within an inch of healing their relationship, of reconciling – and yet, since neither of them moved an inch, nothing came of it in the end, nothing was healed. It had happened several times in those days, at the hospital, when Probo and Letizia dozed off and the two brothers sneaked out of their rooms into the half-light of the corridor. All perfect occasions for them to say what had to be said, forgive what had to be forgiven and forever bury the hatchet: but so many years had gone by that they couldn't quite remember why they were so awkward around each other. Their relationship wasn't the only thing that needed healing: looking at them in that state, withering in their beds, it wasn't easy to see it, but Probo and Letizia were also to blame for the noose that had been slowly choking their family since the day Irene had died.

Then, at the end of January, when the endless rounds of chemo slowed down, Giacomo suddenly dropped everything and went back to the US. He never said he'd be staying until the end – he had his university classes to think of, his entire life – and yet his departure felt abrupt and unnatural: he'd never talked about leaving, and then just like that, he was gone. Perhaps that's why he left such a void, just as he had done in the past. Marco felt it keenly, but in those same days some unexpected comfort came in the shape of a letter from Luisa. After almost four years, completely out of the blue, she wrote him a bizarre letter where she described how the Aztecs believed that the greatest reward for dying in battle was to reincarnate as a hummingbird. At the beginning of the letter though, she told him she missed him – and at the end she apologised for 'messing up'.

Marco spent the night mulling over the meaning of that letter (especially the last sentence), but the following day he decided that, when it came to Luisa, it was no use pondering, interpreting, thinking things over: he could only let himself go, or failing that, end things like he thought he'd done. And since things hadn't ended, after all, he let himself go. He wrote her a long, passionate letter, laying his soul bare, without thinking of the pain she'd inflicted on him four years before, when she'd suddenly backed out of the plan they'd committed to (and they most certainly *did* commit to it, one night, on the

Renaione beach, with the fishing boats' lights shimmering on the flat sea and the fireworks going off over Livorno: they were going to move in together with their kids, one big blended family). She'd accused him of being too dogmatic, of violating her boundaries (which reeked of therapist advice), and had then disappeared to Paris and never contacted him again, and barely said hello to him in Bolgheri over the summer for three years in a row, and then the fourth year, the year before, she didn't come at all, not even for a week, not even a day. Marco didn't think about that, he didn't ponder, he let down his guard one more time (the third? The fourth?), and he told her about the crazy life he was living, filled with love but also sadness, about his strength and his exhaustion, about Giacomo coming back and how having him there felt so strange and yet so familiar – and about the void he left, also strange and yet familiar. He told her about his parents engaged in a race to the end, and the fact they'd swapped roles and turned into each other, and how that moved him. And at the end he told her he still loved her – just like that.

Luisa replied straight away with an equally passionate letter: she still loved him too, she thought she'd ruined everything, she was glad that wasn't the case, she loved him too, she was sad to hear about his parents and really admired him for what he was doing, she'd been there too, two years before when it happened to her father, but both parents at once was crazy, etc. From then on, they started writing to each other again as they'd done for half their lives – old-fashioned letters, written with fountain pens, with lick-and-seal envelopes and stamps that had since become adhesive, letters full of love, of dreams, of anecdotes about their children and even of future plans (although in that respect, experience had taught them both to exercise caution). In short, the wonderful world of Marco and Luisa's impossible love, which shone so bright when they were apart.

Letizia died first, at the beginning of May, a few days before her seventy-fifth birthday. She faded away slowly, meek as she'd been since she'd fallen ill, which gave Giacomo enough time to rush back so he could be there in person, together with Marco and old Ivana the housekeeper (who'd come all the way from Castagneto Carducci so she could be with the *signora* until the end) to witness the solemn moment when her wheezing lungs exhaled their last breath. Not Probo though – he was not present, he was wandering around the house clutching his walking frame like an orangutan, closely followed by his nurse and foaming with rage. A rage Probo had never exhibited in his entire life, and probably never even felt, and yet in that moment – as his transmutation into Letizia reached its peak – it seemed to be the only thing keeping him alive.

Letizia's funeral took place on her birthday. Luisa had come from Paris for the occasion, and she explained to the two brothers that, according to Jewish folklore, those who – like Jacob – died around the date of their birthday were considered *tzadik* ('righteous men') or *tzadeket* ('righteous women'). She hadn't mentioned it in her letters to Marco, but it turned out that in the past few years she had rekindled her interest in her family's religion, precisely because of all the Jewish ceremonies and rituals she had to attend in Paris following her father's death. And at any rate, once she was there in the flesh next to Marco, Luisa appeared hesitant again, so distant from the passionate tone of her letters. Despite there being no real obstacles, they barely touched: they kissed once, on the mouth, clinging to each other as the hearse carried the coffin away – but it was a light, clandestine kiss, tongues barely touching. Talking about such things in those circumstances would have been clearly inappropriate, so Marco let it go, but he was still taken aback by it.

Giacomo left the day after the funeral, with a bag containing a handful of his mother's ashes in his suitcase. He was on the same flight to Paris as Luisa, and from there on a connecting flight to Charlotte, and as a result Marco ended up driving them to the airport and watching them leave together – his brother and the love of his life. It was only after he'd said goodbye – as they walked away and Giacomo said something to her and she shook her head to one side like she did when she laughed – it was only then that he realised that the same radiant aura that surrounded Luisa when she was with him surrounded her when she was with Giacomo as well, because that aura was made of the same memories, the same light, the same intimacy. As he watched them walk away, for the first time in his life, at the age of forty-five and three days after losing his mother, Marco felt a pang of jealousy for his brother: for the first time (and twenty-five years too late) he realised that it didn't matter which Carrera brother Luisa was with, the result remained unchanged. Everything that was truly resplendent in her, everything he thought he alone could see, came from those distant summers when he'd fallen in love with her as he watched her grow, sunbathe, run, and dive into the sea on that rugged stretch of coast: but Giacomo – he realised – had been there too.

With Giacomo gone, it fell to Marco to manage Probo, now almost entirely consumed by cancer too, yet still angrily clinging to life. Stupefied by his pain management regime and tormented by Letizia crossing the finish line before him, he couldn't find peace, day or night. For Marco, that was the second-to-last Station of the Cross, the one where both invalid and carer find themselves wishing for the end to come soon. In his morphine-induced hallucinations, Probo kept demanding to be 'taken away' – take me away, you promised you'd take me away, I want to go away, you hear me? But when Marco tested the waters with Dr Cappelli (the pain management specialist assigned to

Probo) and asked him about the possibility of 'speeding up the process' so to speak, Cappelli pretended not to understand and replied that there was no telling how long it would take. Marco, being a doctor himself, knew that wasn't true. And so, caving in to Probo's relentless pleas (you promised you piece of shit, take me away!) – incidentally, he hadn't promised anything except not to let him die in a hospital – Marco decided to take matters into his own hands. It was the final Station of the Cross, the one only the truly blessed (or truly wretched) few get to experience: to send off the very people who had brought you into this world, out of pity, or obedience, or exhaustion, or desperation, or a sense of justice. Thus Marco knew exactly when he would speak to his father for the last time: he told him to calm down, and not to worry, because this time he was really taking him away. Then he gave him a first injection of morphine sulphate (not included in Dr Cappelli's pain management protocol), laid down next to him on the bed, and asked if he was ready to move to Marylebone. Probo (compliant at last) mumbled that he was, adding a mouthful of names that Marco couldn't understand, and his last words – which Marco did hear rather clearly, but still couldn't understand – were 'Goldfinger House'. Then he fell asleep, and at that point, Marco Carrera – qualified medical practitioner since 1984, ophthalmologist since 1988 – did what he had to do with his father's cannula and Dr Cappelli's morphine.

The following day was exactly a month since Letizia had died. The following day was Probo's birthday. The following day Probo was dead – which, according to Luisa's religion, meant two *tzadikim* out of two parents. This time, however, Luisa didn't rush down from Paris for the funeral, and neither did old Ivana from Castagneto Carducci or Giacomo from North Carolina: they couldn't make it. To the few who came to pay their respects and asked him how he was, Marco replied 'tired'.

Despite coming from the same furnace, the ashes delivered to Marco after the cremation were much darker and much coarser than his mother's.

# Giving and receiving (2012)

FRIDAY 29 NOVEMBER

Dr Carradori? Is this still your number?
**16:44**

Hello, Dr Carrera. Yes, this is still my number. How may I help?
**16:44**

Good morning, could you please let me know when I can call you?
**16:45**

Well, right now I'm in Palermo waiting to board a flight to Lampedusa. If it's not urgent, you could call me tonight after dinner, once I'm settled. Is that all right with you?
**16:48**

Of course, I don't want to bother you. You're going there because of last month's shipwreck?
**16:48**

Yes. But not just because of that. That island is a pretty incredible place, both for giving and for receiving. But how are you?
16:50

Not well, sadly. There's been a shipwreck here too. I need to ask your advice.
16:51

I'm sorry to hear that. If you call tonight I'll be at your disposal.
16:51

Thank you, Dr Carradori. Speak soon.
16:52

Goodbye. Speak soon.
16:54

# Oxygen mask (2012)

– Hello?
– Hello, is this Dr Carradori?
– Yes, hello Dr Carrera. How are you?
– Well, not great.
– What's the matter?
– . . .
– . . .
– . . .
– I don't know how to tell you, I really don't. I mean, I don't know how to tell you without being brutal.
– Then be brutal.
– . . .
– . . .
– Adele . . .
– . . .
– . . .
– Adele?
– Is dead.
– Dear God, no . . .
– She is, sadly. Died eight days ago.
– . . .
– . . .

– . . .
– An accident on the Apuan Alps. One of those freak accidents that shouldn't happen, according to climbers . . .
– . . .
– . . . and that in Adele's case is really horrific. It'll horrify you, Dr Carradori, I'm sure.
– Why?
– Because her rope broke, that's why. While she was climbing. It was rubbing against the rock. Snap. Broken. Except the rope is not supposed to break. Ever. It's made of polyester, with a high-tensile strength core for Christ's sake, it *can't* break! And all the more so for Adele, because you know what ropes meant for her! What they represented!
– The thread . . .
– Precisely! She'd spent half her childhood protecting that fucking thread, making sure it wouldn't tangle up, that it wouldn't snap. And then . . .
– It's awful.
– . . .
– . . .
– I mean. It's not like I would have been happy if she'd died in a car accident. But this, honestly . . .
– . . .
– . . .
– Someone might want to go after the rope manufacturers . . .
– That's what her friends are doing, those who were with her. They want to sue the company that makes the rope, take them to court. They blame them. But I told them I don't want anything to do with it, I told them to leave me alone and go to hell.
– Well yes, I said 'someone might', but it goes without saying that I meant—
– And then there's the police, investigating, seizing evidence,

being a pain in the arse. I've been summoned by the public prosecutor in Lucca but I told her loud and clear I wouldn't go, I don't even want to hear about that accident.

– You're right, Dr Carrera.
– Yes, I know I'm right. However . . .
– However?
– However, there's a reason I bothered you, Dr Carradori.
– I'm listening.
– Adele's mother. My ex-wife. Your former patient. I don't know how to handle her.
– Ah, yes. And how is she?
– Not well.
– Is she still in Germany?
– Yes. She's at a private clinic, some sort of luxury psychiatric ward. Her disorder is now chronic, it seems. Although lately it looked like . . .
– . . .
– . . .
– I'm sorry, I think I've missed something – lately it looked like what?
– No you haven't missed anything, I haven't finished the sentence.
– Oh. OK.
– Well I haven't told her yet. And I don't know how I can I tell her without—
– But it's not you who should tell her, Dr Carrera. It should be her physician, in Germany.
– But I don't know him. I've never met him.
– Who pays for her to stay at that clinic?
– The pilot. Their daughter's father. And actually, speaking of her – Greta, Adele's sister – she has a right to know too, and that's another problem because lately they'd been, well, getting closer.

– You need to talk to that man, I think. Have you ever met him?
– The pilot?
– Yes. Do you know him?
– No. I mean, I met him when I took Adele back, thirteen years ago, because I picked her up from his house, but I've never seen him since. On top of that, he and Marina are divorced too.
– But he still pays for her to stay at that clinic.
– Yes.
– Then he must be a decent man. You should talk to him.
– But I really don't want to, Dr Carradori. That's the point. That's why I bothered you. I don't want to talk to anyone. I don't want to inform anyone. And how would I do it anyway? Over the phone? Am I supposed to go all the way to Munich to tell the man who stole my wife that my daughter is dead? I just can't.
– I completely understand.
– I haven't even got her body back yet because it's still being held by the police, and I barely have enough strength to face the funeral when I do eventually get it back. How am I going to tell those people?
– Then don't. Don't do anything you don't feel like doing.
– On the other hand . . .
– On the other hand?
– . . .
– . . .
– I'm sorry . . .
– . . .
– There's something else, but . . .
– . . .
– . . .
– . . .

– I'm a bit . . . I'm sorry. I'm on anti-anxiety medication.
– Don't worry.
– I was saying, there's something else.
– . . .
– . . .
– Yes?
– Well, two years ago Adele had a little girl. We don't know who the father is, Adele never told anyone. The child is just wonderful, Dr Carradori, believe me – I'm not saying this because she's my granddaughter, it's just that she really is a new, different kind of person: she's dark-skinned, well, mixed race, with Japanese features, curly hair and blue eyes. As if all the world's races somehow came together in her, do you see what I mean?
– I do. Very well.
– I'm not being racist, I hope you understand – I'm using the word 'races' because I can't think of anything else right now.
– I understand.
– She is African, Asian and European, all at once. She's little, but quite far ahead in terms of development: she talks, she understands everything I say to her, draws superbly – at the age of two. She grew up with her mother and with me, because we lived together. I'm her grandfather but also a father of sorts.
– Of course.
– And clearly it's only because of her that I'm still here, fighting, Dr Carradori. If it wasn't for her, I'd have jumped off a cliff already.
– Well, thank God she's here then.
– So anyway, Marina has met her, the little girl. Adele would always bring her along when she visited over the summer. You know just now, when I stopped talking and I didn't finish the sentence?

– Yes.

– I was about to say that being around her granddaughter seemed to be really beneficial for Marina. She was getting better. Or at least that's what my daughter told me. So much so that she'd decided to visit her more often – this year we were supposed to spend Christmas in Germany, because Adele had asked me to accompany her and the child and I'd said yes. Therefore, even if I didn't tell her anything – because I don't feel like it, because I'm not up to it – Marina would get in touch for sure, and at that point I'd have to tell her that Adele is dead and that I didn't even tell her . . .

– I understand, Dr Carrera. You're right.

– She hurt me, that woman. But she suffered and is still suffering a lot and this tragedy could . . .

– . . .

– . . . Well, I can't pretend she's not there, but at the same time I don't have the strength to handle this. Do you understand?

– I do, and you know what? You did the right thing calling me, because I can help you. I'll talk to your ex-wife's doctor in Germany, and I'll talk to her too if possible. And to the girl's father, and to the girl herself. How old did you say she was?

– Who, Greta?

– Your daughter's sister.

– Greta, yes. Twelve. But you don't have to—

– I don't speak German but I imagine they all speak English, right? He's a pilot, he surely does. If you agree I'll take care of this and speak to everyone, so you don't have to worry about it.

– But how? You're in Lampedusa and you've got work to do. I was thinking about a lawyer, a representative, I just wanted to ask you if you could point me—

– Look, I got here tonight but I'm actually not due back at

work until next week. It's just that there was nothing for me to do in Rome, and there's always something to do around here, the refugee camp is bursting at the seams and the survivors from the shipwreck are all still here. But if you give me all the details, I'll get on a flight to Palermo tomorrow and then on to Munich to speak to these people.

– But that's too much. I really wouldn't know how—

– It's my job, after all. Looking after people in an emergency.

– Well yes this is an emergency, for sure, but . . .

– And above all there are fragile people involved.

– Yes, that too, of course. Marina is in a bad way, Greta is still a child . . .

– It's not them I was talking about.

– Who then?

– You, Dr Carrera. You have to look after yourself now. You have to look after yourself first and foremost, you're absolutely right not to be bothered about other people. Do you understand what I'm saying?

– Yes . . .

– I'm telling you this as a therapist but also as a friend, if you'll allow me. Right now you have to look after no one but yourself.

– And the child.

– No! Don't mix things up, Dr Carrera. Right now *you* are in danger, because what happened is terrible and could well do away with you. Forget about the others, you're the one who's in danger. You know what you're supposed to do on a plane in case of emergency? You know what they tell you to do with the oxygen masks?

– Put yours on first, then the children's . . .

– Precisely. Earlier you said that if it wasn't for your granddaughter, you'd have jumped off a cliff already. And I said well thank God she's here then, so you can't jump off a cliff.

But you can't give in either and you can't give up. You can't, because of the child. What's her name?
– Miraijin.
– I beg your pardon?
– Mirai-jin. It's Japanese.
– Mirai-jin. I like it.
– It means 'new man', 'man of the future'. 'Man' because Adele didn't want to know the sex in advance, and she was sure it was a boy.
– I see. But it works for a girl too.
– Oh, yes it does.
– Well, you have to look after yourself now, you have to find a reason to get out of bed every morning.
– Well, for that I've got Miraijin.
– No! You have to find that reason inside you. That's the only way you can properly look after your granddaughter. Children are incredibly perceptive creatures, you know? If you were to look after Miraijin while dead inside, that's what she'd learn from you. But if you fight to keep yourself alive – and it doesn't matter if you succeed or not, *trying* is enough – then you'll pass on that determination to her, and that determination is, quite simply, *life itself*. Believe me. Every day, I look after people who've lost everything, they're often the only survivors in their whole family. They have all kinds of material problems, sometimes they're even gravely ill, but you know what we work on?
– No.
– We work on desires, on pleasure. Because even in the most disastrous of situations these things endure – yet we actively try to suppress them. When we're overcome with grief we suppress our appetites, whereas that's the one thing that can save us. Do you enjoy playing football? Play football. Do you enjoy walking on the beach, eating mayo, painting your nails,

hunting lizards, singing? Do it. It won't solve a single one of your problems, but it won't make them worse either – and meanwhile you'll have escaped the dictatorship of pain.

– So what should I do?

– I don't know, these are complicated matters, hard to resolve over the phone. But basically, you have to bear in mind that right now you are fragile, you are in danger. And you must salvage all the things you cherish from the shipwreck. Do you still play tennis?

– I do.

– And are you as good as when we were kids?

– Well. I get by.

– Play tennis then. Just an example.

– Easy for you to say – and what about Miraijin? I don't want to leave her, ever, do you understand? Not even to play tennis. I never want to leave someone I love with anyone else – surfers, climbers, babysitters . . .

– Of course, that's perfectly reasonable of you. But nothing's stopping you from bringing her along when you play.

– Is that what I'm supposed to do to find a reason for living again? Drag Miraijin along when I go play tennis?

– I'm not saying it'll give you a reason for living. It probably won't. But you'll still be living. You'll still be doing something that your grief is trying to suppress, because it gives you pleasure.

– You know, my father was a huge fan of sci-fi literature. He had an almost complete collection of Urania sci-fi novels, from n.1 to n.899. He was positively obsessed with it, there were only four volumes missing. Since my sister Irene died in 1981, until he himself died eight years ago, he never bought nor read a single one again.

– That's precisely what I'm advising you *not* to do. You know what gives you pleasure: do it, don't punish yourself. Bring the child along and look after her while you do what you love. There's no other way. Of course, the ideal thing would be for someone to help you along this path, but if memory serves me well, you're not a big fan of us psychiatrists.

– Psycho*therapists*. All my life I've been surrounded by psychotherapists, and in spite of that everyone around me was still in so much pain – except in the end it always turned out to be my fault. It's psychotherapists I've got a problem with, not psychiatrists.

– You don't have a problem with psychotherapists either, believe me. Either way, I wouldn't advise you to act against your nature right now. If you don't want to be helped by one of my colleagues, then go it alone. The most important thing is that you look after yourself. Put the oxygen mask on. Breathe. Stay alive.

– Thank you for your advice. I'll try.

– Please do. And text me names and contact details for the people I need to speak to in Germany so I can leave tomorrow morning.

– I am so very grateful for this, Dr Carradori. I really am.

– As I said, this is my job.

– Indeed – and I'm going to pay you for it.

– Don't even mention it, Dr Carrera. I meant it's my job in the sense that that's what I'm good at.

– Well, let me at least cover your travel expenses—

– Not to worry. I haven't had to pay for a plane ticket in years. This is not going to bankrupt me.

– I don't know what to say, Dr Carradori. I'm really touched.

– Don't say anything. More importantly – I know what to say to the pilot, to the girl, and to my colleague at the clinic, but I need to know how you wish to proceed with your ex-wife.

– How so?

– If she wanted to come to Italy for the funeral, would you be happy to see her again, to have her stay with you?
– I don't think she can travel, Dr Carradori. I don't think she's self-sufficient.
– I understand that, but you never know. Experience has taught me that in some cases a big shock can result in the temporary suspension of a debilitating condition: that is not to say the condition is cured, but the physical impediments associated with it are momentarily removed.
– It wouldn't be a problem for me to have her stay here.
– And as for the child, Mirai-jin – do you think you could take her to visit your ex-wife over there, like your daughter did? I understand this is premature right now, but sooner or later the problem will arise.
– I think I could, yes.
– Only when you'll feel better yourself, obviously. For now, listen to me and focus on that oxygen mask.
– I will, Dr Carradori. Thank you so much.
– Text me everything I need then, please. Names, addresses, phone numbers. Better via WhatsApp actually, the phone signal is even worse than the internet connection over here. The sooner you do that, the sooner I can get going.
– I'll do it straight away, Dr Carradori.
– Good. And tomorrow I'll be on my way.
– Thank you, really.
– You did the right thing calling me, you know?
– Yes, I'm beginning to realise that.
– And this means you do want to put on that oxygen mask.
– I put it on once before, Dr Carradori. When my sister died.
– True. And now you have to put it back on.
– There's no other way . . .
– Indeed. And I do . . . care about you, if you understand what I mean.

– I care about you too, Dr Carradori.
– And if I have time, on my way back from Munich I could stop in Florence if that's all right with you? So I can report back in person.
– Of course. Although please don't change your sched—
– I said 'if I have time' – I'm due back at work in a week.
– All right then.
– So you can introduce me to Miraijin. And maybe we can play a few sets?
– You mean tennis?
– I rarely play these days but you know, just for fun. And at any rate, even when I played regularly as a kid you still beat me 6–0 6–1.
– Ah, come now. That was forty years ago.
– We'll go play tennis and bring the child with us. What do you say?
– OK.
– Goodbye for now, then. I'll be waiting for those contact details.
– I'll send them right away.
– Goodbye, Dr Carrera.
– Goodbye, Dr Carradori. And thank you for everything.
– Hang in there. See you soon.
– See you soon.

# Brabanty (2015)

Bolgheri, 19 August 2015

Dear Luisa,

For years now I've felt that when I was talking to you, I wasn't talking to you alone. By 'you' I mean the girl I've loved for twenty years, who became a woman, a mother and now even a grandmother. For a very long time now, whenever I talked to you, as well as talking to that girl (or to whatever is left of her) I've felt like I was talking to a stranger, too. To be perfectly honest, I've felt like I was talking to your therapist – what's her name again? Madame Brazily? Or is it Brassery? I can tell, Luisa. I can tell because by now I recognise the voice of all the therapists talking to me via the people I love. I've had to deal with that all my life. I can tell.

Yes, what you told me about Giacomo yesterday – after all these years – really horrified me. But what you said afterwards, my dear Luisa, was worse – much worse than that. Because in your inability to tell me about Giacomo I can (with a little effort) still see the girl I love: I can tell myself 'that's life' and accept it. I am fifty-six years old, and I've had to swallow far worse. But when you finally decided to come clean, you just couldn't handle my surprise (and my anger too – rather justified anger, you have to give me that): instead of simply apologising, you started this elaborate dance to defend yourself, because suddenly *I* was the danger you had to escape from (no less!), *I* was 'violating your boundaries' and 'projecting my own guilt onto you'. That wasn't you talking. That was her – what's her name? Madame Brambly? Broccoly? What the hell is her name again? Aren't those her words, your tirade about heroism? About my 'heroic vision of life' that manipulates and crushes everyone around me?

Am I wrong, Luisa?

The truth is I am the way I am, I have always been like this, since I was a child: I've changed very little and no one knows that better than you do. You say I always have to see myself as a hero? That may be, but I've always been like this, there's nothing new about that. There's never anything new about me – now *that*'s something you can accuse me of. 'You're boring, Marco.' I'll take that. Although things have always changed so brutally around me that I never really had the privilege of living a boring life. Now, for instance, I have to look back on a big chunk of my life and re-process it from scratch in light of what, until yesterday, you had kept from me all these years.

Because I blamed him, I blamed Giacomo. I blamed him entirely for what happened on that awful night. Irene had been in a bad way for a while, and it showed. I never lost sight of her all summer except for one evening, *that* evening, to see you: but Giacomo was with her, so I felt safe. I was relaxed when I left the house because he was there with her. That's why I blamed him afterwards. I can still see his stricken face when I blamed him. I told him he was a coward. I told him it was his fault Irene had died. I said those things, I did – and I know it's terrible, and I've regretted it for the rest of my life. But I would never have done that if I'd known he was in love with you too.

Now, I can see why you didn't say anything back then. You were fifteen, it was all so much bigger than you. And I can see why you still didn't tell me before we found each other again – you'd moved to Paris, we'd lost touch, how were you going to tell me? It's harder to understand why, however, you didn't say anything when we rekindled what it was we had. Why didn't you say anything in all those years? Shall I make you a list of all the occasions you could have told me? All those moments are etched in my memory, and you weren't a little girl then, you were a woman – you had two children, you were about to divorce, you could have told me. Why didn't you? Why did you let me believe Giacomo was running away from me, when in fact he was running away from you?

And then during those messy years – divorces, relocations, us getting back together, then splitting up again – I can see why you wouldn't tell me then. But for crying out loud, when we started writing to each other again, when my parents were dying and Giacomo came back: why didn't you say anything *then*, why didn't you put it in writing, at least? Or when they died, and you came to Mum's funeral, and Giacomo was there, and I even drove you to the airport together – why didn't you tell me then? Or that summer? Why didn't you tell me those three days we spent in London? Giacomo had disappeared again, and I was hurt again. Why didn't you tell me, in that wonderful room at the Langham Hotel, that he hadn't come to Dad's funeral because he was afraid he'd find you there? Or that August, in Bolgheri, after you came back from Kastellorizo and we spent the rest of the summer together? Why didn't you tell me when the two of us went scattering Mum and Dad's ashes in the sea, by Mulinelli beach, and Giacomo's absence was so conspicuous? Why didn't you tell me, as we scattered the ashes at sunset on Dr Silberman's pedalo, that Giacomo had always been in love with you too? That *that* was the real reason he'd run away? And that while he ignored all the emails I kept sending him year after year, hoping he'd forgive me, he was writing to you instead? And why didn't you tell me on any other occasion in all those summers we spent together in Bolgheri since? All you had to do was take me to one side one morning, like you did yesterday, and tell me all the things you'd never told me.

But above all, seeing as by then I'd learnt to live with my guilt, just why did you take me to one side yesterday morning and tell me? For what insane reason are you now forcing me to revisit the rift between me and my brother? After everything that's happened to me? Never mind if I was angry or not – all I asked you yesterday was this: why-are-you-telling-me-now?

And lo and behold, she comes to the rescue, this Madame Whatsherface, Brazenly, Brainwashy. Am I right? 'How dare he protest, how dare he blame you? He's the one who's been causing all this trouble, always, with his wretched family and his wretched life: how dare he accuse you? With his heroic vision of life, with his impossible expectations about people – no mistakes allowed, everyone must be a hero, always.'

Am I wrong, Luisa?

'Don't let him blame you, don't let him project his guilt onto you, you are the victim, you were fifteen, that family ruined your life.' Isn't that what she said?

Brabanty. That's her name. Brabanty.

I tallied it up, Luisa, and it turns out we broke up one more time than we got together. I swear. So, technically I wouldn't even need to tell you this, but in one hour I'll be driving you to the airport, you will leave, we will say goodbye – anyway I'm telling you all the same, and this time we better consider the matter closed once and for all.

Farewell.

Marco

# On everyone's lips (2013)

After Irene's death, years went by before any of the Carreras could breathe easily again – some of them never fully recovered. Pain shattered their family and then scattered away the pieces. When Adele died, thirty-one years after Irene, the family had already disintegrated: Probo and Letizia's ashes scattered in the Tyrrhenian Sea, Marco and Giacomo unable to speak to each other. There was nothing to break that hadn't been broken already, and even though it was just as tragic, Adele's death somehow seemed less significant, mostly because Marco alone had to suffer the consequences – and Marco, alone, managed to cope with his daughter's death in a way his whole family had not been able to cope with Irene's. Dr Carradori stepped in with two life-saving acts of kindness, and that was enough for Marco to weather the storm and keep living a life he never would have wanted to live.

First, Carradori took it upon himself to inform his former patient – Adele's mother – of Adele's tragic death, going all the way to the clinic where she was staying in Bavaria. Despite being the bearer of such awful news, he managed to win back her trust like he'd done fifteen years before, he managed to get through to her and above all he managed to put to use one of the golden rules of PTSD management – namely that among survivors, mutual compassion trumps every other emotion. Thanks to him, for the first time since their divorce Marina and Marco were able to rebuild a rapport of sorts. Dr Carradori knew how risky it was to meddle in the lives of people so close to breaking point, but he wasn't surprised by the fact that – to use a slightly unorthodox term – he'd *pulled it off*: it worked for communities that suffered large collective traumas, and it worked for smaller individual traumas as well. He was relieved too – it was proof that the theories he'd devoted his life to were indeed sound.

For the sake of their granddaughter, therefore, Marco and Marina started talking again. From time to time, Marco would visit Marina in Germany with the child: he'd take Miraijin to the clinic and sit with them and Greta (Marina's other daughter) in Marina's room, or in the garden. At times he'd even take them out for a walk in a nearby park. He didn't resent his ex-wife anymore; on the contrary, he pitied her for her diminished life and for having lost a daughter, like him. On those occasions, he performed what he felt was a necessary task, a task his daughter had diligently and affectionately carried out while she was alive, and that now fell to him, as if by some sort of reverse inheritance.

Dr Carradori's second act of kindness was to give Marco Carrera a hammock. He gave it to him in Florence, on his way back from visiting Marina at her clinic: it was a hammock with a foldable frame, made in Japan, which could be carried around in a bag and assembled anywhere in just a couple of minutes. A small hammock. A child-sized hammock. He'd found it in a sports equipment shop at Munich airport while he wandered around waiting to board his flight, and in a stroke of genius he decided to give it to Marco. It was the offer of the week – 62.99 euros instead of 104. 'Hanmokku' it was called (or ハンモック,

which means 'hammock' in Japanese). It was available in a variety of colours and sizes, for adults and for children: ultra-light steel frame, extremely easy to fold and carry, roughly the same size as a tennis bag. Carradori knew rather well how the human psyche behaved under the cruel rule of grief, and he knew that in order to stoke the fire of rebellion, it was necessary to commit small, marginal acts of rebellion – even meaningless, perhaps dangerous ones. He felt the urge to give that hammock to Marco Carrera hoping he'd make it his own instrument of revolt – if not against grief itself, at least against its tendency to suppress all forms of pleasure. Whatever he felt like doing he wouldn't have to sacrifice it to be with his granddaughter. Since he didn't want to leave her with a babysitter, he could just bring her along and she'd sleep right where he was, in that hammock. That plan, of course, didn't really bear scrutiny. First, what was the point of a hammock when prams already fulfilled that purpose and – second – where Miraijin would sleep wasn't the real problem. The real problem was indeed the desperation howling inside Marco, his inability to even talk about the things in life that gave him joy – and both he and Carradori were perfectly aware of that. But precisely because they were both aware of that, it was rather convenient to pretend that it was only a matter of logistics. That hammock created the bubble inside which Marco was able to follow Dr Carradori's advice. Because it was a hammock, and there's something exciting about hammocks, and it was portable, and Marco never knew portable hammocks existed, and it was even Japanese, and Miraijin was a Japanese name, and Japan had definitely something to do with her mysterious father. In short, the hammock was a clever decoy (and that's all hammocks ever are, really, in gardens, sheds, even in bedrooms: decoys) but a decoy was precisely what Marco Carrera needed to start his own rebellion. Because of the sheer defiance of that object, Marco was able to defy his own grief.

So he started playing tennis again: over-50s tournaments across Tuscany, then over-55s, and then the doubles. His opponents were the same as when he was a kid, except they had less hair, and they played without a referee, at night. He'd pitch the hammock directly on the court (under an air dome in winter) and place the child who'd already fallen asleep in the car in said hammock (wrapped in a blanket in winter); she'd sleep, he'd play – and win almost every time – then he'd pack it all up and head back home as brazenly as he'd arrived, often holding a trophy. Because of that, *he was on everyone's lips* – as they say in Florence when you're being talked about by a lot of people. Yes, he was on everyone's lips, and he liked it – but that's not what saved him.

He began attending conferences again. He hadn't kept up to date with the latest scientific developments; for years, he'd been just a regular ophthalmologist with no fervent interest in research and it was too late to catch up now. But he was friends with neurologists, psychiatrists and art or music enthusiasts who organised conferences to bring together their various passions, and at those conferences Marco could still hold his own, while also combining his interests in ophthalmology, photography and wildlife. They'd get together two or three times a year to examine the mystery of seeing and being seen, to come up with a theory that would encompass, say, strabismus, total refraction, and the cow on the cover of Pink Floyd's *Atom Heart Mother*. Getting on a stage to present his theories to the attendees in Florence, or Prato, or Chianciano Terme was very gratifying for him. He'd bring the child along even during the daytime sessions, shamelessly advertising her presence by pitching up the hammock on the front row (even though she wouldn't sleep and preferred to sit next to him). He'd listen to other speakers' talks, give his, then pack everything up and head back home, skipping cocktail receptions and dinners. Once again, because of that hammock, he was on everyone's lips, but he didn't care: all he cared about was being with Miraijin, and that – as Carradori would have it – was the transgression, the pleasure he derived from his effort to break free from the yoke of grief. But that's not what saved him, either.

He started gambling again. That was the real rebellion, that's what saved him. Because it's no use pretending otherwise: Marco Carrera had never, in his entire life, experienced anything that even came close to the thrill of gambling – a thrill he had long ago sacrificed on the altar of family. But not anymore. His passion for gambling had never really gone away in all those years, and he always had to exercise considerable restraint to keep it at bay, without ever really succeeding. He always felt like it was lying there *waiting for him*, buried under a pile of more wholesome pursuits he'd favoured in the meantime, ready to spring out and show the world his real nature – a bit like the wolves howling at the end of that agonising song by Joni Mitchell that nobody liked apart from him, and he liked it precisely for this reason, right from the beginning (it was released in the seventies, when the world was still young). His passion for gambling was still there throughout the years he spent in Rome with Marina, and it was still there when he moved back to Florence where, during a tennis tournament, he'd met Luigi Dami Tamburini. Unlike most scions of old Italian aristocratic families, he wasn't entirely destitute but managed instead a large fortune consisting of Brunello di Montalcino vineyards, real estate across Tuscany, commercial rights to a mineral water source on Mount Amiata and a small family-owned business bank, complete with its own charitable foundation dedicated to twentieth-century iconography, to which Marco had donated his mother's entire photo archive. Helping Dami Tamburini win a few charity doubles earned Marco the first dinner invites at his villa in Vico Alto, and as their tennis partnership consolidated, the invites became more frequent. Adele was still alive at the time, and those dinner parties worried her because Dami Tamburini was also on everyone's lips, on account of his well-known habit of turning his villa into a gambling den twice a month. Marco reassured her that the invitations he received (let's call them 'type A') were strictly to formal dinners where – if anything – you'd end up rubbing elbows with a few Freemasons, but no gamblers.

That said, all Marco had to do was mention his past gambling exploits and his desire to rekindle his interest to be catapulted into the dark side of Dami Tamburini's life. From the very first party though (let's call it a 'type B' evening), Marco sensed there was something wrong. There was nothing dark about that side of Dami Tamburini's life, those evenings were just a slightly more sparkling version of the type A dinners. There was nothing different except for the roulette and chemin de fer tables positioned between the sofas, where the guests would indeed gamble, but in a completely disinterested manner, laughing and chatting away. Amateur gambling, in short: no professionals, no all-consuming obsession, no damned souls. Many guests were the same as the type A diners, and the fact that Marco would turn up with his hammock and pitch it in a small study with the child asleep in it was considered endearing. The guests were relaxed, there wasn't even the slightest whiff of financial ruin, which was precisely what he missed most from his gambling days: the scent of ruin. Without it he didn't feel any pleasure at all, and above all – he couldn't help but think – without it Dami Tamburini wouldn't be on everyone's lips. Therefore, just like a scientist who demonstrates the existence of invisible matter by establishing the impossibility of its non-existence, Marco Carrera became convinced that there must necessarily be 'type C' evenings.

As it happens, the only aim of those fake gambling soirées

was indeed to act as a cover for the real ones: Dami Tamburini often invited scores of public prosecutors, financial crime detectives and judges with a passion for the finer things in life, waging that they would surely do everything in their power to prevent a raid in a place they regularly visited. Those type B gambling parties were nothing but a smokescreen, expertly devised (together with the complete secrecy surrounding the type C invites) to disguise the real ones.

Thus protected, the real gambling den could be as sinister and feral as Marco Carrera had imagined. He couldn't care less about high society – the only thing he was after was a fire in his loins roaring louder than the pain devouring his heart. He wanted to debase himself to the same level of those damned souls – he wanted filth, depravity, and the bitter consolation of finally doing something to deserve all the punishment he'd already received in life.

Things were dead serious. For starters, all guests had to adopt a nom de guerre, regardless of whether they knew each other or not. Dami Tamburini styled himself 'Drago' after one of Siena's historic *contradas*. A public prosecutor from Arezzo (the only 'type B' high-ranking officer to successfully transition to type C evenings) went by Desperado. The sexy, buxom wife of the German consul in Florence was Lady Oscar. A nice restaurant owner from San Casciano Val di Pesa with an Africa-shaped birthmark on his neck was called Rambo. A ninety-something former government minister was 'The Machine'. Then there were others whose real identity Marco ignored, and who therefore were simply El Patron, George Eliot, Pulcinella, Girl Interrupted, Negus, Philip K. Dick, Mandrake – all with a distinctive stench of ruin about them. There were dandruff-sprinkled shoulders, sweaty brows, loose ties, nervous coughs, frantic superstitious rituals and the frenzied look of those who are about to bet more than they can afford to lose. And then there was

Maranghi the notary (who never gambled himself but was there to provide emergency legal aid on those occasions when properties and other possessions had to change hands) and Zorro (a doctor who both gambled and ensured emergency medical aid in case of heart attacks, strokes and fainting fits). That suited Marco Carrera just fine. The fact that Dami Tamburini had kept those evenings from him suited him just fine. The fact that he'd earned his invite through behaviour that stopped just short of blackmail suited him just fine. He'd got to the point in his life beyond which there was nothing but howling wolves, just like that Joni Mitchell song. That suited him just fine.

Meanwhile Miraijin always did the right thing, namely sleeping away in the little study where Marco Carrera deposited her. He'd check on her from time to time, and if by chance he found her awake, he'd stay with her a while, ever so slightly rocking her hammock until she fell asleep again, then he'd go back to the main room to continue gambling. And just like when he was young, he'd win: roulette, chemin de fer, Texas Hold 'Em – he almost always won. But above all, whether he won or lost, the child in the hammock was the perfect excuse to quit at the right time (which gamblers almost never do) and that was his real strength. After all, he wasn't looking for a big win to turn his life around. He was looking for a reason to carry on living.

His nom de guerre was Hanmokku.

# To look is to touch (2013)

To: enricogras.rigano@gmail.com
Sent: 12 February 2013 22:11
Subject: Conference talk
From: Marco Carrera

Hello Enrico,

I've attached the text of the talk I'm planning for the conference. I'm very excited to take part in a conference again after all these years – thank you for this opportunity, and please do be honest if you think the talk's not good enough.
Hugs,
Marco

> Conference title: VISUAL PERCEPTION – FROM EYE TO BRAIN
> Pecci Museum Auditorium, Prato – 14 March 2013
> Title of talk: TO LOOK IS TO TOUCH
> Duration: 8–9 minutes
> Speaker: Dr Marco Carrera, Careggi Hospital, Florence

'Grandpa-grandpa-grandpa-grandpa . . .' I'm lying on my bed with my granddaughter Miraijin, who is twenty-six months old. I'm trying to get her to sleep. I'm holding her tight and stroking her curls with one hand. My mobile's in my other hand, I'm reading a text – and Miraijin does not like that. 'Grandpa-grandpa-grandpa-grandpa . . .' she protests, on a loop. I stop reading the text and look at her: she smiles and immediately stops complaining. I get back to my text, still holding her and stroking her hair, and she resumes straight away: 'Grandpa-grandpa-grandpa-grandpa . . . ' I look at her. She stops. Back to my text. She resumes. It's not enough – my body, my hugs, my warmth, my cuddles are not enough. She wants me to look at her, otherwise you're not here, she's saying, and if you're not here you can forget about me falling asleep.

I'm at a service station, I've just filled up my car. I'm paying with my credit card. Once the amount has been keyed in, the card reader (I've recently learned it's called 'POS', which stands for Point Of Sale) asks for my PIN (which stands for Personal Identification Number, as I've known for some time). The guy at the till hands me the POS device and then pointedly looks away in the direction of the windswept countryside. He does so in such an ostentatious manner that his action stands out in a context of otherwise small, routine actions of no real consequence. He has absolutely no reason whatsoever to behave in such a conspicuous manner, other than to signal that he's not looking at me while I key in my PIN, and hence he's not to blame if my card details get stolen.

Canto n.13 of the *Purgatorio* in Dante's *Divine Comedy* is dedicated to the souls of the envious, who are found on the second terrace of Purgatory. These souls are huddled together, clothed in coarse fabric the same colour as the rock they lean against, pleading with the saints and the Virgin

Mary to help them. Virgil invites Dante to look closely at them, and Dante sees their eyes are sewn shut with wire, tears streaming through the seams. The poet then looks away in a wonderfully generous and modern gesture: 'To me it seemed, in passing, to do outrage / Seeing the others without being seen / Wherefore I turned me to my counsel sage.' That is, he turns away to look at Virgil, and not because he is horrified by the sight of that terrible punishment, but so he doesn't offend those souls by looking at them when they can't look back at him. It is as though he was saying that you can't shoot unarmed people, that you can't strike those who cannot strike back.

According to a former member of Prince's staff, the artist wouldn't let his employees look at him. In an anonymous interview to fashion magazine *Notorious*, a staff member said: 'I've literally seen him fire a guy once, because he'd looked at him – Why is this guy looking at me? Tell him to go away!'. There is even a specific term for such a provocation: eye *contact*.

In 2008, French philosopher Baldine Saint Girons published a book called *L'Acte Esthétique – 50 questions* ('*The Aesthetic Act – 50 Questions*') in which she introduces a rather extreme philosophical concept, that of aesthetics as an 'act', precisely. This term turns the traditional concept of 'looking' on its head, associating it not with a passive, contemplative state but with action, with doing. The aesthetic act, claims Saint Girons, implies a degree of 'meddling': to look is to touch from a distance. A look possesses material substance. It is anything but passive.

Hundreds of people hit us with their eyes every day. We, in turn, hit hundreds of people with ours. Most of the time it goes unnoticed: we don't register being looked at, other people don't register we're looking at them, and as a result nothing happens. These looks have no consequences, but that's not to say they're any less substantial than the ones I mentioned earlier. Come to think of it, are we sure that when our gaze is not returned it has no consequences? Some people fall in love just by looking at a certain person walking down the street from their window. Others fixate on TV presenters. No, there are no second-class looks: from the moment our eyes home in on someone or something, we are meddling – and the consequences of this meddling will be determined exclusively by the particular combination of events (i.e. by chance).

Such consequences belong almost exclusively in the realm of emotions. Take the cashier at the petrol station, for instance: let's assume that instead of making such a show of looking away he stared at my fingers while I keyed in my PIN – or even just looked me in the eye instead of gazing at the countryside. I'd be annoyed, that's for sure and my reaction (whether I'd say that out loud or not) would be similar to Prince's: why is this guy looking at me? Even if I didn't suspect he was trying to memorise my PIN, I'd still feel violated. It goes to show that our eyes are extremely powerful weapons, even when they're not intended as such. Who hasn't felt humiliated when the person they were talking to glanced at their watch? What makes the difference – what makes knowing that people are constantly looking at us more or less bearable – is the quality of the attention paid to us. Imagine a guy on the motorway, standing by the roadside next to his car: as we drive past at seventy miles per hour, we suddenly realise he's urinating. He's probably a very honest, respectable, mentally stable person – and yet, faced with an irrepressible urge, he had no choice but to commit such a 'socially extreme' act. 'Oh what the hell,' he must have thought, 'it's got to be better than wetting my pants.' But nothing could induce him to do what he resolved to do facing us as we drive by. By facing away from us he withdraws his attention, which in turn neutralises the impact our eyes would have on him. Whether he looks away or not makes very little material difference (as it's quite unlikely we'll know him) and yet it makes all the difference to him. It follows that in this context, the most salient action is not so much his urinating by the roadside, but us seeing him do it. If he was somehow prevented from looking away, the most salient action would be his seeing us, as we see him urinate. The act of looking is anything but passive.

'I am what I see,' said Alexandre Hollan – and it's indeed no surprise that a painter should identify with his field of vision. Similarly, a model could arrive at the diametrically opposite conclusion that 'I am what others see in me'. Either way, existence is predicated on the same concept – that of seeing. The electronic gaze of a machine, on the other hand, is by definition uninvolved and blameless – making it the ideal repository for the gravest of responsibilities. US bombardier Thomas Ferebee asked his eyes to tell him when to drop the atomic bomb on Hiroshima from the *Enola Gay*. A few moments later, those very same eyes saw the terrifying mushroom cloud generated by the explosion: he meddled all right. Nowadays, bombs are dropped by unmanned drones piloted by algorithms. No one is looking, no one is meddling, no one is to blame.

And then there's the most creative and mystifying of all aesthetic acts: contemplation. Now, for instance, Miraijin has finally fallen asleep, and instead of reading my text I'm contemplating her: she's a child, just a normal child, asleep – and yet my eyes transfigure her into the most beautiful of creatures.

# Wolves don't kill unlucky deer (2016)

It didn't hit home at first: Drago introduced him to the new guest (Blizzard, meet Hanmokku, Hanmokku, meet Blizzard) Marco shook his hand without giving it much thought, made a faint attempt at a smile and moved on. He's distracted, perhaps reflecting on his own baseness: he's dragged Miraijin there again, even though she has a fever. But it's 29 February – a special day – and Marco couldn't resist. He is not the superstitious kind, but he does believe in the power of numbers and recurring events, and a day that only comes along every four years is a good day to gamble. And so there he is. After all, he thought, 38°C is not that bad, and she doesn't look like she's in pain. He gave her some paracetamol, calculating that in a worst-case scenario, if the fever spiked, he could always take her to the nearest hospital in Siena. For all that, everything went off without a hitch: as usual, Miraijin fell asleep in the car and slept the whole way from Florence to Vico Alto. As usual, she woke up as they arrived at the villa, just in time to make it easier for Marco to get her out of the car (with the help of Dami Tamburini's colossal Filipino servant, Manuel, who as usual was waiting for him at the end of the drive). As usual, she promptly went back to sleep as soon as she was deposited in her hammock, which as usual was pitched in the 'Suffering Room' – thus named because it was there that one of Dami Tamburini's ancestors (Francesco Saverio, Viscount of Talamone) wrote his memoirs, entitled *My Suffering*, where he chronicled his wife Luigina's infidelities and the unspeakable pain they caused him.

Everything as usual then – nevertheless, the child still has a fever, and Marco Carrera is still wallowing in his own baseness. That explains why he didn't realise Dami Tamburini had introduced him to The Omen. But then, suddenly, his eyes find that spindly figure still standing next to the host at the other side of the room – and he sees, at a distance, what he couldn't see up close. While he's at it, he recognises his nom de guerre too (Blizzard), which had also gone unnoticed earlier. Amazed, Marco walks back towards him. Blizzard, however, had recognised him straight away, and now looks at him, smiling and waiting.

– You . . . – Marco mumbles, immediately interrupted by The Omen.

– Could you please tell me where I can find a bathroom? – he interjects, grabbing his arm and leading him away from Dami Tamburini, who is still greeting his guests.

They leave the room. Marco Carrera actually makes for the bathroom. He looks at his old friend, still astonished – astonished that he should crop up there after all those years, and that he didn't even recognise him. His heart is pounding. The boy who saved his life almost forty years ago now looks like a walking scarecrow in a ragged, frayed suit: his hair is white and dishevelled like that of a mad scientist, he has the wrecked skin of an addict, a hunched back the shape of a shepherd's crook, yellow teeth, and tattoos snaking up his neck like tentacles. They look *out of place*, so to speak, those tattoos – as if someone had tattooed him against his will.

And yet he's still smiling.

– Duccio . . . – says Marco.

The boy he had betrayed almost forty years ago: betrayed, humiliated and effectively forced to disappear – and disappear he did, which at the time became a source of agonising guilt for Marco (short-lived guilt though, superseded after just two years – like everything else – by Irene's death, and never resurfaced since, completely obliterated as it was by the various calamities that had befallen him – so much so that for decades, until that moment, there had been no trace of that guilt, or of Duccio, in his memory). But now that he's standing right in front of him, so old and haggard, Marco is wondering why he didn't think of him every single day. How could he forget him? How was that possible?

– Are you the one they call *Ammoccu*? – asks The Omen.

– Yes – answers Marco – but what are you—

– Then go home. Now.

He seems to have trouble speaking, as if his language abilities might be somewhat impaired – which might well be the case given the way he looks. Yet, precisely because of the effort he has to make, he appears to savour every word intensely.

– Listen to me – he insists – You'd better not play tonight.

– But . . . why? – asks Marco Carrera.

They're now inside the bathroom, where two mirrors on opposite walls endlessly multiply their reflection.

– Look at me – says The Omen – and try to understand what I'm saying: don't play tonight. Go. Home. I'm saying this to you as a friend.

He smiles again, baring his yellow fangs – a broad, crooked smile.

Marco Carrera's mind goes into overdrive: several contrasting reactions to Duccio's words jostle for space, producing a gridlock. Should he listen and just leave – immediately, without even asking why, simply interpreting that warning as another bad omen, on top of Miraijin's fever? Or should he question Duccio's rather dramatic reappearance instead: why was he there, in what capacity, what were his intentions? Should he apologise to him, thirty-seven years too late? Or, on the contrary, antagonise him and tell him to fuck off (as he is really tempted to do). Come to think of it, why is he so angry all of a sudden? Is it because Duccio's words sounded less like friendly advice and more like a threat? Or is it because when you hurt someone, you end up hating them (rather than the other way round) and anything they do or say becomes insufferable?

Duccio – he says in the end, trying to stay calm – I come here every week. I know this place, I know all the players, I'm on my turf. And now you come out of nowhere telling me to leave? Why? Where have you been all these years? What have you been doing? Why are you here? And what the hell are you wearing?

Duccio's black suit seems to get more tattered with every mirror reflection. Not even a gravedigger would wear that, thinks Marco. Not even a bloody gravedigger.

– I'm here to work – says The Omen – and this is my uniform. I was born ugly, which helps, but my job requires me to come across as very unpleasant, and clothes play a crucial part in it.

– What are you talking about? What is it that you do?

Duccio looks away for a moment, lifting his head towards the ceiling, and in that moment Marco catches a glimpse of the boy he used to know, the ski champion they called Blizzard. Or maybe it's just his imagination.

The Omen takes a long breath.

– Right – he says – I'm a jinx, that much you know. And you also know that I bring bad luck to everyone except those who are close to me. What did people call it again? The eye of the storm and all that . . . Well, seeing as at some point my reputation became rather . . . inescapable, so to speak, I decided to put it to good use.

– What do you mean?

– I mean this is how I make a living now.

– Like how?

– Like I'm a professional jinx. I bring bad luck for a fee. I wouldn't laugh if I were you, because tonight I've been hired by your friend here to bring bad luck to this Ammoccu, as he calls you. *Very* bad luck. *The worst.* That's why I'm telling you to leave. Listen to me – it's not a joke.

Once again, his strained, slurred words seem to add poignancy to everything he says.

– Wha-what are you talking about? – stutters Marco, struggling to hide his astonishment.

– Marco, I live in Naples now – do you know what that means? It's like being a bullfighter in Seville. People tell me who they want me to bring bad luck to, and pay me for it, and I do: I've been doing it for years, and it works every time. I work every day, in Naples and elsewhere. Gambling, business, love, sports, family feuds. I'm like a magnet for bad luck, and I'm telling you this morning I got on a plane from Naples expressly on account of this Ammoccu. 'Make him cry,' was his request. He's paying me good money, this friend of yours.

– Friend of mine?

– Your friend, the host.

– But why? We are friends, as you say – why would he want to hurt me like that?

– Listen, I never question my clients' motives. I don't know what's going on inside this guy's head, I'm flying back to Naples tomorrow and I'll never see him again. He's crazy, if you ask me – but not like he can't count the fingers on his own hand, if you see what I mean. A different kind of crazy.

But I don't know him at all, it's just the impression I got – I could be wrong. All I know is that he wants to see you cry, so I'm telling you, go home . . . I keep my deposit, forget about the rest, and no one gets hurt.

One reaction is gradually gaining the upper hand in Marco's gridlocked mind. Far from subsiding, the adrenaline that's been pumping since the morning in anticipation of the evening's exploits is pumping faster than ever. But Marco still can't find the right words, so he remains silent.

– That's enough now – insists Duccio – Go away. My mother told me what happened to you. Go home.

Marco shuddered.

– Your mother's still alive?

– Yes.

– How old is she?

– Ninety-two.

– And how is she?

The Omen's ravaged face crumples into a feral expression – bitter and feral.

– She's fine – he replies – not that I can take any credit for that. I neglect her. My lovely cousins, they look after her, hoping to get their hands on the inheritance. Such eager beavers: they take much better care of her than of their own mother, who died alone in a nursing home. They don't know it's theirs already – the inheritance – because I'm not interested in it. If they knew they'd feed her rat poison. It's my way of protecting her: letting them believe they need to get into her good graces so she'll write me out of her will.

He pauses. The grimace vanishes.

– She's always kept an eye on you, all these years – he continues – she's always kept me informed. She's very sorry about what happened to you. Now go home.

And this is how Marco Carrera found out he was an object

of pity. He'd never given it much thought: he'd moved back to the town where he was born, taken up with his old friends again, rejoined the old sports clubs – but he never mentioned what happened, what kept happening to him. Irene. Marina. Adele. He didn't look for a shoulder to cry on. He kept it together and carried on, and now he realises people had been pitying him all along – even an outcast like The Omen. In that moment, the right words come to him.

– Listen, Duccio – he says – thank you for warning me, but I'm not going home, because I don't believe you're a jinx. I never believed it and I always fought those who did. I made a mistake, many years ago, just one mistake – a pretty serious one, I'll give you that – because I was in shock and stupid and lonely, and you're the one who had to pay the consequences, and for that I apologise. If I could go back, I swear I wouldn't make that mistake again. But even then, I never believed what they said about you. Plus, I owe you my life, so I can't be afraid of you. And if you're telling me that Dami Tamburini, my friend as well as my doubles partner – which incidentally is the only reason he's won a couple of tournaments in the past few years, apparently the thing he values most in life – if you're telling me that Dami Tamburini, instead of kissing the ground I walk on (like my mother used to say) hired you to make me cry . . . well that's all the more reason for me to play. You know what they say, when the going gets tough . . .

Now it's Duccio's turn to be surprised. He's clearly not used to interacting with someone who *doesn't believe* he's a jinx – the first time in God knows how many years.

– Besides – he continues – now you've told me why you're here, this gives me a huge advantage, and I intend to make the most of it. And in terms of good and bad luck, let me show you something – come.

Followed by The Omen, Marco leaves the bathroom and heads towards the Suffering Room. He puts a finger on his lips to signal to Duccio to be quiet and gently opens the door. He lets him in, then sneaks in behind him and carefully closes the door. Miraijin is asleep, one arm dangling out of the hammock. Marco places the arm back on her lap and gently kisses her on her slightly damp, cool forehead.

– She's my granddaughter – he whispers – her name is Miraijin. She's five and a half. Wherever I go, she follows. Always. My nom de guerre is Hanmokku, after the hammock where she sleeps. See the frame? It's portable. Did he tell you about this, that friend of mine?

– No.

– Well then.

Marco strokes the child's forehead one last time, then opens the door and they walk out without a sound.

– As I said – Marco continues, closing the door behind him – I don't believe in these sort of things, but I promise you that if there was such a thing as the ability to bring good or bad luck, she'd be unbeatable. She's here with me, protecting me. So maybe you're the one who should go home – I wouldn't want to, you know, ruin your reputation or something.

Marco smiles. He and Duccio are the same age. They were best friends when everyone knew him as The Hummingbird. They competed in the same ski races and spent hundreds of afternoons listening to the best music in those years when a new masterpiece would come out every week. They started gambling together – horse races, roulette, dice, poker – messing about in casinos all over Europe. There's something glorious about their shared memories. But then life got in the way, and now they pity each other.

– Don't play with fire – says The Omen – Go away.

Duccio is old, and alone, and finished – Marco could be his

son: he's in good shape, and he has a future, because he has Miraijin. In a flash, Marco sees how it was all meant to be: Carradori's inspired gift, the disgraceful way he'd been using it (so much for the doting grandfather everyone thought he was), everything leading him to that moment, to that twenty-ninth of February. A day that doesn't exist.

All the love he'd given, too, the time he'd wasted, the pain he'd felt: all of it was energy, it was power, it was destiny, and it all led there.

– Wolves don't kill unlucky deer, Duccio, – he says – they kill the weak ones.

# Third letter on hummingbirds (2018)

Marco Carrera
12 Piazza Savonarola
Florence 50132
Italy

Paris, 19 December 2018

Marco,

I'm reading a book about one of your favourite singers, Fabrizio de André. His partner Dori Ghezzi wrote it, together with two linguists. It's an amazing book, and I've just come across this passage where the two linguists explain the meaning of a term they coined, 'emmenalgia':

'From Ancient Greek '*emmeno*' (meaning to 'hold steady', 'persevere', 'valiantly endure') and '*algos*' (pain) – so, a kind of sad, melancholic yearning to persevere to the bitter end. An insidious term though, because '*emmeno*' also means 'not abiding by other people's rules or decisions'. That, however, is every human being's fate (insofar as we are all bound by the laws of time and space), and God's fate as well – because he too has to submit to man's free will.

Marco – this is you. No one can persevere as strenuously as you do, and no one can elude change quite like you do: just as the linguists said in the book, you hold steady and push on to the bitter end while also (fatally) refusing to submit to other people's rules or decisions.

And just like that, out of the blue, I saw it (which is also why I'm writing to you out of the blue, even though I know you won't write back): you really are a hummingbird. It's so obvious. It was a revelation: you really are a hummingbird and not because you were so little. You are a hummingbird because all your energy is spent keeping still. Seventy wing beats per second only to remain where you are. And you truly are formidable at this. You can keep still as time flows around you, you can stop it flowing, sometimes you can turn back time, even – just like a hummingbird, you can fly backwards and retrieve lost time. That's why being with you is so beautiful.

That said, what comes so easy to you is almost impossible for other people.

That said, change (even when, in all likelihood, it won't be a change for the better) is part of human nature – and you can't comprehend that.

And above all, expending all that energy just to keep still can sometimes be the evil itself, rather than the cure. That's why being with you is impossible.

I've spent my entire life wondering why you'd never managed to do what you most wanted to do – why you couldn't take that step you needed to take to be with me. I wondered what part of you would always suck you back every time we got so close to being together (and that happened a few times, over the years) – why you'd suddenly push away everything you'd so desperately tried to grasp up until that very moment. Today I realised I'm the one who never managed to be with you. Because in order to be with you, you have to keep still, and I was never able to do that. The end result, of course, remains the same: we've missed each other (in all the possible meanings of the term) but this new perspective on our relationship fills me with anguish. New, unbearable anguish, because I see now that it had been my fault all along.

Realising this so late is atrocious too, but better late than never.

Marco. I hear loud bangs, ambulances, people screaming outside my window: it's Saturday, and like every Saturday it's the end of the world here in Paris, but that's just the way it is now. Yellow Vests protesting everywhere – but that's just the way it is now. Being without you is just the way it is now.

Merry Christmas
Luisa

## Things as they really are (2016)

– Hello?
– Hello, Dr Carradori, Carrera here.
– Hello, how are you?
– I'm all right, you?
– I'm fine too, thanks.
– Am I bothering you? Where are you now?
– Not at all. I'm in Rome, I'm completing a training course before going back to Brazil.
– Brazil? Why?
– I know, no one's heard about it here in Italy, but four months ago Brazil suffered one of the most devastating ecological disasters in human history. Bento Rodrigues – does that ring a bell?
– No.
– It's a village in the state of Minas Gerais – or rather, it *was* a village.
– What happened?
– It was flooded by a toxic mudflow from a nearby iron ore mine. The tailings dam collapsed. It's been four months now.
– God. Were there many casualties?
– Not that many, considering. Seventeen. The problem is that

an area the size of England has been contaminated, including rivers and a big chunk of the Atlantic coast, hundreds of miles from the village itself. Tens of thousands of people have lost everything and have been evacuated.

– Gosh, that's the first I've heard of it.

– It's barely made the news in Italy – just a couple of articles, no one's talked about it in months. But it's a real catastrophe. The people want to stay, but everything's been poisoned. If you let them, they'll die of cancer. If you take them away, they have nothing to live for. And take them where, anyway? It's a complete disaster.

– I'm sorry . . .

– Anyway. But how are things with you, Dr Carrera? Tell me all is well.

– Well yes, actually, all is well.

– I'm glad. And what about the child?

– Oh, she's just a dream.

– How old is she now?

– Five and a half.

– Blimey! How long has it been since we met?

– Three years.

– Ah yes, she was two and a half then. So all is well with you?

– All is well. Except . . .

– Except?

– There's something I'd like to talk to you about.

– Go ahead.

– But first, I have a confession to make.

– A confession?

– The hammock. The one you gave me.

– What about it?

– I'm using it.

– That's good.

– But not just when I play tennis or go to a conference, like I told you.
– Oh? And what else?
– When I was young, I gambled. Did you know that?
– Yes. Your ex-wife told me when I was her therapist.
– Poker, chemin de fer, roulette. Then I quit.
– Yes, I knew that too.
– Well I've started gambling again.
– Good. Do you still enjoy it?
– I bring Miraijin along. She sleeps in the hammock.
– But of course.
– In the room next to where we play.
– Sure. That's precisely what—
– It goes on all night, sometimes. Until dawn.
– So what? I don't see anything wrong with it. Unless you've lost too much money. Have you lost too much money?
– No, on the contrary . . .
– . . .
– . . .
– Tell me what happened, Dr Carrera.
– Last night – I mean this morning. Well ten hours ago . . .
– Yes?
– I've *won* too much.
– What do you mean?
– I mean I won a ridiculous sum. And I did something ridiculous, too.
– And what would that be?
– I'd been warned, before we sat down to play, by an old friend I hadn't seen in over thirty years. A professional . . . player, so to speak. I should tell you about him too actually, but not now. So, after all this time, I see him at this villa where I've been gambling practically every week for three years now. He takes me to one side and tells me: 'Go away, go home',

and I go 'Why?'. 'Because they're after you, the big boss here – he hired me to ruin you. He wants to see you cry. I didn't know it was you.'

– How come he didn't know – aren't you old friends?

– We don't use our real names when we play. He was told his target was a guy called Hanmokku, and when they introduced us, he realised I was Hanmokku.

– I see.

– Which, incidentally, is the name of the hammock you gave me.

– Right.

– Anyway that's what he said. And the one he called the big boss is the host, Luigi Dami Tamburini. Ever heard of him?

– No. Should I?

– It's a fairly well-known name in Tuscany. An old aristocratic family from Siena. Anyway it doesn't matter, really. What *does* matter is that this Dami Tamburini is my doubles partner in over-50s tennis tournaments. Someone I considered a friend, until yesterday.

– I see.

– Anyway, this old friend of mine tells me Dami Tamburini wants to ruin me. And Miraijin had a fever, which meant I was already unsure whether to play or not. What would a normal person do, in that situation?

– You tell me.

– They'd leave, that's what they'd do. And then they'd try to piece it all back together the following day. Right?

– Right.

– Well not me.

– You stayed?

– I stayed and I played, yes.

– And you won that ridiculous sum.

– I did.

– You won it from your doubles partner or from your old friend?
– From my doubles partner, the one who wanted to see me cry. But I came this close to losing everything. This close.
– How do you mean?
– I mean I bet money I didn't have.
– How much?
– I can't tell you that, I'm too ashamed. So much money that, if I'd lost it, I'd be completely screwed.
– But you didn't lose it.
– No. Because a Jack of Diamonds trumped a Jack of Clubs.
– What were you playing?
– Texas Hold 'Em.
– And what's that?
– A type of poker that originated in Texas.
– Is it very different from regular poker?
– It's more complicated. Each player is dealt two cards face down – your 'hole cards'. Then there are five cards dealt face up in the middle of the table, shared by all players.
– Right.
– It's designed precisely to limit losses, so people don't end up ruined. Last night, however, it didn't work. Last night I came this close to losing everything.
– But then you won.
– I did. And Dami Tamburini is the one who lost everything. He started losing and then playing again to get back what he'd lost, again and again and again, and in the end it was just me and him, and it got personal. And I didn't stop. In twenty minutes – no, in fifteen minutes, I won an outrageous sum.
– How much?
– I'm ashamed to say.
– Why? You're not the one who lost it.

– No, but I'm involved all the same.
– How much?
– Eight hundred and forty thousand.
– Dear God!
– He kept doubling the ante . . .
– And does he have this kind of money, this friend of yours?
– Oh he does all right. His family own a business bank, land, a vineyard, real estate . . . But I didn't take it. That's why I called you.
– You didn't take it! Why?
– Because it's too much! I mean . . . even the notary – he's always around to sort things out when large sums are involved – and even he didn't know what to do.
– You're telling me you won eight hundred thousand euros and turned it down?
– Eight hundred and forty thousand. Yes.
– Wow . . .
– Do you think I'm crazy?
– No. It's just . . . unusual.
– I did ask for something else in return, though.
– You did?
– You see, Dr Carradori . . . the sun was coming up. Next door, Miraijin had drifted off into a drugged sleep. I was sitting there, shattered, together with four others, more exhausted than me. I was due at the hospital in two hours. And I sat there, looking at the table, looking at the man I'd ruined – a man that up until six hours before I considered a friend . . .
– So what did you ask for?
– I was ashamed. Of everything. Ashamed I'd decided to play even though Miraijin had a fever. Ashamed I didn't go home when I was told to. Ashamed I'd got sucked in and kept playing when I started losing – instead of leaving like I usually

do – and got sucked in even more when I started winning, again and again, until I won all that money.

– Well, you were in shock . . .

– I was ashamed of being a gambler – worse, I was ashamed of myself altogether, of the way my life had turned out. Ashamed I'd lost all the people I loved, because one way or the other they all left, Dr Carradori, and I've got no one . . .

– You have the child.

– I was ashamed of her too, parked in that hammock, I was ashamed *for* her even: I felt shame, and pity, terrible, immense pity. And I did something gamblers never do.

– What did you do?

– I told those four wretched souls what I'm telling you now, I'm sure they were as ashamed as I was. And I said something else too, things you're unlikely to hear at a gambling table, even though deep down everyone feels the same.

– And what's that?

– That the more I won the more I hated my life. I won fifty thousand and I thought I should buy a new car because the one I have is a wreck. But I never thought my car was a wreck before – see what I'm getting at?

– Yes.

– It's what gambling does to you, you end up hating your life, you want to win so you can change it, but you wouldn't hate it in the first place if it wasn't for gambling. I was two hundred thousand up and I saw myself at the Maldives, or in Polynesia, in one of those luxury resorts where I've never wanted to go before. Four hundred thousand and I fantasised about hiring assistants, servants, cooks, chauffeurs, nannies – as if that's what I lacked in my life, as if all I wanted was to stop taking care of myself and Miraijin. Six hundred thousand and I was going to retire – as if the job I've been devoting so much time and effort to for thirty-five years had been nothing but a nuisance. But it isn't. I don't hate my life. Quite the opposite in fact: I like my life, because unlike other people I have a purpose, which is raising the Man of the Future – an immense privilege.

– You said all these things?

– I did. And then at the end I said what every gambler knows: that it's not possible to make good use of the money you win at the gambling table. And that for all these reasons, I didn't want my eight hundred and forty thousand euros.

– And what did your friend say? What did the others say?

– They all started crying. I swear. They wanted to see me cry and I made them cry instead. But they weren't upset, they were moved. It was pathetic really, but it's the one thing I'm not ashamed of.

– So what did you ask for instead of the money?

– I asked for my mother's photo archive back. I had donated it to a foundation run by this Dami Tamburini a few years ago, and I asked for it back.

– Why?

– Because last night I finally saw things for what they really are. I realised the only valuable thing this man owned was that photo archive I'd given him.

– Good on you.

– Truth is, I hadn't *donated* those photos, I'd *got rid* of them. I told myself the foundation would take better care of them, but I was simply throwing away what my mother had left behind, erasing every trace of her life. Tomorrow I get her archive back. That's what I really won last night.

– No regrets?

– Not even for a second. You see, money's not an issue for me. I always enjoyed working and I never wanted to live off private income or anything like that. That money would have ruined me. And gambling was just this bullshit I got sucked into as a teenager and never managed to escape since: it was always there, all my life, threatening to destroy me, until last night I saw it for what it is. I saw everything for what it is last night. I saw things as they really are. I needed to tell someone and I thought of you.

– You were right.

– I'll let you go now, I've kept you long enough.

– Nonsense! You did well to call me.

– Thank you, Dr Carradori. I hope to see you soon.

– I'll come visit so you can show me your mother's photos.

– I'd love to. They're beautiful.

– I don't doubt it.

– Goodbye, Dr Carradori.

– Goodbye, Dr Carrera.

# One last time (2018)

Luisa Lattes
23 Rue du Docteur Blanche
Paris 75016
France

Florence, 27 December 2018

Dear Luisa,

As you can see, I'm answering your letter. But perhaps you knew I would: all that stuff about hummingbirds, that made-up word (what was it, emmenalgia?), the reason we never managed to be together . . . I couldn't just let that sit there. This doesn't mean I'll start writing to you again, mind you. One thing's for certain: I can't afford to be in any kind of relationship with you.

First of all, on the subject of moving or keeping still, I notice you've moved house again. Why? Have you broken up with that Jewish philosopher too? And if so, why? Or is this some kind of office space you're renting out to work? And if so, why get a place so far from home? I can't think of any other possible reasons, as I don't believe you've simply moved together: I really can't see a Jewish philosopher who's lived in the Marais all his life (as you yourself told me) suddenly upping sticks and relocating to the sixteenth arrondissement.

The fact is, when things change it's easy to see that they change for a reason, but it's not as easy to understand that there's a reason things stay the way they are, too. This is because we've been glorifying change for such a long time now, that all everyone wants is change – even when it's just change for change's sake. Therefore – inevitably – those who move on are brave and those who stay still are cowards, those who change are enlightened and those who don't are ignorant. It's the zeitgeist. That's why I was glad to see you've realised (if I read your letter correctly) that it takes a lot of effort and courage to keep still too.

Take a look back at your own life: how many times have you moved house? Changed jobs? How many relationships, husbands, partners, children, abortions, holiday homes, routines, obsessions, good times, bad times have you lived through? Countless, as far as I know (and I don't know everything). How much energy have you invested in doing all that? An awful lot. And now, at the age of fifty-two, here you are writing to me – and yes, I've mostly kept still all this time.

I say 'mostly' because there have been changes in my life too, as you know: shockwaves that threw me off course and left me for dead.

All the changes I've known, Luisa, have been changes for the worse. I know that's not the case for everyone, quite the opposite: we're all familiar with those uplifting, edifying stories where change is doggedly pursued to improve someone's life – everyone's life in some cases – no need to mention that. But that's not how things went for me.

I'm not asking for your pity, Luisa: just to say that I haven't managed to keep still either, sadly. I wish I had. If it had been up to me, I would have. But it wasn't to be, and every single change I've endured was like a collision that knocked me off and sent me careering into another life, and then another, and then another – and I had to learn to adjust to these lives from scratch, and learn fast, with no guidance whatsoever. Do you see why I hold on to things as tight as I do?

Yes, I too believe we could have been together if only you'd been able to keep still. But we cannot change who we are, and if I'm a hummingbird, you're the lion or the gazelle in the savannah or however the fuck the saying goes – the stupid one about waking up in the morning and running, regardless of who you are.

I have a mission now, something that gives meaning to everything I ever did and didn't do, including you: I'm raising the Man of the Future, that is, the eight-year-old girl who lives here. She will become a woman. She will become the Man of the Future. This is what she was born to do, and I won't let change throw her off course. That's all the strength I've got left now – just enough to raise her (and answer you one last time). I'm sorry, Luisa, but this is the last letter I'll write to you. I have loved you so much, you know I have: for forty years you have been the first and the last thing I thought about, every single day. But not anymore. My first thought is for her now, and the last, and all the thoughts in between. This is the only way I can live now.

Hugs,
Marco

# The New Man (2016–2029)

There are those who strive all their life to learn, improve, move forward, conquer new heights, only to find out they were just trying to recreate the burst of energy that brought them into this world. For them, life is a full circle where starting point and end point coincide. Then there are those who – not moving at all – still manage to cover great distances, because life itself seems to glide under their feet and transport them very far from where they'd started: Marco Carrera was one of them. It was clear to him by now that his life had a purpose. Not all lives have one, but his did. All the pain he'd lived through, that too was for a reason, nothing had happened by chance.

His life had never been 'normal' by anyone's standards: he had always been the odd one out. There was his abnormally small size, for starters, which set him apart from the other kids – and then the treatment that brought him back in line with everyone else at the age of fifteen. The results, in fact, had far outstripped what the specialists had anticipated: Marco had grown much more, and much faster than expected. No one had bothered looking into it, but the treatment Marco underwent in the autumn of 1974 had triggered an abnormal growth spurt: over six inches in eight months. He went from 5' 1" in October (much lower than the 5' 5" average for boys his age) to 5' 6" (i.e. bang on the average) the following June. And then, suddenly, his miraculous growth stopped – or rather, it stabilised right on the fiftieth centile: 5' 7" the following year, then 5' 8" the one after that, and finally 5' 9" when he turned nineteen, just about half an inch above the national average.

And no one had a clue why. According to Dr Vavassori's forecast, Marco could expect to grow about four inches (rather than six) over a period of fifteen months (rather than eight), which would have made him just a regular short guy. Letizia, for her part, ever faithful to D'Arcy Wentworth Thompson's theories, remained convinced that the treatment had nothing to do with her son's development, and that everything was already written in his genetic code. Quite simply, it was all meant to be: his insufficient growth, then the sudden burst and, finally and most bizarrely, the fact he had ended up back on an average development curve (this last detail in particular could *only* be explained by Thompson's theories, she maintained). Probo, however, was torn: he was happy the treatment had been successful beyond measure, but he also wondered whether such an unexpected result should be cause for concern. He worried something might have got badly out of control, and he was afraid his son's body would suffer the consequences. He never stopped worrying (although after Irene's death nothing seemed to matter all that much anymore). He worried that, with time, Marco would have to pay the price: infertility, degenerative diseases, cancer, deformities. He asked Dr Vavassori, who replied that, as with all experimental treatments, there was of course the risk of unexpected collateral effects further down the line (a risk which, he reminded Probo, had been clearly outlined in all the authorisation documents he had signed). That said, Vavassori maintained there was no reason to believe an unexpectedly successful outcome implied an increased risk: Probo was just being paranoid. That was the first time Probo had ever been called 'paranoid'.

Marco, for his part, hadn't had the time to think at all, bowled over as he was by his miraculous progress: he simply 'inhabited' – so to speak – this phenomenon, and tried to keep up with it. Between November and June, he had grown almost an inch (and three pounds, and half a shoe size) a month – and that had been his sole occupation. He wasn't worried, he wasn't scared, he wasn't ashamed and he was in no hurry either: he abandoned himself to this transformation, demonstrating a remarkable degree of flexibility and resilience (qualities which would come in useful in the future). It was as if his body had decided to skip adolescence and jump straight from child to grown man. After a few years, his time as a hummingbird had become just another childhood memory.

From then onwards, his life continued to follow that pattern: frozen in one spot for years while others moved on, only to erupt out of the blue into an unexpected event, hurling him into completely uncharted waters. Those were almost invariably painful transitions, prompting Marco to wonder, angrily and with a hint of self-pity: why me? *Why me?*

Often, the most valuable of the six honest serving men we all keep (What and Why and When and How and Where and Who) turns out to be *When* – the one question that can truly save us. Marco Carrera never asked himself that question until he had the answer, and that's the only reason he managed to cover so much distance and overcome so much suffering without collapsing (when all he ever wanted was to stay where he was). The revelation came at the right time; that is, in his darkest hour. It was all meant to be, everything had happened for a reason, and that reason was clear, and simple, and fascinating. Miraijin. Miraijin was the New Man. She had always been the

New Man, since before she was born. She was born to change the world and he, Marco Carrera, had been granted the privilege of raising her.

Miraijin's destiny had never been in question while Adele was alive. She kept saying it all the time: the human race would start anew with that child, the human race would start anew with Miraijin. Marco liked to humour his daughter, like when he played with her thread many years before. Ah well – he thought – Adele has been through so much, so what if she needs this Man of the Future fantasy to cheer her up a bit?

But Adele passed away too soon and Marco was completely unprepared for the void she left behind. He reacted to change like he'd always done in the past: he simply stood still in the middle of the desolation that surrounded him and inhabited that desolation. It wasn't a conscious reaction – in fact, he didn't even realise he was doing it. But it wasn't enough anymore. This time, he felt he needed more strength, a new determination to keep fighting. For a while, at the beginning, he followed Dr Carradori's advice and lived recklessly: his only purpose was to look after Miraijin and beyond that he just clung to whatever life he had left. He was far from being a model father figure – what with all the nights he'd spent gambling while Miraijin slept in her hammock – but that too had to happen for him to be able to take the next, decisive step.

The revelation came as he did something that would have otherwise been hard to explain, i.e. as he turned down the ridiculous sum he'd won from his friend Dami Tamburini in a ferocious game of poker. That was the time to ask the right question, to ask *all* the questions. That was the time to summon the most challenging of the honest serving men: *Why?* Everything finally became clear to him. All the pain he'd suffered was the very foundation of the world to come, his memories were his destiny, his past was his future. Turning down all that money (Why me?). Narrowly escaping a plane crash (Why me?). His sister taking her own life (Why me?). Surviving an acrimonious divorce (Why me?). Helping his father die (Why me?). Burying his twenty-two-year-old daughter (Why me?).

Now he had an answer, and the answer was the name that had barged into his life – Miraijin. Miraijin who, as Adele truly believed – always – was the New Man: the human race will start anew with Miraijin. Now Marco Carrera believed it too. He had suffered for a reason, the most noble of reasons: his destiny was to raise the Man of the Future, but only after suffering the slings and arrows of outrageous fortune (as Hamlet would have it). This rather fanatical idea fit in surprisingly well with his otherwise sober and painful existence, even completed it in a way – and for this reason, it immediately ceased to be a fanatical idea.

Miraijin, after all, was rather exceptional. Her beauty grew day by day, a supernatural kind of beauty only previously seen in videogame avatars: taller than most girls her age, slender, soft brown curls, dark brown skin, almond-shaped eyes the colour of deep water . . . She really looked like she'd been assembled choosing different options from a menu. And it was through her eyes that Miraijin reminded Marco of her uniqueness, every single day. An experienced ophthalmologist, he had been studying the anatomy of the visual apparatus for over forty years, and yet he had never seen eyes like hers in anyone – human or otherwise. He felt like an astronaut seeing the earth from outer space from the first time. The one thing that came remotely close to Miraijin's eyes he had observed – and photographed – only once, in a cat belonging to an American friend of his. He dug out that photo (from 1986) and printed a detail of his eyes, captured just as he looked at the camera, but even that didn't quite cut it, because the cat (a Ragdoll called Jagger) was white, whereas Miraijin was black.

And yet, despite her extraterrestrial looks, there was something wonderfully familiar about her. Her eyes were the exact same shade of blue as Irene's – and that was quite something in and of itself. Her athletic, perfectly formed physique was the same Marco remembered in Adele as she was growing up. The dimples in her cheeks were the same as Giacomo's, but unlike his, they didn't seem to disappear as she grew older. Most movingly of all, she had a minuscule birthmark between her ring finger and her little finger in her right hand, the exact same as Marco's and Adele's. Invisible to the rest of the world, that little dot was the Carrera trademark: how many times had he slotted his hand into Adele's so that the marks would meet – their 'power spot', as they called it. That's how they held hands in the birth pool too. Now Marco could keep doing that with Miraijin, because miraculously, in the midst of the genetic storm that made her so *new*, that minuscule birthmark had somehow managed to survive.

But beside her looks (which were the literal embodiment of the utopian ideals of multiculturalism), Miraijin's most striking trait was her uncanny ability to always do the right thing. Always, ever since she was a baby and only cried when she was supposed to cry, ate when she was supposed to eat, and learnt what she was supposed to learn straight away – which made looking after her a remarkably easy task. And growing up she kept doing things right, and always at the right time. Every now and again she would surprise Marco (or Adele, or her teachers, or her paediatrician) with something unusual, but even then, it was unusual in that it was always considered *above* average. It was precisely this phenomenon that convinced Marco she was destined to change the world: because technically speaking, when her behaviour diverged from the norm it wasn't necessarily above average – it was only a different way of doing things. It just *looked* better because she was doing it. Miraijin's body, in fact – her smooth skin, her halogen eyes, her crystalline voice, her expression and her smile and her dimples – her whole body in short, still small and rapidly evolving as it was, already possessed the charisma of a leader. It was one of those bodies whose natural talent is to persuade. One of those bodies that other bodies tend to imitate.

There was nothing Miraijin didn't show an aptitude for, right from the beginning. Every time she tried a new sport – from tennis to judo – she would astonish her instructors with her natural talent. The first time she came across a horse, she walked right behind it and started stroking its tail: no darling, you can't stand there, it's dangerous, you're going to get kicked, horses hate it when you— And yet the horse (the mare actually) seemed exceedingly pleased with Miraijin and was more than happy to let her brush her tail, which, according to the riding instructor, was a sign they had built a deep connection. Except, of course, that was the first time Miraijin had ever seen a horse. (The mare, incidentally, was called Dolly. She was a thirteen-year-old bay quarter horse from Texas, docile but skittish and extremely sensitive to the bit. Just the day before, she had unceremoniously thrown a gentleman from Arezzo who tried to ride her like he was pushing a pram, yanking the bridle left and right. From that day, Miraijin continued to ride Dolly for seven years until she was put out to pasture, waiting to go to Horse Heaven.) At school, teachers were amazed by her ability to focus and to help her classmates focus too. Her drawing skills were outstanding. She'd barely learnt to write and already she could tell 'your' from 'you're' and 'its' from 'it's' (which is more than can be said for many adults). What everyone kept saying every time Miraijin tried something new was: 'She's a natural!'

And so Marco asked her, one day: 'Miraijin' – he asked – 'do you realise that every time you try something new, you can do it straight away? How do you do that?' Her reply was 'I just look at how my teacher does it.' That body of hers was so charismatic precisely because it knew how to imitate other bodies itself. Engrossed in his role of primary educator, Marco began experimenting with this theory. He made her watch NBA games on TV every day for a week, then gave her a basketball: and lo and behold, Miraijin could faultlessly replicate the players' moves – feints, pivot foot, layup – without even knowing the rules. On her first snowboard lesson (which she chose over skis), she could already perfectly imitate her instructor and got safely down the slope without falling, not even once. Next up was dancing (not that Marco liked children who dance, quite the opposite, he found them grotesque, but it was all for the sake of his experiment): just two afternoons spent watching videos of an Iranian girl shuffle-dancing on the street to protest against the regime, and Miraijin had learnt to shuffle. After dancing came music: on her very first piano lesson, the teacher asked her to just randomly hit keys but to try and do a different thing with each hand. She followed the instructions – and sure enough, her hands were on two different beats altogether, completely independent of each other. An excellent start, commented the teacher, quite the little prodigy. Less than a year after that first lesson, Marco walked into her room to ask what she was listening to: it was 'River Flows in You' by Yiruma, and she wasn't listening to it, she was playing it. It beggared belief. And so it was that Marco, at the tender age of sixty, began scrupulously checking his behaviour, his moves – even the way he spoke – like he'd never done before: he was determined to purge his life of all the faulty elements that might sully her purity. Starting with him then, starting with Marco Carrera, Miraijin had begun changing the world.

Ah Miraijin, you're growing so fast! Nine! Ten! Eleven! Twelve! What a joy to throw you a birthday party every twentieth of October! What an adventure to teach you about the world as the world is going to the dogs! Never mind sports, even though you're so good at them – you'd be wasted as an athlete. Piano, dancing, drawing, riding: keep doing the things you love but don't let that dictate who you are, don't become just another child prodigy – you are meant for far bigger things. Good girl – never be competitive. Good girl – be afraid of global warming. Good girl – watch stupid videos on YouTube with your friends and get some of the answers wrong on purpose at school, so you don't leave them too far behind. Remember you are the New Man and everything comes easy to you, but the point is not to stand out, to leave others in the dust as you climb higher and higher – quite the opposite, the point is to lift them up too as you climb, and that is the most difficult part. Thirteen already! Monday is movie night with Grandpa: old films watched the old way (on DVDs) and sushi prepared by you (because it goes without saying, you'll be a great cook and you'll be able to make everything from pasta to dim sum). *The Big Lebowski, The Great Gatsby, One Flew Over the Cuckoo's Nest, Donnie Darko, Ghost World, Persons Unknown, The Usual Suspects* (which will bore you to death, because after five minutes of close-ups and other camera tricks you'll understand that Kevin Spacey is Keyser Söze). You'll watch films with your friends too: *Spring Breakers, Coyote Ugly, Juno, Me Before You, A Star Is Born* – or the old TV shows, *Stranger Things, Black Mirror, Money Heist, Breaking Bad*. You'll be streaming those on tablets, of course, and you'll never go to a cinema, because cinemas are dead and no one can save them, not even you. Fourteen now! There's no rush, Miraijin (you're getting so beautiful) there's no rush (all those boys hovering around you) there's no rush, give it time, trust me: you'll fall in love, you won't be sure, you'll say no, you will be sure, you'll say yes, you'll be happy, unhappy, happy again – it'll all happen when it's meant to happen. Good girl, take your time. Good girl, get bored, and start reading novels – *Dr Zhivago* (that's my girl), *Martin Eden, Wuthering Heights, Harry Potter* – good girl. And then books your grandpa has never even heard of: *The Power, LaRose, His Dark Materials,* Susan Cooper's *The Dark Is Rising* sequence. You'll like comics too, especially manga (you take after your mother) so why not start with *Miraijin Chaos*, and then Tezuka's most famous sagas – *Astro Boy, Next World, Dororo* – and then other series by other authors, like *Sailor Moon* (oh you'll love *Sailor Moon*, just like your mother), and then you'll poke around your great-grandfather's sci-fi collection (893 volumes!): good girl – you're the Man of the Future but you'll want to know your past, so your grandpa will tell you to read Heinlein's short stories (*The Roads Must Roll, The Man Who Sold the Moon*) because they are the most beautiful sci-fi stories he's ever read. And it won't matter that they are the only ones he's read, actually, because you'll like them, and you'll understand how long we've been waiting for this New Man, how passionately and naïvely we've been imagining him, dreaming of him.

You're fifteen, Miraijin – why don't you try and start your own YouTube channel? Come on, what have you got to lose? Do it! And your grandpa (who you always thought was so strict, but he wasn't, because being strict with children is supremely useless: the ones who have any use for authority – like you – will find it where they want, and the ones who don't will just challenge it) even your grandpa, surprisingly, will agree – encourage you even – and so you'll start your own YouTube channel. Just videos you made on your phone to begin with, where you'll talk about the things that make you so popular with other kids, things you can share with them: films and TV shows to watch, books to read, clothes to wear, food to taste, dance moves to learn, hairdos to try, games to play and places to visit and ways to protect the environment. This means strangers will be able to do what everyone who's met you in real life is already doing: imitate you. In short, you will become *that thing*, you know, which has a very specific name that your grandpa will forbid you to use (so he is strict after all – or is he joking? Either way you will never use it. Ever). Sixteen! Seventeen! Your destiny will catch up with you, and you'll be famous, very famous: your videos will be watched millions of times, which is insane considering you'll only be talking about simple things, normal things – and as your country is going to the dogs so many teenagers will look up to you, so many kids too, and they'll want to do what you do, be like you, see the world through your unbelievable eyes. And they'll follow you, so many will follow you.

This means money will come, a lot of money, but it won't seduce you or send you off course: you'll give away a good chunk to those who need it most, of course, and the rest you'll save, because being rich while everyone else is getting poorer is a huge advantage if you're trying to change the world. Your grandpa will have retired by then: he'll be taking care of the money side of things so you can stay focused on your life, on school, and school trips, and your piano lessons, and the trips to London to improve your English, the parties, the festivals, the holidays in Bolgheri with him and the holidays with your friends (because they can't get enough of you and they'll always invite you everywhere). Grandpa will be looking after all the practical details now that you're so famous, because (he thinks and he's right) otherwise fame will swallow you whole, because (he thinks and he's right) otherwise you'll just become another business, another brand, and then the agents will come, the entrepreneurs, the producers, the promoters, the sponsors, the parasites. He'll keep them away from you so you can be surrounded only by real people: the boys and girls that look up to you and fight against the carnage caused by their parents. Marco Carrera, therefore, will keep doing what he's been doing all his life: he will stand still, his feet firmly planted on the ground, and he will try as hard as he can to stop time. But time won't stop for you, Miraijin – and now you're eighteen, hard to believe Miraijin, you're a grown woman, a young woman, so beautiful, so cathartic and so formative (formative in that – it's no secret anymore – you are shaping a brand-new generation capable of surviving the devastation caused by the previous one). Because real change, change even your grandpa can get behind, will come when those like you, Miraijin – the chosen ones, the New Men, the Women of the Future – will be identified, located, drafted and deployed to save the world (before you can start changing it).

Because the world by now is in great danger, exactly as many had feared. Exactly as it had been imagined thousands of times a century ago – in books, films, comics, cartoons, songs. And yet there are so many people who still refuse to see it, and many others who saw it too late and were caught by surprise. At any rate, you, Miraijin, and those like you, will be drafted and trained for a war no one had the courage to fight before, and it's clear by now that it is indeed a war – a fight to the death between truth and freedom. You, those like you and your army of children and teenagers (mostly) but also young men and women (many), adults (a few) and elderly people (very few) will be fighting for truth. Because meanwhile freedom has been turned into something hostile, feral, plural: there are many freedoms now, an infinite number, like chunks of rotting flesh torn from the carcass of Freedom. Freedom to only ever do as you please, freedom to ignore any form of authority that tries to limit that freedom, freedom to disobey the laws you disagree with, to disregard the founding values of society, to despise institutions, to break the social contract, freedom not to honour past agreements. Freedom to defend the indefensible, freedom to rebel against culture, against art and against science, freedom to choose alternative medicine – or to choose no medicine at all, freedom not to vaccinate, not to use antibiotics, freedom not to believe indisputable facts, freedom to believe fake news instead and freedom to create fake news even, freedom to generate carbon emissions, to produce toxic waste and radioactive waste, freedom to dump plastic into the sea, freedom to contaminate water sources and ravage sea beds. Freedom for women to be misogynists and for men to be chauvinists, freedom to shoot trespassers, freedom to turn refugees away and send them back to concentration camps or let them drown, freedom to hate religions that aren't yours, traditions that aren't yours, freedom to despise vegetarians and vegans, to hunt elephants, whales, rhinos, lions, wolves, foxes and badgers. Freedom to be cruel, politically incorrect, ignorant, antisemitic, Islamophobic, homophobic, selfish, racist, fascist, negationist. Freedom to say nigger and spaz and gyppo and retard and fag and be proud of it. Freedom to only ever pursue your own personal gain, to do what's wrong knowing it's wrong, and to oppose those who try to right those wrongs, because all these freedoms are based not on the rule of law, but on the freedom to be wrong. And while some will be fighting this fight in real life (which is hard enough) you, Miraijin – and those like you, with your charisma – will go behind enemy lines, that is online, that is the petri dish where all these freedoms proliferate and metastasise. Your mission will be to protect and preserve the old values that are fading away: rationality, compassion, generosity, the generosity of nations that were once nations of migrants, of exiles who died away from home, of servants, of farmers, of miners, of labourers, of dockers who worked like dogs so their children could have a better future, of intellectuals, of poets, artists, architects, engineers and scientists persecuted by tyrants. You will fight to keep all this alive online, for your young audience, with your games and your relatable stories, teaching them to see right from wrong – that is, with *critical thinking*.

And for this reason, Miraijin, simply because you will fight for and in the name of truth (even the most insignificant, trivial of truths), because you will fight against the freedom to ignore the truth, you will be in danger. Nineteen now, Miraijin, and everything will change (the first real change for you, yet another change for your grandpa): you'll have to leave your home, your town and your life behind, you'll have to hide, and move often. You'll be threatened, slandered, admired, treasured and protected so you can keep reminding people that the world was once a beautiful place, a healthy, welcoming place full of joys that don't cost a thing and that it could be that place again. You'll keep contributing to the programme created by the brightest minds of your generation, *Remember Your Future* (programme not just in the sense of online broadcast, but in the sense of a plan, an agenda, with clear objectives and a roadmap). You'll keep promoting it from your hiding places, but also from poppy fields, from glaciers, from the open sea, and more and more people will follow you, and the world will have begun to change, because the kids who started following you years ago will have grown up, and they'll break away from their parents – fight them if necessary – and they'll care about others, and because of your hybrid beauty they'll be attracted to everything that is 'other', and they'll be interested in culture, and they'll look for each other and find each other and get together and stay together, and they'll know what to do as the old world fades away.

All this thanks to you and those like you, but *mostly* thanks to you according to your grandpa, who will be alone now – proud and alone, worried and alone – and will follow you like everyone else on his phone, and he'll find out that since you've left you talk about him often, which will move him, and he'll think of all the years he spent raising you (seventeen!), years that have flown by, and he'll barely remember the years that came before, when you weren't there (just a blur to him now) and he'll wait for you in the old house in Piazza Savonarola, or in the old house in Bolgheri – both still standing thanks to him – where you'll go visit him as often as possible, with your *security detail* (because you'll need a security detail, Miraijin). You'll go see him and you'll find he's still keeping well, still keeping active – keeping still, in short (what he does best) while everything around him changes, and yet knowing all too well that change will come for him too, all at once, all of a sudden. And change will come, and it won't be a change for the better, because it will take the shape of a medical report, and the diagnosis will be cancer (pancreatic carcinoma to be precise, in so many words), an aggressive cancer, already at a quite advanced stage. But how is it possible? Your grandpa always goes and gets himself checked every six months, and six months ago there was nothing there! How can a tumour grow so fast? How? The same way his body grew when he was fifteen, Miraijin, because that is how Marco Carrera grows. Maybe it was always written in his DNA (as his mother believed), or maybe the day of reckoning his father feared has finally come: either way, he's seventy, and he's got cancer – and it's a tough one, dammit – and your knees will buckle when he tells you Miraijin (he'll have to tell you), and that world you're carrying on your shoulders will crumble around you. He'll tell you he wants to fight, but you'll know he knows he's dead already, just like his mother knew when it was her turn. That's what he'll think because he's a doctor, so he'll know, but he'll also know his life had a purpose, he'll know he should have died on a plane many years ago – it was all set, his name was on the list, but then at the last minute, he was spared, Miraijin, because if he'd died that evening he couldn't have seen you being born in the water, he couldn't have raised you, he couldn't have gifted you to the world.

# Here for you (2030)

Dear Grandpa,

Please ignore what I said yesterday. I kept crying all the way back to my place, I was desperate, I couldn't sleep, but now I understand. I understand everything, I completely understand. I understand and I'm ready. All these years, you have given me everything and never asked for anything in return – so if for once you ask something of me, even something as huge as this, I won't let you down. I'm sorry about yesterday, forget what I said. Today I'm here. I'm here for you.

I'll be back with you in a few days. I've taken some time off from the programme so I can look after you. I want you to know I'm proud of you, proud of how brave you've been these past few months, and proud of the decision you made – so clean, so raw – but above all I'm proud that you, my role model, my idol, should ask me for help. I'll help you, my dear, dear grandpa, I will: you don't have to worry about anything. I know what to do, I've dealt with this kind of situation before for the programme. Oscar knows the right people, you won't have to do anything – and I won't have to do anything either, don't worry. I'll get you to where you want to go – simple as that. And we'll be together.

Yours,
Miraijin

# The Barbarian invasions (2030)

– Are you awake? – asks Miraijin.
– Yes.
– Carradori is here.
– Finally. Where is he?
– I told him you were resting. He went for a walk on the beach with Grandma.
– Oh.

Miraijin kneels by the bed.

– I have a confession to make.
– What confession?
– I can't keep it from you.
– What did you do?
– Promise you won't be mad?
– I promise.
– I've started seeing a therapist.

Marco Carrera is tempted to answer, in the dying words of Julius Caesar, 'You too, Brutus?' but then thinks better of it. Miraijin doesn't deserve his sarcasm. If she told him it's not so he could make fun of her: she is being honest with him. How much strength is she summoning right now just to be there by his side, smiling? She deserves a real answer.

– Lucky guy – he says in the end – I envy him.

Miraijin lowers her eyes, as always when someone pays her a compliment. Marco lifts his arm towards her and pain shoots all the way down his right side. But it was worth it, because now (for the last time? Second to last?) he can stroke that hair. He strokes it and something indescribable happens: her curls feel almost liquid, no not liquid, fluid, no they're not fluid either, it's like sticking your hand in a bowl of cream. Jet-black cream.

– And how is it going?

– It's going well.

– I said lucky him, but is it a man or a woman?

– It's a man.

– And what does he look like?

– Thin, beautiful. He looks like you, actually. I'm already quite fond of him.

– I see. So we've invited him too? (He couldn't help himself this time, but that wasn't too sarcastic.)

– Silly . . .

Miraijin gets up.

– Call Rodrigo when you're ready – she says – he's outside the door, he looks like he's guarding it. I gave him a chair but he prefers to stand.

Miraijin walks out of the room. It's Probo's room, the most beautiful in the house, with French windows overlooking the garden. Curiously, after he died, Marco didn't claim it for himself and opted instead for his mother's. Why? He can't quite recollect. Lucia, the housekeeper, immediately dubbed it 'the guest room' – but no guests had slept in that room for over twenty-five years. Marco Carrera can't remember anyone occupying that room since Probo died. Could it be? Back when Miraijin still invited friends over, they'd always stay in her room. Perhaps Luisa? The last time she came, her house next door had already been sold, so she stayed with him: did she sleep in that room? Marco Carrera can't quite recollect. It was many years ago. Everything, in that house, happened many years ago.

He could open the French window though, and ask her directly: 'Luisa, the last time you were here, did you sleep in this room?' Because Luisa is there, in the garden, Marco can see her through the thin curtain. She's talking to Giacomo, he's there too. Actually, Giacomo is the one talking, and Luisa is listening. What is he saying to her? Miraijin walks by and brushes against her great-uncle (whom she only met the day before), and then walks on, past Marco's visual field. Is she headed to the beach to join Carradori and her grandma?

Inviting them was Miraijin's great idea. 'Like in that film we watched together,' she said, 'what was it called again?' Marco Carrera couldn't remember the title. He couldn't remember the film either. The tumour had reached his brain and his memory worked only intermittently.

Inviting them was a great, unsettling idea. Marco hadn't even remotely considered it – he'd lived his life and that was that, the thought of *improving* it right at the end hadn't even crossed his mind. He hadn't spoken to Luisa in so long . . . how long exactly? He couldn't remember, but it had been quite some time. And Giacomo? Even longer. He'd ended it with Luisa – that much he remembers: in the past few years she'd written to him a few times, but he never wrote back. With Giacomo it was the other way round: Marco had written to him for years without ever hearing anything back, and in the end he'd resigned himself to his silence. He remembers that too. How could he *invite* them, now? 'But would you like to, Grandpa?' asked Miraijin, 'Would that make you happy?' Marco didn't know what to say. 'I'm not sure that's what I want,' he answered, but he wasn't sure he wasn't sure, either. A rather fitting quote came to mind: 'Ubi nihil vales, ibi nihil velis.' He couldn't recollect where he'd read it, but he did remember its meaning, because it perfectly described how he felt: 'Where you are worth nothing, there you should want nothing.' Miraijin, sensing his confusion, countered with the irresistible logic that made her who she was: 'I'm not asking for you, actually,' she said, 'it's for me, really – for those of us who'll stay behind.' *For those of us who'll stay behind*: she'd thought of everyone, even the ones she'd never met. She knew her grandmother, and Greta, and Carradori (vaguely) – she knew of Giacomo's and Luisa's existence only from Marco, but she had never met them. And yet she'd thought of them too – that was Miraijin Carrera for you. From that perspective, inviting them was a gift from Marco *to those who'd stay behind*, and his feeling of powerlessness vanished. There was also something obscene and shameless about the whole scheme that appealed to him – and so in the end he said yes, he would like that very much, but he doubted they'd come. 'Leave it to me,' replied Miraijin. That was twelve days before, in the living room of the house on Piazza Savonarola, which had been turned into a makeshift hospital. It was unclear how she'd managed that, but all five of them had come, even at such short notice. That girl could do anything.

Giacomo had come from North Carolina, Luisa from Paris, Marina and Greta from Germany, and Carradori from Lampedusa. Then there was Oscar (Miraijin's boyfriend who'd come from Barcelona), Rodrigo (the nurse who'd come to do the deed), and Miraijin's security detail (also from Spain, all three of them). The house in Bolgheri had never seen such an international crowd. Guido, the nurse who looked after Marco in Florence, couldn't make it: he couldn't leave Florence as he was also looking after his disabled mother. Which was just as well actually, because otherwise they'd have had to make up an excuse for him to stay in town: he was a devout Catholic and wouldn't have approved. It had been an emotional goodbye, because Guido sensed Marco wouldn't come back; although he didn't suspect what was going on, Marco's decision to stop the treatment and move to the seaside at the end of May spoke volumes. He was so very sorry he couldn't go with him to Bolgheri (he was crying, too) but he couldn't leave his mother.

The whole thing, come to think of it, was in serious danger of turning into one big teary, emotional goodbye, so much so that Marco, as a point of honour, refused to shed a single tear. No – he thought – if this thing is to have any meaning at all, then we must make it a celebration of sorts, a joyful, life-affirming experience. Maybe not an actual celebration, given the circumstances, but the guests Miraijin had invited were alive, and alive they'd return to where they'd come from: their hospitality, therefore, had to be impeccable. The rooms were carefully prepared, there was freshly caught fish, homemade pasta, and vegetables from the garden – even though Marco, in his current state, wouldn't be able to partake. He hadn't eaten in months, in fact, all the nutrients he needed came from a thin pipe they'd stuck into his stomach. He had still helped Miraijin prepare dinner and lunch though, as if they were just having people over for a party. After all, he knew exactly what everyone liked to eat: Giacomo loved seafood, Luisa liked scampi, buffalo mozzarella for Marina, and so on. Or at least that's what they enjoyed eating thirty years before – but people's taste in food doesn't change. At worst, there may be new dietary requirements due to health conditions he wasn't aware of and in that case the sight of him, sitting at the head of the table with his feeding tube, would make them feel less sorry for themselves. But it wasn't necessary in the end: everyone was able to enjoy their favourite food, which was really rather lucky.

And there lay yet another obstacle that threatened to derail Marco's plan. We mentioned cynicism and sarcasm already: Marco, a product of the old world, had always made liberal use of both, but there was no room for them in Miraijin's new world (there was room for irony, nothing else). We also saw there was a risk the whole thing would end in tears. And then there was self-pity – if not downright envy (look at them, happily scoffing scampi while I'm dying). Marco, therefore, had been extremely vigilant both during meals and as he welcomed his guests to the house: no tears, no sarcasm and no self-pity. If this really was to be a gift to those who'd stay behind, then there must be no awkwardness or discomfort. He wanted them to have fond memories of their presence there, which meant he had to be perfect.

He hoists himself up into a sitting position. Stabbing pain, again. It's time for his morphine tablets, but that wouldn't make much sense, given the circumstances. Pain aside, Marco could still be self-sufficient; he's very far from the actual end yet, he hasn't yet turned into a zombie like his parents did, and he never will. He wants to leave before he becomes a nuisance.

On the first day, as soon as they arrived, he insisted on going on a bike ride in the pine grove with Miraijin. And he managed, somehow, to stay on the saddle, even though he was very frail and very slow and very wobbly (Miraijin's security detail were following them on foot, ready to pounce and catch him if he fell). Now, *that* they could laugh about – and they did, later, at home: there was no cynicism, no sarcasm.

If he took the morphine tablets now, he ponders, he could probably walk into the garden on his own two feet. Once there, however, he'd still have to sit in the wheelchair, and on top of that the tablets might interfere with the other drugs. Something else he wanted to avoid at all costs: being pathetic (look at me, I can manage all by myself!).

But he can still get from the bed to the wheelchair without help – that much he can manage. He has to cross the length of the room because Rodrigo left the wheelchair far from the bed, precisely to discourage any such initiatives on his part. Marco Carrera gets up and totters unsteadily towards the wheelchair, half dragging, half leaning on the IV stand. Don't fall now, he thinks. Don't you go and break a leg now, he thinks. He gets to the chair and checks the brakes are on. They're not on. He puts them on, then slowly, carefully lowers himself on to the padded seat to avoid any aftershocks. Done. It was painful but easy. Only then does he call the nurse: 'Rodrigo,' he says, softly. Too softly maybe? No: Rodrigo comes in right away. He can see Marco got up and walked to the wheelchair by himself, but says nothing. 'Take me to the garden, please. I want to do it there.'

It's a bright, balmy afternoon. The hedge is in bloom, as are the bougainvillea and the jasmine. The lawn was mown that very same morning, and the freshly cut grass adds to that intoxicating combination of scents. Luisa steps away from Giacomo to meet him. Marco looks at her, radiant in the sun that has just about begun to set: how old is she? Sixty-four? Sixty-three? Sixty-five? She hasn't had any work done on that face and that body that Marco so ardently desired for all those years, and she's still incredibly beautiful. Giacomo walks behind her. He, too, loved that body and that face. He, too, is still beautiful. Something else to watch out for: melancholy. Luckily, here comes Miraijin back from the beach, followed by Oscar, Marina, Greta and Dr Carradori. Good, we're all here – thinks Marco – let's proceed.

He's nervous. His heart is pounding.

Carradori greets him affectionately. As always, without his magnetic gaze he would cut such a diminutive figure – he's the same age as Marco, but looks older. Or maybe it's Marco who looks younger: despite losing weight, despite the cancer and the chemo, he still doesn't look seventy-one. His hair is still there – thick, straight, grey hair gently ruffled by the afternoon breeze. That's the whole point, in the end: for him to go while he still looks passable. For him to leave before the horror sets in.

No one is talking. No one knows what to say. Marco nods at Rodrigo, who walks back into the house. He thought many times about how he should behave in his final hours, what to do, what to say. He'd discarded everything that might come across as pathetic, meaning there was to be no music (at first, he thought of 'Don't Cry No Tears' by Neil Young, but immediately caught himself). There was to be no speech either (God forbid), no solemn words, no tears, no melancholy, no self-pity. Just a hug – no harm in that – with those who wanted to, as if he was simply going on a trip somewhere. And a few technical words to remind everyone they were not complicit in (and least of all to blame for) anything.

No one says a word until Rodrigo returns from the house carrying the drugs. As he hooks the bags on the IV stand and plugs them into the cannulas, Marco begins to speak.

– So – he says – thank you for coming, I am very happy to have you here with me. As you know, inviting you was Miraijin's idea, and since you're all here I assume you thought it was a good idea. Now, however . . .

Suddenly, Giacomo starts sobbing: two loud, consecutive sobs in the space of two seconds. Marco is sitting right in front of him, and in those two seconds he can see Giacomo's beautiful, lean face twist into a harrowing grimace, then immediately go back to the vaguely preoccupied look he'd been wearing ever since he got out of the taxi the day before. He'd held it all together admirably, from the challenging moment when he and Marco saw each other again after all those years, to them talking – just the two of them, after dinner – about Giacomo's daughters and Miraijin. He'd held it all together admirably and then seemed to crumble with those two sobs, but luckily he caught himself in time.

– I'm sorry – he whispers.

And he looks up at Marco again, contrite, his hands between his legs, as if nothing had happened. In the end, it was almost comical.

– I was saying that you don't have to watch if you don't want to. I'm very happy to have seen you and talked to you all. Anyway, if you'd rather go back into the house now, or to the beach, or wherever, please do, don't feel you have to stay.

He stops talking and scans his audience. Giacomo is holding it together. Miraijin is holding on to Oscar, his strong, tanned arm wrapped around her golden shoulders. Luisa looks sad but steady. Marina returns his gaze for one second, then buckles and shakes her head.

– I . . . – she says – no, maybe it's better if I go back to the house.

She looks at Marco again, smiles, and leaves. A wounded gazelle. Thanks to Miraijin she has improved a lot in the past few years and can now live and travel independently. Marco watches her disappear through the kitchen door, then looks at Greta, Adele's half-sister.

– What about you?

Greta is a beautiful girl, approaching thirty now, with a buzz cut and tattooed arms. Adele had just about started to get close to her before she died, and Greta and Miraijin had subsequently built a beautiful, deep, almost sisterly relationship – all thanks to Marco's determined efforts to have Miraijin spend time with her grandmother and Greta in Germany, year after year. Those trips to Munich are the reason Miraijin will still have some family left.

– No, Marco – says Greta – I'm staying.

Her features are as stark as her voice – but also bright, and vaguely triumphant – as if they'd been cut into steel. Marco takes a deep breath, bats away the thought of Marina crying, alone, in the house (this is so bloody hard) and continues:

– I'd like to say a few words to explain the medical side of things, and so you understand that this is entirely my own decision, which I have made in full possession of my mental faculties. Rodrigo, here, is just going to help me out and give me twenty, maybe thirty seconds of peace. But I could do it all by myself.

He points at the two bags Rodrigo has hooked on the IV stand and plugged into the cannula inserted in his right arm.

– The first bag contains a combination of midazolam – a benzodiazepine medication – and propofol, which is a powerful drug causing loss of consciousness. Both are commonly used as general anaesthetics. The dosage is generous enough to ensure I'll be under strong sedation. The second bag contains concentrated potassium – that's going to do the dirty work. I'm not going to tell you how I obtained these substances, but I can assure you that no one knew what use I intended to make of them. Quite simply, having worked in a hospital for over forty years meant I was able to get my hands on these drugs without needing to involve anyone else.

That's a lie – and Marco tells it well, sticking to the script he'd prepared. The concentrated potassium is not something he could have easily obtained, which is why he asked for Miraijin's help. And she found some. Well, she found Rodrigo and Rodrigo found some. But Marco doesn't want anyone to know.

– In a little while, once I've said goodbye to everyone, I'll open the red tap and the anaesthetics will begin flowing through my veins. Once they've kicked in, Rodrigo will kindly open the other tap, the blue one, which will let the potassium in – and it'll all be over in a matter of minutes. All you'll see is me nodding off. As I said, Rodrigo is here to give me twenty seconds of peace because, if I wanted to do all this by myself, I'd have to make an effort to stay alert so I can activate the blue tap before losing consciousness, which would be a shame. I'd miss the best part, that is, softly sinking into oblivion.

As he'd hoped, his dry, technical words appear to have cooled things down and neutralised all the obstacles that threatened to derail his plan. His heart is beating regularly now, the emotion is gone. He's talking about his death, but he might as well be describing a cornea transplant.

– The potassium will produce arrhythmias, which in turn will lead to a ventricular fibrillation and eventually to cardiac arrest. That shouldn't make for a gruesome spectacle though: worst-case scenario, if tachycardia sets in, there may be a few jolts before the ventricular fibrillation, but it is highly unlikely.

A treacherous thought crosses his mind: Irene. Irene would be proud of him right now. Irene took her own life when she was only a little older than Miraijin.

Deep breath. He bats away this thought too and continues:

– Once it's all over, Miraijin will call an ambulance, which will come from the hospital in Castagneto Carducci. They will pronounce me dead at the scene. Miraijin will explain what my situation was, she'll show them my medical records, and no one will ask any questions. The way I see it, there's no reason you should stick around when the ambulance arrives, but anyway if you choose to stay, don't worry, you won't be questioned and you won't have to give false testimony.

No one – I can assure you – will want to investigate the matter.

Done. His speech is over. Marco is very proud of himself: proud he remembered everything, proud he explained everything professionally. Except for Marina, no one left and Giacomo's sobs were the only minor ripple in an otherwise perfectly smooth performance. Miraijin slips out from under Oscar's arm and joins him, leaning over to hug him.

– Well done, Grandpa – she says.

Marco suddenly remembers something – as we said, his memory comes and goes.

– *The Barbarian Invasions* – he whispers in her ear – you know that old film you asked about? That's what it's called.

– That's it – Miraijin whispers back – *The Barbarian Invasions*.

She strokes his hair (like he stroked hers so many times before), then moves to stand next to his wheelchair on the opposite side to Rodrigo, who – silent, enigmatic – holds the IV stand like a spear. He's ready.

Greta approaches. She leans over too, like Miraijin, and hugs him affectionately. Marco breathes in her citrusy scent, then looks at her: her eyes are ever so slightly teary, she's smiling.

– Farewell, Marco – she says.

– Goodbye – he answers.

Greta walks back to her seat. Everyone's got their own seat, it really is a performance.

Carradori's turn now. He steps forward and offers Marco his hand to shake (or do whatever he pleases with it): Marco opts for a vigorous handshake, of the kind you'd give after a tennis match. Smack – and here comes the pain, again.

– I've grown very fond of you, you know, Dr Carrera – says Carradori.

– Call me Marco, from now on – he replies. They both laugh.

He can afford to be sarcastic with Carradori, they're the same age.

Oscar's up next. Marco only met him a few months before, in the midst of his chemo, when he'd come to visit Miraijin who had moved back to Florence to look after her grandfather. Frail and suffering as he was, he'd found solace in Oscar's strength – delighted in it even, because it was contagious. He was like a male version of Miraijin: a leader, a captain, another great hope for a brave new world.

– Hang in there, all of you – says Marco, hugging him.

– *Claro* – he answers. You bet.

Then he adds something he wasn't obliged to say:

– *Su vida es mi vida*. Her life is my life.

He squeezes Miraijin's hands, kisses her lips ever so softly and steps aside.

And now what?

Not that it really matters anymore, but Marco is wondering who'll come next – Giacomo or Luisa? What's the hierarchy? Maybe that's what they're wondering too: there's a moment of awkwardness as they both hesitate. Then Giacomo comes forward. They hug. That lump in their throat again – Giacomo's brief meltdown earlier scared them both, if they start crying now it'll be a disaster, it'll ruin everything. They're still holding on tight to each other.

– I'm sorry – says Giacomo.

– No, I'm sorry – says Marco.

They let go. Deep breath. That's it. Done. It's Luisa's turn now.

Here she comes. Marco's heart starts pounding again. Her silver-green eyes. Her sun-drenched brown hair, still glowing. Her soft neck, her scent which is the scent of the sea, the same as all those years ago. Marco hasn't prepared anything to say, he decided he was just going to say the first thing that crossed his mind, and in this precise moment, seeing her, he knows.

– Do you know what day is today? – he asks.

– No.

– It's the second of June. And what day is that?

She smiles, puzzled.

– The anniversary of the Italian Republic?

– Yes, and what else?

Luisa shakes her head, smiling.

– It is the furthest day of the year from my birthday – he continues – we're exactly six months away. What's that thing about righteous men dying on their birthday? What's that Hebrew word again?

– *Tzadik.*

– That's it. Well I'm not a *tzadik*. I'm the opposite of a *tzadik*, in fact.

Are these really the last words Marco Carrera will say to Luisa Lattes? Perhaps – he thinks – I should have prepared something after all.

– Oh but you are – she says.

– What about Jewish folklore?

– Jewish folklore is wrong.

She strokes his head, his forehead, his face.

– *Mon petit colibri* – she whispers. My little hummingbird.

And then, and then, her head tilted to one side, her hair falling on her shoulder, that languid look, Marco knows it well, the same as all those years before, when she . . .

A kiss! On the mouth! Tongue and all! She holds his head in her hands, passionately, who cares if they're old, if Giacomo sees them, if everyone sees them!

Well done, Luisa – if it's meant to be obscene, then let it be truly obscene. Marco grabs her head too and holds her close, and God bless the jab of pain down his side. He wanted to kiss her too. It's what he always wanted, always. He wanted to kiss her for the first time in that very spot, half a century before, and he never stopped wanting it since. He would never have dared though, not on that day – but she did.

It's over. Luisa stirs, straightens her back and retreats to her seat, head bowed, as if she'd just taken communion.

It's time. Nothing else left to do. The afternoon is intoxicating, brimming with light, abuzz with life. A light breeze blows in from the sea and casts an aura of luxuriant peace around the garden, gently stirring the hedges, playing with people's hair. The way he is sitting right now Marco can't feel any pain. He's felt so much pain in his life. His was a life full of pain, no doubt about that. But all the pain he suffered never prevented him from fully enjoying moments of unadulterated perfection like this one – and there were many of those moments in his life, too. It doesn't take much, after all: decent weather, a few hugs, a kiss on the mouth. There could be more moments like these, after all . . .

Ah! Something else to watch out for (it never ends) – having second thoughts. Maybe that's what they're all secretly hoping for, that he'll change his mind. That he'll pretend to believe he can beat cancer, that he'll start another round of chemo, start fighting again, that he'll endure the endless nausea, and the diarrhoea, and the mouth sores. That he won't be able to leave his bed anymore, that he'll turn into a wheezing larva covered in bedsores, that Miraijin – instead of saving the world – will rush to hire water mattresses and night nurses and buy massage oils and various other ointments, and morphine tablets, and morphine injections, more and more morphine because after a while it's not enough anymore, but not too much because it's not allowed, and that he'll beg Miraijin to 'take him away' like Probo, and that Miraijin – instead of saving the world – will have to . . .

Marco turns towards Rodrigo and shakes his hand.

– Thank you, for everything – he says. Rodrigo squeezes his shoulder.

Marco reaches for the red tap – jab of pain – and opens it, then rests his hand back on his thigh – jab of pain. He takes a good look at the five people sitting in front of him, then glances up at Miraijin and gestures for her to lean forward. She does. He looks at that incredible girl for the last time, then lifts his arm – pain, again – and sticks his hand into the enigma that is her hair. Miraijin holds his gaze wearing a resolute, knowing expression. The drugs are beginning to kick in, everything starts pulling away from him. If he'd chosen to do everything by himself, he would have had to muster all his strength to open the potassium tap now. But that's Rodrigo's gift to him. Wait, what is Miraijin doing? With infinite tenderness she pulls out his right hand from her hair and replaces it with his left hand – no more pain. Everything's so far away. What on earth is she doing? Oh, of course. She slots her right hand into Marco's between her ring finger and her little finger, and their identical birthmarks touch. Of course. Their 'power spot'.

Everything is so, so far away. Fluctuating, aquatic peace. Irene. Adele. Dad. Mum. This creature is my gift to the world. Are you proud of me?

Irene.

Adele.

Dad.

Mum.

How many people are buried inside us?

He's asleep now. His head flops to one side. Miraijin holds it up, protects it. It's Rodrigo's turn now, he came all the way from Malaga to do this. He's had a crazy life – his father is blind, his mother is a Romani singer, dancer and street artist who (allegedly) dated Enrique Iglesias before he started seeing Anna

Kournikova, his twin sister he never sees because they both travel the world with various NGOs, his boyfriend is a Basque pelota champion, and his adoptive son lives in Benin: but this is not his story. He's only here to open the blue tap.

Let us pray for him, and for all the ships out at sea.

# This tired old sky (1997)

Luisa LATTES<br>Poste Restante<br>59–78 Rue des Archives<br>75003 Paris<br>France

Rome, 17 November 1997

If this tired old sky came crashing down on us
Luisa Luisa my Luisa,
Before we had a chance to say these words –
  The two of us we're in love,
  If I say so myself.
  Let us write it like that, all wrong,
Your mine and I'm yours
Let us write it like that,
Luisa Luisa my Luisa
On every surface on God's green earth.

# The Hummingbird

# (Rome and many other places, 2015–2019)

## ACKNOWLEDGEMENTS

First of all, the chapter called 'Mulinelli' isn't simply a homage to Beppe Fenoglio's short story *Il gorgo* ('The Whirlpool'): it is an actual cover, so to speak. That story – possibly the most beautiful ever written in Italian – is so inherently perfect, and that perfection wouldn't have come across if I'd simply borrowed the idea behind it, without reproducing its structure as well. Because it is precisely in the structure that its perfection lies, that combination of candour and desperation that makes it sound so natural. Therefore, I decided I'd rewrite that very same story adapting it to the characters in this novel and trying to preserve the structure and tone as much as possible. It was a powerful exercise for me. In the end, to clearly signal what I was doing (as well as my admiration for Fenoglio) I decided to reproduce the first and last line exactly as they were – and sure enough, they turned out to be the best lines in the whole chapter.

In the chapter called 'The eye of the storm', one of the traits I attribute to The Omen comes from one of my favourite authors, Mario Vargas Llosa: '*El hombre era tan alto y tan flaco que parecia siempre de perfil*' ('The man was tall and so thin he seemed to be always in profile') is the opening line of his novel *The War of the End of the World*, published in Spanish in 1981 and translated into English by Helen R. Lane (1986, Faber & Faber). The skiing accident I describe in the same chapter actually happened, to a young talented skier from Florence called Graziuso – I can't remember his first name. It was during training (not a giant slalom qualifier) on Mount Gomito at the Abetone ski resort. Blood, snow, the boy screaming in pain – every time I think of it, I feel faint.

The whole chapter was published as a preview in the Italian magazine *IL* in July 2017.

In the chapter called 'Urania', the lines scribbled on the sci-fi novel title page were actually written by my own father, as I was being born in a hospital in Florence (not sure which one), on the title page of one of those very same Urania sci-fi novels: 'Good morning Ladies and Gentlemen! I'm about to introduce you to my new friend, Miss Giovanna Veronesi . . . or perhaps Mr Alessandro Veronesi . . . who knows . . . Ah here we go . . . Here comes the nurse . . . Can't quite see yet . . . Ah yes . . . Ladies and Gentlemen, say hello to Alessandro!' The novel in question was *Eye in the Sky* by Philip K. Dick, which – for reasons I explain in the chapter – was said to be published in Italy on 12 April 1959, even though I was born on 1 April.

The film I mention at the start of the chapter entitled 'Gospodineeee' is *Amarcord* by Federico Fellini, released in Italy on 13 December 1973.

In the same chapter, the phrase Marco underlines in a novel he's reading ('with the darkness and confusion in him') comes from Salman Rushdie's *The Golden House* (2017, Random House).

★

In 'A thread, a wizard, three cracks' I pay homage to Sergio Claudio Perroni's wonderful lyrical prose from his novel *Entro a volte nel tuo sonno* ('I sometimes visit your dreams') – and specifically from the chapter '*Sapere la strada*' ('Knowing the way') – published in Italy by La nave di Teseo (2018). I didn't think much of my homage, actually, so I'd decided to leave it out, but then on 25 May 2019, while I was still working on this novel, Perroni took his own life in Taormina, Sicily, where he lived. He was a friend, so I decided to keep my mediocre homage after all, if only so I could acknowledge him here.

The article mentioned in 'First letter on hummingbirds' was written by Marco D'Eramo for the Italian newspaper *Il Manifesto* and published on 4 January 2005. It is indeed a review of the Aztec Empire exhibition which ran from 15 October 2004 to 14 February 2005 at the Guggenheim in New York.

The 'Discourse on dhukha' from the chapter called 'Weltschmerz & Co.' is from *Nidana Samyutta: Group of Related Discourses on Causal Factors (Suttanta Pitaka/Samyutta Nikaya)*, published by Burma Pitaka Association/Sri Satguru Publications, 1993.

A few words about the song 'Gloomy Sunday' after which the chapter is named. It was written in Hungary in the 1930s (original title: '*Szomorú vasárnap*'; lyrics by László Jávor and music by self-taught pianist Rezső Seress). It was first recorded by Jazz singer Pál Kalmár in 1935 and instantly achieved worldwide success, becoming one of jazz's most iconic pieces (especially Sam Lewis's 1936 English version).

As its popularity grew, a rumour (complete with names and gruesome details) started circulating according to which this incredibly sad song had pushed several people to commit suicide:

'Gloomy Sunday' became 'the Hungarian suicide song', and was consequently censored in a number of countries. It was precisely to counter this sinister fame that new lines were added to Billie Holiday's 1941 version, in an attempt to disguise the original lyrics as nothing more than a bad dream.

The song, however, was still banned by the BBC in what were already extremely challenging times for Britain, under constant attack from Hitler's Luftwaffe (incidentally, the ban was only lifted in 2002). Over the years, the song was covered by many great artists and musicians, with or without the additional lines. Besides the 1981 punk version by Lydia Lunch that Irene listens to in the novel, these (among many, many others) are also worth a mention: Elvis Costello (1994), Ricky Nelson (1959), Marianne Faithfull (1987), Sinead O'Connor (1992) and Bjork (2010).

There is also an Italian version ('*Triste domenica*') with lyrics by Nino Rastelli, sung by Norma Bruni, Carlastella, Myriam Ferretti, Giovanni Vallarino and, most memorably by Nilla Pizzi in 1952. The Italian version doesn't attempt to soften the original rawness of the lyrics or in any way muddle the clear allusion to suicide following the death of a loved one.

In 1968, Rezső Seress jumped from a window in his house in Budapest.

In the chapter called 'Shakul & Co.', the analysis of the various terms referring to parents who have lost a child was partly inspired by Concita de Gregorio's *Mi sa che fuori è primavera* (*The Missing Word*) Feltrinelli, 2015.

The lyrics quoted in that same chapter are from '*Amico Fragile*' by Italian singer-songwriter Fabrizio de André who – for Marco as for so many of his generation in Italy – was indeed a cultural icon. Incidentally, these lyrics are themselves a homage to Oscar Wilde, and specifically to one of Lady Bracknell's caustic rispostes in *The Importance of Being Ernest*: 'To lose one parent, Mr Worthing, may be regarded as a misfortune; to lose both looks like carelessness.'

The book by David Leavitt mentioned in the chapter called 'Via Crucis' is his first one, *Family Dancing*. It's a great book – read it, or read it again.

The Joni Mitchell song in 'On everyone's lips' is 'The Wolf That Lives in Lindsey' from her 1979 album *Mingus* – there really are wolves howling at the end of the track, it's haunting.

The chapter 'To look is to touch' was originally published as an essay in 2017 for *La Lettura*, the literary Sunday supplement of Italian newspaper *Il Corriere della Sera*.

The sentence 'Wolves don't kill unlucky deer. They kill the weak ones' is from Taylor Sheridan's 2017 film *Wind River*. A gruesome, unsettling story set in an Indian reservation in Wyoming, it reminded me of Louise Erdrich's novels. The problem is that the chapter 'Wolves don't kill unlucky deer' is set in 2016, i.e. the year before the film was released. I couldn't postpone the chapter by a year, so I decided to keep the sentence despite the slight anachronism. I just want to make clear that the words are not mine – they're Taylor Sheridan's, who wrote as well as directed the film.

In the same chapter, the story of Duccio Chilleri a.k.a. The Omen is inspired by Pirandello's 1911 short story '*La patente*' ('The Licence'). The protagonist, called Rosario Chiàrchiaro, is rumoured to bring bad luck, but instead of fighting his reputation, he decides to profit from it and acquire an imaginary licence to operate as a professional jinx. In Luigi Zampa's 1954 screen adaptation (the four-part film *Questa è la vita / Of Life and Love* inspired by Pirandello's short stories) the character of Chiàrchiaro is played by celebrated Italian comedy actor Totò.

The book Luisa mentions in the chapter 'Third letter about hummingbirds' is *Lui, Io, Noi* (*He, I, Us*) published by Einaudi Stile Libero in 2018. It's a long collection of memories of life with Fabrizio De André written by his widow Dori Ghezzi together with Giordano Meacci and Francesca Serafini (the two 'linguists'). It's essential reading for all De André fans, but also for those who are passionate about the Italian language – as demonstrated by the new term they coined ('*emmenalgia*').

In 'The New Man', the mare I describe (Dolly) belonged to my brother Giovanni.

In the same chapter, the concept of a war between truth and freedom is borrowed from a formidable essay by Rocco Ronchi called '*Metafisica del populismo*' ('The Metaphysics of Populism') published in the 12 November 2018 issue of the Italian magazine *Doppiozero*. It is truly enlightening. While I was browsing *Doppiozero*'s archive, I came across another essay called '*Ricorda il tuo futuro*' ('Remember Your Future') by Mauro Zanchi, and before I even read it I decided it was going to be the name of Miraijin's programme. It describes a visit to a 2017 exhibition in Reggio Emilia, Italy, called *Fotografia Europea 2017 – Mappe del tempo. Memoria. Futuro* ('European Photography 2017 – Time maps. Memory. Archives. Future') curated by Diane Doufour, Elio Grazioli e Walter Guadagnini. That essay also proved useful.

The Latin quote Marco remembers in the second-to-last chapter ('*Ubi nihil vales, nihil velis*') is by Flemish philosopher Arnold Geulincx (1624–69). It's from his monumental posthumous work *Ethics* which, apparently, saved young Samuel Beckett's life when he was tormented by suicidal thoughts. Beckett describes coming across this maxim in a letter dated 16 January 1936 to his life-long friend Thomas McGreevy (incidentally, do read *The Letters of Samuel Beckett – Volume 1 1929–1940*, Cambridge University Press, 2016). The quote makes an appearance in his 1938 novel *Murphy*, which he wrote while he was in therapy with celebrated English psychotherapist Wilfred Bion. Geulincx himself also makes an appearance in *Molloy*. The radical idea of suppressing human will in order to eliminate all conflicts and suffering generated by it – which is found in all of Beckett's characters – stems from precisely this maxim. Note the (deliberate) affinity with the concept of dhukha in the chapter 'Weltschmerz & Co.'.

Finally, these are the people I would like to thank from the bottom of my heart (and they all know why):

My wife Manuela, my brother Giovanni, my children Umberto, Lucio, Gianni, Nina and Zeno, Valeria Solarino, Elisabetta Sgarbi, Eugenio Lio, Beppe Del Greco, Piero Brachi, Franco Purini, Marco D'Eramo, Edoardo Nesi, Mario Desiati, Pigi Battista, Daniela Viglione, Marinella Viglione, Fulvio Pierangelini, Paolo Virzì, Karen Hassan, Marco Delogu, Teresa Ciabatti, Stefano Bollani, Isabella Grande, Domenico Procacci, Antonio Troiano, Christian Rocca, Nicolas Saada, Leopoldo Fabiani, Giorgio Dell'Arti, Paolo Carbonati, Stefano Calamandrei, Filippo de Braud, Vincenzo Valentini, Michele Marzocco, Francesco Ricci, Enrico Grassi, Ginevra Bandini, Giulia Santaroni, Pierluigi Amata, Manuela Giannotti, Mario Franchini, Massimo Zampini.

# About the Author

Sandro Veronesi was born in Florence in 1959. He is the author of nine novels including *Quiet Chaos* (2005), which was translated into twenty languages and won the Strega Prize, the Prix Fémina and the Prix Méditerranée.

*The Hummingbird* was an instant bestseller in Italy, winning the Premio Strega and selling over 300,000 copies to date. It was voted best book of the year by the *Corriere della Sera*, Italy's most widely read newspaper.

Sandro is only the second author in the Premio Strega's seventy-four-year history to win the prize twice.

# Translator's Acknowledgements

I would like to thank my husband Sam, who patiently tended to me every day and put my soul back where it needed to be whenever it got lost. Most importantly, he put his dreams on hold for a little while so I could pursue mine.

I would also like to thank my baby son Dorian who – like a certain character in the book – always did the right thing, namely, sleeping away in his room.

# About the Translator

Elena Pala's love of all things language took her to many weird and wonderful places throughout the years. After a somewhat convoluted journey which included shepherding tourists up and down the Eiffel Tower, a PhD in linguistics at Cambridge University, and a stint at a busy creative agency in London, she eventually found her calling. A commercial as well as literary translator from Italian and French, *The Hummingbird* is her first book-length translation, and she is currently working on two forthcoming publications.